THE KNIGHT'S SHADOW
PROLOGUE
Pat

Summer moonlight filled the cir
It rested on the shields of the b
wrinkles of concentration on their faces and reflected silver from the
tips of their spears.

In their centre of field, Lucius peered through the surrounding
border of trees, beyond the moonlight's reach, into the unknown
darkness. Shivers ran from his heels to his neck. *Something's glaring
back*, he sensed.

An owl hooted. *Oh God,* Lucius thought. Silent, still, the woods
never made any sound. *The owl could only mean trouble.*

Corvus, a young scout, emerged from the shade between two
trees.

'Scout returning,' someone called.

A gap formed to let him through.

'Nine,' the scout reported.

Nine is not many, Lucius doubted the number of enemies.

Scipio, a centurion who stood beside him said, 'When?'

'Now.'

'STAND READY.' Scipio commanded.

The front line stepped forward and rested their spears on their
shoulders.

Everything is wrong, Lucius reasoned. Scipio and his mercenaries
did not come into the woods to fight men. They came to hunt the
thing that took the people. It all began when individual workers

who laid the path from the new city in the west to the mountains in the east went missing. And then whole work parties vanished. Eventually, legionnaires and the labourers under their protection disappeared.

Lucius had read through records of the events and spoken to the sole survivor from the last work party yet had never suspected people lived out here. *It was all wrong.*

From the woods, a voice, loud and angry, roared a battle cry. All around them, all at once, hundreds more joined the call.

Nine is not the number of enemies. Lucius realised his mistake. *Nine is the number of times Scipio's forty mercenaries are outnumbered by.*

A man ran from the woods. The mercenary in line with him held out his shield arm so his fist aligned with his target. He leaned back before throwing himself forward. His spear sailed up, glided down, then punched into the charging man's chest. The impact flung him backwards.

Staring at the spear standing upright in the corpse, Lucius squeezed his crucifix, 'Jesus Christ.'

Wild men poured out of the woods in a charge towards them.

The front-rank of mercenaries threw their spears into the horde. Connecting their shields, they drew their swords and rested them on their flexible barricade. The inner rank positioned their spears over the front line's shoulders.

'FIGHT FOR EACH OTHER!' barked Scipio, his order the sole Roman response to the roar of the approaching mayhem.

Hit *enmasse* and squeezed inwards, the mercenaries braced against the weight their attackers whilst meeting them with sharpened iron. Waves of blood splashed over the swordsmen's shields. One mercenary's sword cleaved into a man's neck and through another's arm before slicing back and forth through a third barbarian's chest.

The Knight's Shadow

Sam Heslop

Published by Sam Heslop, 2025.

THE KNIGHT'S SHADOW

First edition. February 3, 2025.

Copyright © 2025 Sam Heslop.

ISBN: 979-8230493563

Written by Sam Heslop.

For Kimberley.

Scipio shoved Lucius out of his way. He gripped the shoulder of an inner-rank mercenary. 'I'M MOVING YOU LEFT,' he roared.

The mercenary's spear withdrew. Scipio's spare hand grabbed the bottom of the shaft. 'ONE, TWO, MOVE!' Pushing the back end down, lifting its shaft clear of the fighters, the centurion manoeuvred the man into position, released his weapon then slapped him on the helmet in a gesture which said, *'Get into them.'* The moved man thrust the tip of his spear into the swathes of wildmen.

Hands grasped the shield of a man at the front. He tried to manage the pressure building around him with frantic hacks. Attackers pulled at the desperate mercenary's shield. Others lunged through the gap, grabbing him and dragging him into their swarm. The mercenary's sword swung and slashed in a doomed effort to escape the inevitable.

A wild man leapt through a gap in the shield barricade plunging the sharp point of a bone into a defender's eye whose scream paled into the uproar of battle. The biggest of Scipio's men drove his spear into the bone wielder's chest. His hands slid along his weapon's shaft as he leapt ahead to thump his shoulder into the savage's screaming face. His body tilted into his enemy as he drove the onrushers back. After collecting his sword and shield, he fought his way forward, to take his place in the blockade.

Barbarian after barbarian slammed into the defensive wall. Weaponless, armourless, Lucius got in the way of the men surrounding him. The blunt end of a spear sprung into the side of his head. As he grimaced, rubbed and checked his skull, more spears hit him. Their feet stamped on and planted on top of his feet.

The surrounding slaughter reminded Lucius of his father, a centurion like Scipio. On his death bed, dying of malaria, he had told him, 'Give yourself to God, not a general.' His father had remoulded his sword—a three-foot-long Spatha, once the pride of his life—into a half-inch thick crucifix, with a foot-long shaft and half-foot broad arms.

Lucius descended into the woodsmen called "The Abyss of Trees", because of this piece of Roman iron. The thought of his father dying with the weight of his sins on his soul drove him to seek a way of cleansing the burdens. Now, witnessing the hell around him, he understood, *Some sins cannot be washed away.*

Beyond the havoc, a shadowy figure directed the horde to the weakest part of the defences. *That person is organising the Barbarians,* Lucius recognised, *it is their version of Scipio.* As though hearing his thoughts, the organiser's head snapped straight. The glare from eyes he could not see exposed him as the weakest lamb in a flock inspected by wolves. He lifted his cross into the air in an attempt to engage the intelligence.

The enemy's organiser retreated into the deeper shadows. The roar of aggression lowered, and the chaos dimmed as the attack pulled back. For the first time, the defenders caught their breath.

A voice, not civilised, gave instructions.

'Prepare yourself!' Scipio warned.

Barbarians hit the shield wall in an arrowhead thrust. They forced a breach. Hordes of barbarian hands grabbed hold of Lucius. They hauled him away from the mercenaries. Shoved to and fro, flung to the ground, they dragged him through lukewarm blood and mud. He hid behind his arms, expecting to be mauled. When they left him on the ground, he thought, *Why are they standing back?* The sound of fighting continued.

What do you want? He asked.

A wild woman straddled his hips. When she blinked, one colourless eye still looked at him. Lucius clenched his iron, his tongue struggling, attempting to form a prayer. The woman said something with strange words. A wild man rushed past and booted Lucius in the head.

'Jesus Christ!' Lucius implored.

Another ran past, this time connecting a foot to his nose. His eyes rolled. A rush of blood flowed down his face. The woman inspected his crucifix. She blinked. Through the gap of a round hole in her left eyelid, a dead eye, resurrected with moonlight, glared at him with a hunger for his soul. The living eye opened to complete a stare demented by madness.

She grabbed his crucifix. Lucius held it tight. She pulled his hand to his mouth and bit. He tried to push her face away. He wrestled his cross from her hand and drove it into the side of her head.

'HELP ME!' He screamed as he struck her again.

Her mouth let go. A barbarian ran at him. The attacker's leg reared. Lucius braced for the impact. Before the blunt force connected, the wild man's chest pushed out, his arms flung back, and a spear burst through his stomach. After he glimpsed the biggest of Scipio's mercenaries step over him, with his sword hacking at the enemy, Lucius passed out.

***

Sunlight transformed the temperament of the woods. It became warm, windless and pleasant. Lucius' skin tightened and chills caught in his chest as he plunged into the cold shade to drag the body of a man, whose name he could not remember, to the growing heap of the dead.

Underneath the high canopy of the towering trees, nothing lived. No natural sounds indicated life somewhere unseen. No movement disturbed the shadows which thickened into the deepening darkness of the abyss. Even the clouds above passed silently from their origins over the mountains to the east.

The emptiness sharpened yesterday's surprise discovery of human tracks. When the men prepared themselves for conflict,

Lucius believed them to be joking, teasing him. *How could wild people live out here?* He thought. *What are they eating?*

The fifteen bodies they managed to retrieve came to rest in a mass pyre made of broken shields, shattered spears and dead branches. Twenty-eight of Scipio's men remained missing after the battle.

'Why does each mercenary have a sword in their hand?' Lucius questioned Scipio.

'Because in the next place,' the centurion grunted, 'their enemies will be waiting for them.'

Stunned by the answer, Lucius hesitated before proposing, 'I would like to bless them with a prayer.'

'Why bother?' The centurion dismissed the request while igniting the pyre. 'None of them will go to heaven.'

Lucius held a silent vigil while the white smoke from the masses of foliage built upwards. Once the flames became established, whiffs of burning flesh seeped out into the air. None of the men discussed this. They only stepped back.

While reviewing the small part of the territory the men had defended, Lucius tried not to think about the loss of all their carting mules and rations. *The other men must also be hungry*, he thought, *but if they refused to discuss it, neither will I.*

The men retreated to sleep in the shade from shields which were propped against their spears.

Lucius remained to keep vigil. The mercenary who rescued him, Barfant, fuelled the pyre with branches.

'Thank you for helping me last night,' Lucius said.

Barfant's grisly ginger and grey beard embarrassed Lucius' similar aged whiskers.

'Why are you not sleeping, Padre?' Barfant asked while he worked.

Lucius said, 'Last night I dreamt a terrible nightmare. When I awoke, I discovered it to be true...now I hope I never sleep again.'

Barfant stopped his work and smiled but offered no words.

'How come you are not sleeping?' Lucius countered.

'I stand guard.'

But Lucius knew the men did this. He was tired, he forgot. He tried another question. 'Why do you men come to this place?'

'We used to be legionnaires, Padre,' Barfant informed him. 'The legion no longer required us, so we become mercenaries. Then our business became tusk hunters. The pay is good, but this hunt will make us all rich. This beast in these woods is different. He preys only on men. The legionnaires they first sent couldn't track or kill it. These men were lambs. Now they send Scipio and his Tusk-Takers because we are the wolves. If we cannot slay this beast, no men can.'

'You did well last night Padre,' Barfant continued. 'When this is over, you come trophy hunting with us. You become very rich.'

Lucius did not realise he cringed at the thought of more killing. Barfant laughed at him.

I should not be here, the thought ran in a loop around Lucius' mind.

They continued to feed the fire throughout the day. When noon came, and Barfant did not leave to wake a replacement, Lucius understood the mercenary did so to look out for him.

Mid-afternoon, Scipio awoke. The way he measured the sky made it clear the sun sat too close to dusk for his liking.

Corvus returned an hour later. Having trailed the retreating barbarians, he looked exhausted.

'Get ready men.' Barfant, clapping his hands, mustered the others.

'We're surrounded by tribes.' Corvus spoke without permission or even saluting Scipio. 'This morning, they made a feast of our mules and our supplies. Afterwards, a wild woman, a witch of some kind—' Lucius pictured the woman with the halfway eyes. '—Performed a ceremony on our dead. She used a bone to pry open their chests and take out their hearts. She led a group of them to a cave in those mountains.' Corvus pointed east. 'She went inside alone. She...'

'Tell me about the cave?' Scipio interrupted.

'Human hands cut into the mountain to make this place. It is a man-made shape, not natural. Twenty paces in, the cave ends and a hole goes into the ground. How deep? I do not know...'

'Is it the beast's lair?' Scipio asked.

'The witch took buckets inside, filled with offerings. When she and her people left, I went in. I followed a blood trail leading to the hole. When I dropped a torch down the hole, I glimpsed something large and black.'

'Can we smoke it out?'

'With more time and daylight, yes,' Corvus had already considered this. 'But the wild people will come again tonight.' He did not say the words, *and finish us*, but the silence whispered them.

'Can we reach the cave before nightfall?' Lucius interpreted Scipio's question to mean, *Can we at least kill the beast?*

Corvus, assessed the sun, close to setting and answered, 'If we hurry.'

***

Two weeks after they started marching, Scipio and the Tusk Takers came to the end of "The Abyss of Trees". The mountain facing them presented a world of rock and wind. Thick, exploring roots from the woods pushed out into a stone border. A passage between two cliffs led to the cave. The dusk breeze brought a chill to Lucius, rousing the hairs on his neck.

'Forward march.' Scipio whispered his command. The men held their spears and shields in one hand, their torches in the other. They ranked eight at the front, four at the back, including Scipio. Behind them all, holding a torch, Lucius squeezed his crucifix. A trail of blood on the ground led towards the end of the cave. *We should not be here.* He kept this thought to himself, for even if he displayed the courage to say something, the men would not listen. *I am not one of them.*

Scipio paused and patted Corvus on the shoulder, giving the scout the silent instruction to lead the front line on. Each man placed his torch on the ground. One step at a time, the eight men advanced to the end of the cave. They set up a shield wall around the hole and readied their spears.

Scipio elbowed the man next to him. The mercenary exchanged his shield for a torch then approached the line. Transporting the sphere of light over the shields, he peered down while he leaned. His shoulders sprung backward. The torch fell from his hand. A black hand grabbed his head, whipped him through the shields and took him into the hole. The light of the falling torchlight faded alongside the descending scream.

The mercenaries engaged the enemy below. Scipio, Barfant and the man beside them ran forward. A black claw broke through the shield, grabbed its holder's calf and yanked him down into the hole.

'GET BACK, DAMN IT!' Scipio screamed. He gripped one of his men by their collar and heaved him away. 'GET BACK.'

They retreated while facing the danger. Two men fell before being pulled into the hole. The rest made to run away.

'FORM A LINE,' Scipio regained order. 'Right-hand marker, left-hand marker, stay where you are. The rest, pull back one step from the man to your side...MOVE!' He said whilst retreating seven steps.

The line tilted inwards to make a V shape, with Scipio and Barfant in the centre.

'Padre.'

'Yes?'

'Drop your torch in front of me.'

After doing as instructed, Lucius glanced at the hole. Blood spurted out and hit the cave top. Red droplets fell like rain. Scratching, climbing noises ascended over the rippling sound of torch flames fighting the wind.

'Fight for each other!' the centurion encouraged his men.

We should not have come here! Before Lucius did not speak for fear of being ignored, now terror bonded his tongue to the bottom of his mouth.

Hands the size of forearms covered in black fur with pointed, clawed fingers, pressed against the edge of the hole. Stupid with fright, Lucius recoiled, slipped, fell on his back and banged his head.

More paralysed by fear than stunned by the fall, he laid still staring at the firelight on the wall. On it, a silhouette rose out of the ground. Standing erect, it became far bigger and wider than the shadows of the mercenaries. A claw swept away the first man to attack. The silhouettes merged. Blood sprayed everywhere. Flame light flickered. Lucius tried to listen to Scipio's commands, but the centurion's voice became muffled amongst screams and roars of the beast.

When the blur on the wall divided enough to identify the silhouettes, he recognised Corvus. He pressed his spear into the beast's claw, then attempted to push back. The spear snapped. The claw slashed forward. A dying grunt came from the mauled scout.

'BASTARD,' Barfant barked. The shadows showed the big man to be dwarfed by the creature. He threw his weight behind his sword. The beast pushed his blade aside, thumped a claw into his body and lifted him up. The beast's opening muzzle showed long, sharp teeth that plunged into the mercenary's shoulder and neck. Warm blood soaked the floor and ran through Lucius' hair.

Rushed by another mercenary, the beast dropped Barfant. A looping claw slashed up and into its attacker. Thrown to the ground beyond Lucius, the man looked at him with eyes which revealed his panic as they searched for an alternative to dying. His hands ran over the fatal slices in his body. He gasped for breath. Lucius crawled to help him. He grasped his hand. The man gazed at him with fading attention. His eyes stiffened. His breathing stopped.

Too scared to turn, Lucius witnessed the things happening behind him in the hazed reflection of the dead man's eyes. Only one mercenary still lived.

Scipio moved his feet, shield and sword in a rhythmic dance of defiance. By stepping away from the beast's claws, trying only not to be hit, he created an attacking opportunity and slung his sword across with all his weight. Though loaded with the intention of killing the beast, his iron sword may as well have been wood powered into stone.

A claw cut into the centurion. His helmet whipped back. The beast raised him from his feet. Its jaws snapped forward. Scipio's sword stabbed into its mouth. Rebellious laughter filled the cave until the jaws returned. This time, no sword stopped them.

Chapter One.

The rider headed through the darkness, into the wind and rain. A lightning strike exposed fields of crops swirling around him. He checked behind. The next flash showed his trail of horses. In single file, their heads down, they followed the hooves of the horse in front. At their rear, another rider hid from the rain within his hooded cloak. The darkness returned. The thunder growled.

Caught without shelter, the rider and his team suffered in the bitter weather for an hour. The village, his destination, flashed alive. Brought forth from the darkness, it materialised as though from memory. The next glimpse showed the shapes of thatched cottages. Another twenty paces and another sighting revealed the church at the village's centre.

A black and tan hound ran past his horse to beat him to an emerging path. The dog's tail cut through the rain as it wagged. The sound of running water increased. In another burst of the storm's energy, the rider glimpsed the stream that flowed beside the village's muddy footpath.

A crack of illumination showed the village's sole stone building. A three-foot-tall wall surrounded an aged church. The spiritual barrier for the graveyard within added no fortification. Gentle pressure on his reins stopped the rider's mount. Momentary light caused the crucifix on top of the church to cast its shadow over him.

The rear rider trotted through the stream to take the leader's reins and hold his horse still while he dismounted. The front rider stood aside waiting for his team to pass by. After striding over the stream, he walked the pebbled pathway through the graveyard. Another flash of light showed him the silhouette of an elevated mill beyond the church and far wall. He knocked on the church door with four overhand thumps.

'Who is it?' The voice within sounded wary of the night time caller. 'What do you want?

'Fetch Father Monroe,' the rider instructed. 'Tell him his son has returned.'

A muffled conversation took place inside. The door's locking bar slid. Candlelight streamed out of the opening door. A short, stocky, old man rushed to peer up into the rider's hood, 'You're home.'

Instead of inviting his guest inside, Father Monroe stepped outside to embrace him. He squeezed as hard as he could.

'It's good to see you, Father,' the rider said.

'Why are we standing out here?' Father Monroe replied. 'Come in, come in, get yourself out of the storm.'

***

After hanging his hooded cloak, the rider unbuckled his belt, which he wrapped around until his dagger rested next to the sword. While he took off his sheepskin coat, he alternated the weapons between his hands. Next, he kneeled and placed his forehead on his sword. He closed his eyes and whispered, 'May the Lord guide me.' He made a cross with his hand before kissing the engraved brass pommel which showed a man carrying a child across a river. Though bulled for a sheen, scratches and dints distorted the Saint Christopher portrait.

Standing, he handed the weapon to the priest's aide who gazed at it from behind his brown, draping hair. Hid inside the stiff, fleeced scabbard, were three-and-a-half feet of double-edged sharpened steel. Above the black strapped handle—which allowed single- or double-handed use—the hand-and-a-half sword's polished cross-guard there was an etched inscription, "Reap thy Lord's vengeance".

'William!' Father Monroe's agitated voice dragged his aide's attention away from the sword. 'Hang the clothes and fetch something to eat.' The smiling priest shook his head to disregard the incident. 'He is not deaf, he just pretends to be.'

Though he tried to hide his emotions, proud tears welled in Monroe's eyes. Christopher understood, *I have stirred memories of the orphan boy this man raised.* He towered over the priest. The features of his once boyish face had matured, had become chiselled and masculine. His arms, shoulders, back and legs boasted of power.

Pride shamed the priest into burying his eyes into his robes.

Christopher clutched Father Monroe's shoulder.

'You deserve your pride father.' He comforted. 'Without you, I would never have become the man I am now.'

'For six years I have wondered about you.' Monroe's shaky voice expressed emotion. 'My arms are tingling with the joy of seeing my son, standing before me as a man. The strong roots Our Lord gave you have grown well.'

'Having said that,' Monroe continued, 'my correspondents inform me, you have achieved remarkable things. Come...' he nodded his head to indicate towards a door at the far left of the church hall, 'Tell me of your adventures.'

After giving his guest a cup of mead, the priest sat beside a fire. The fish hanging inside the stone chimney reminded Christopher of the Thursdays he spent with his childhood friends, fishing at the river in the valley near Spearhouse forest.

William selected choice pieces of stew from the same cast iron pot Christopher had tended during his time there. Watching the flame light on the walls change shape, he remembered following the fire's flickering as a boy while Monroe read scriptures to him.

'Though I've always wanted to come home,' Christopher explained, 'tis duty which drew me back.'

Light footsteps on the floor switched his attention. William handed him a hot bowl.

'This looks good,' Christopher said. In the glance he gave William, he evaluated the deacon's physical potential by comparing him to himself to at the same age. *He is tall and has a decent range. His shoulders are built from the labour of lifting bags of grain to and fro from the church mill. The sinew of his arms has swelled with strength derived through working the village's surrounding fields. Yes, his body would respond well to training.*

'Can you wait by the door to greet Christopher's squire, Richard, please?' Monroe said dismissing his aide. 'He will be joining us soon.'

A rumbling stirred in the pit of Christopher's stomach. After thanking God for his meal, he asked a question to keep Father Monroe talking while he ate.

'You've done well with the lad, Father,' Christopher said. 'He's far healthier than the boy I brought to you. Tell me, does he ever speak about what happened to him?' He relished the first mouthful of the stew for its warmth alone. With his second bite, he savoured the freshest meat he had enjoyed in days.

'William reminds me of you,' Monroe stated. 'He's got those same strong roots in him. He will blossom into quite the man. But no, I never pushed him for answers about what happened to him, and he has never volunteered them to me.' Monroe lowered his voice, so Christopher understood to keep the information confidential. 'He has trouble sleeping. I catch him sometimes, outside in the graveyard, sleeping in the sunlight. I pretend not to notice. The boy works hard. For that, I owe him respect.'

'I see you have not grown out of your old eating habits.' Monroe changed the subject. 'I remember the time you ate twenty eggs. And the time you ate half a deer.'

'Oh *deer,*' both men said together, 'oh *deer,*' they laughed. *Oh deer*, Christopher thought.

'The boy can read and write,' Father Monroe returned to the previous subject. 'He acts as though he would like to take my place here when I am gone, but he possesses no love for the church. He is more of a physical person, like you. Though he may seem shy, not one visitor is allowed to pass through the village without being pestered for news about you, or the tournaments you compete in.'

Carried away with the excitement of seeing his son returned, the priest lost track of his tongue. 'The boy wants to know when you shall leave for Barbarous...' Monroe stopped himself when he realised what he said. Both men's eyes clashed. Father Monroe grasped Christopher's arm and leaned close to confess a secret. The seriousness that came over his voice conveyed a tone of respect. 'You say you returned because of duty, yet I fear my prayers drew you home. Trouble weighs deep into my heart. But your arrival confirms our Holy Father has granted my request. For in my prayers, I begged him to deliver a champion of the light and behold, he sent me you, the finest of his knights.'

***

'As a child,' Christopher said, 'my hardships became yours. So, it is fitting that as a man, your hardships shall become mine. Please, Father, tell us what troubles you?'

'Men say the Lord's ways are mysterious,' Monroe's smile faded, and his eyes hazed as his mind drifted from the room. 'But so too are the ways of time. I imagine you can all remember your childhoods. For me, trying to recall my youth is like grasping at dreams. I see half-images and hear half-forgotten voices. The only thing I remember...' Though his words stopped, his thoughts seemed to continue. In the absence of his voice, the rain outside grew louder.

'As children, my brother Theodus and I went through a great deal.' Monroe sighed. 'Weeks after our mother died, our father chose to follow her to the grave. Without her, Hell seemed better than life. My grandfather took me and Theodus into his house. He was a wealthy man, religious, wise, but more importantly, very kind. My brother and I basked in his affection. Because tradition decreed our uncle and cousins inherit his lands and title, and because we enjoyed our worship, Grandfather secured for us religious educations.'

The younger men waited in silence while their distant-eyed friend smiled.

'Oh, how I have lost such wonderful years to memory,' he continued. 'When we came of age and finished our education. Grandfather secured the position at this church for me, but Theodus refused the position secured for him. Rather than serve the Lord through the church, he dreamed of preaching the Lord's Word to the poor and needy. We have not spoken since my grandfather's funeral when he told me of his plans to take the Word of God to the people of Barbarous. Though he remains in my daily prayers, a lifetime has passed since we said goodbye.'

Father Monroe stood and left his audience to the sounds of wind and rain beating against the church, and the fire crackling on its feast of wood. He returned carrying three letters. His audience leaned forward.

'Three months ago, after Sunday morning mass, I found a traveller asleep at the back of the church. I woke him with food and drink. A stranger to the village, who walked many a road, for many a day, to get here. He identified himself as an envoy to a monk called Gaston. He sailed for weeks and walked for days to deliver his burden to me. When I opened the box he carried, I discovered these three letters inside.'

'This is the first.' Monroe presented his visitors with a white cloth embroidered with writing. 'Before the envoy left, refusing payment or reward for his task, he told me that this carried the last ramblings of a dying man, recorded on his death bed. What is not noted is that this man named me and the location of this church.'

Christopher held the cloth at arm's length to allow Richard and William a view of it.

'*Call me a soldier of the Word, a bearer of the Eternal Light, who drove Christianity into the forgotten trees of Barbarous.*

In the beginning, we experienced winters of endless ice. Suffering and Death sang the first seasons' songs. Our task is the Word, and we stayed true to it.

When our toils in the virgin soil bore a harvest, we prospered; we reached out to our savage brothers and sisters. Thus, we shared the light.

In exchange for our charity, we became educated in the true meaning of misery.

The light we brought grew too strong. The love we shared awoke a slumbering evil. A creature of darkness. We unleashed the shadow of all fears.

I returned from hell, to seek a champion of the light.'

Christopher and Richard exchanged confused looks. In response, Father Monroe spoke some more, 'I understand the strangeness of this letter. But there is also this,' he passed over another letter.

Christopher read aloud,

'*Monroe, Brother, if my prayers are answered, you are still alive. It is the only hope I have not yet mourned.*

I saw you in a dream, Brother. Your hair reflected time's change. The brown crop of your youth now boasted a white crown of wisdom. It pleases me to believe you are still as strong as you used to be.

In my dream, you told me our brotherhood shall be my salvation. You showed me a weapon you held in your hand. Both a crucifix and a sword shone with white light.

This vision of you brought me a taste of happiness I fear I cannot afford. My prayers have since convinced me to send for your help. The last of our fighting men will brave the night to reach you. He takes with him the last of our hope. May the Lord deliver him.

I pray, do not abandon me, Brother,
Theodus'

Father Monroe said to Christopher. 'From the moment you came to me, I knew the Lord held a purpose for you. I am as certain as I am of the Lord's wrath that you are the weapon of light my brother wrote of. However, a soldier is only a mercenary if he does not believe in the thing he fights for. Therefore, before we go any further, I must ask, "Do you wish to champion this cause?"'

Christopher held out his hand to receive the wax-sealed envelope, addressed to 'Monroe's Champion.'

'I did not open it,' the priest explained, 'because I have no right to.'

William admired Father Monroe's respect for others. Christopher's smile showed he did too. Without hesitation, the knight broke the wax seal. He passed the letter to Richard, who understood to read it aloud.

Champion, I am Brother Gaston, a monk of Saint Constantines monastery, the last outpost of Christianity and civilisation. Beyond our walls lie the forsaken lands of Barbarous, the so-called "Abyss of Trees".

I was twelve years old, in the middle of my schooling, when Theodus' mission took pilgrimage through our gates. Many seasons passed and, eventually, the mission withdrew from our memories. Three nights ago, an old man appeared from the woods and forced us to remember it. He carried many wounds which needed urgent attention, yet he refused aid until I agreed to a letter delivered to Father Monroe. As you now know, I fulfilled my duty.

The man referred to himself as the last knight of Theodus' mission. After I treated his physical wounds, he revealed to me the sickness that plagued his mind. His tale is one of ungodly terrors.

In the beginning, the mission struggled against the weather. Cold and hunger took the first lives. Those who survived, harvested the rich earth. Then they converted the barbarians to true faith. The man's voice trembled as he confessed the path which led the settlers away from their light. Of the sins that turned their children into demons and the dead being refused their graves.

Before I left him, his eyes became taken with fear. They searched the growing shadows of dusk, expecting death itself to emerge. Those who cared for him shaped his last words into the cloth which accompanies this letter. By the end, his mind became lost to terror.

During the night, a flame caught alight inside his room. His tenders told me he cried of ghosts that haunted the night, feasting on the blood of men. They believed he started the fire on purpose.

I instructed my man, who delivered these letters, to await you in the dock town of Ullumber, in a small church administered by Father Mullens. I am told is easy to locate. Once you find Mullens, tell him you seek Ellrick. He will guide you to him. My man is capable. Only when he ensures your safe arrival will I know I have done God's work.

I hope my plans are to your satisfaction. I assure you I constructed them through much-troubled prayer. I am certain it is the Lord's will that I accompany you, and our guide, as you take this journey into darkness. Then at last, may we hope to earn the Lord's forgiveness for our sins.

To Father Monroe's champion,
From his devoted follower,
And loyal servant of Saint Constantines monastery,
Brother Gaston.

Richard finished reading the letter and looked at Christopher. 'What do you think?' he asked.

'I think Theodus needs our help,' the knight answered.

Chapter Two.

The sack of grain weighed heaviest in the swing from the ground to his shoulders. William lifted himself from a squat and charged to the mill's platform. The sack's weight increased as he climbed the four, foot-high steps. The night and rain increased his chance of slipping. He kept one foot planted at all times.

He balanced the sack on a chest-high platform. In a swift rotation, he shifted his hold from his shoulders to his chest before shoving the sack forward to secure it on the deck. Instead of going further around the mill to the ladder, William grabbed the platform, jumped, curled his left leg on the surface and raised himself to his feet. He gripped the sack one-handed, then dragged it inside next to six others.

Back outside, he dropped to the ground and walked around the graveyard wall. While passing the miller's cottage shed, he checked the grain sacks remained covered from the rain. Further around the wall, he glanced at the barn across from the church but saw no sign of activity.

Inside the church, William stamped clogs of mud from his boots into the puddle that settled inside the doorway. Father Monroe slept now after spending most of the night entertaining his guests. More than a spiritual leader, Monroe's authority spread across the church lands, from the river to the south and Spearhouse forest to the north. Two hundred people belonged to his congregation. He collected taxes, in grain from any who used the church's mill, and in wheat, meat, milk, game, fowl, mead, cider, ale and wool from peasants who lived on church lands. What the church demanded they received but from his allocation, he kept nothing. Someone always needed his help, and he always found ways to give it.

To provide for himself and William, Monroe made his living from the skills he learnt as a child. Fluent in Greek and Hebrew, he translated old and eastern orthodox scriptures into Latin and Anglo-Saxon. The skill allowed him to live independently off the generosity of his people. His keen eye for imagery matched with a sensitive hand. He designed beautifully written and illustrated manuals of worship, which he bound in fine leather.

William hated how the priest needed to sell the books, which he poured love into. Every time he did, his father said to him 'The heaven is in the work.' Then he would wink and smile, and William understood the priest's wisdom. For some people, pleasure came from creating fine things rather than owning them.

The first time William sowed wheat during a damp, cold, hazy October, the labourers he worked with made a point of telling him about his adopted father. How during the dark days referred to as "The Burning", when war and horror raped the kingdom of more than its harvest, when a wind of terror drew men away from the village, never to return, the land turned on the people. Father Monroe earned his place as the parish patriarch.

By begging favours from noble relatives and his superiors in the church, he scraped together the funding to build a spiral windmill and to employ an experienced miller. He reorganised his congregation into an effective workforce and motivated their labours by being the first to wake and last to sleep.

One older woman worker told William how Monroe would call out sermons while he worked the fields, netted the rivers and streams, and picked berries. When the wolves of famine circled his congregation, Monroe shepherded his people and saved them from starvation.

William stripped and hung his wet clothes on a rack two metres away from the fire. The warmth from his replacement clothes felt comforting. He poured himself a cup of hot water from a pot hanging from a hook in the chimney and supped. Heat built around the fire until he needed to step back. The dance of shadows from the flame light created the only change within the silence of the church. His head nodded forward into a sleeping position.

Wake up William told himself, shook his head, took a sip of water and rubbed his face. Tiredness, the nightly enemy, caressed his eyes. *There is no escaping it, I have to sleep sometime, but it is better not to wake to darkness.*

From behind the rectory door, he collected the church's broom and brushed both sides of the altar. He then pulled sixteen pews into the swept space before sweeping the floor towards the puddle in front of the entrance.

Opening the door, he brushed the muck and water outside. The wet patch left on the ground afterwards showed goose bumps as prickles of rain landed on it. William checked outside.

Earlier, while bidding courtesy to Monroe's departing guests, he spotted a shape on the wall. In the dark, it looked as if one of the gargoyles that decorated the drains on the roof came to life. Only when it moved within the approaching lantern light did the form of a hound reveal itself.

It should be natural for William to take the church over from Monroe. Despite his education and the guilt of going against the priest's investments of time and effort, the deacon told his father that he did not want to become a priest. Events earlier in his life already shaped his longings.

When he confessed his ambitions, Father Monroe understood, as he always did. He requested only that William stay on at the church until God showed him his purpose.

The next day, a knight, attended confession with Monroe. Intrigued by the man, William followed him to the outskirts of the village. There, the knight sparred with his squire.

He examined the display of aggression. A man attacking another with a sword, then a hammer and then an axe. He recognised how the knight, who displayed genuine power, possessed the ability to pursue whatever ambition he wished. William believed that moment to be God showing him his purpose: and with it, the path to retribution.

***

Christopher stirred to the sound of wind whistling through a wet hole in the barn's wall. *It's not morning yet,* the thought tempted him to return to sleep. Due to his unexpected quest, he needed a head start because his plans for the winter needed to be compressed into a single day.

Beat the sun, the knight forced open eyes which wanted to remain closed, *beat the day.* Christopher stood, dropped his fleece cover, pulled on his leather leggings and boots then strode outside. Though the rain ebbed throughout the night, the wind remained vigorous. While he urinated, the damp wind chilled his naked torso.

Back inside, he finished dressing in the faint moonlight which shone through the open barn door. Over his riding leathers, he wore a thick sheepskin coat. His guard dog, Argus, stretched his legs as he stood. The knight took his sheathed sword from the belt next to his bed and placed its handle in the dog's mouth. The dog walked close to the door, dropped the sword, *Reprobus,* flat to the ground and rested his head on it.

Christopher buckled his belt so that his dagger rested in the middle of his back, next to a purse. Before leaving the barn, he collected one of two wooden training swords.

Lifting his shoulders and tucking his chin into his collar, he looked around at the sleeping village as he walked along its mud path.

In the dark, the underbelly of the scattered clouds shone brighter than anything at ground level. Deep shade curtained the thatched cottages. Christopher's cold feet splashed in the stream which still overflowed because of the dispersed storm.

At the end of the village, the water cut across his path and flowed downhill. The moonlight showed the streams which divided the fields beyond. As a teenager, he used the water trails as routes to his friends who lived outside the village. He spent days running these fields or swimming in the swelled waters. He enjoyed the nostalgia of encountering the landscape of his youth.

Deep into the field, the knight stabbed the air in front of him three times with his training sword. Flicking its handle into his left hand, he repeated the process. Mentally, he pictured one of the six bandits who attacked his camp a year ago, charging at him. He stepped right to evade the phantom's sword while twisting his own towards it. After stabbing the phantom, he dodged the attacks of another man from a different fight. With this phantom slain, his memory replayed another threat.

The view from the peak of the hill beside the village showed faint trees from Spearhouse forest over to the far right. Stubborn and sour, the wind threatened to chill his body should he stop. The knight switched from swordplay to a march. His pace increased to match the emerging light until he reached a jog.

The orange from a rising sun reflected on the river that flowed through the fields into the forest. He visualised three men emerging from the trees. Though far away, he recognised their dirty faces. Predators on a trail they raced each other to discover what prizes the path beside the river might lead them to.

Christopher's first projected memory disappeared. Another began. The shepherd's dog, Marshall, ran past him tracking the predators' departing trail. The shepherd's son Thomas, followed him, the Knight himself, as a fourteen-year-old brought up the trail.

Alive only for a moment, they flushed his heart more than the exercise.

What did I expect? Christopher thought. *I must anticipate encounters with more phantoms for this is the territory of memories; in such landscapes, ghosts are as real as men.*

***

William stood by the door listening to birds, who beginning their labours, whistled to one another. In the still dampness, he witnessed the moment of nature's transformation from night into day until a thin scratch of high-speckled ice discoloured the otherwise clear sky.

Rain flowed from the church drains through the graveyard and into the village stream. Last night's storm defused with nothing more than a distant splash from where it collided with a stream from the field. A muddy road ran beside it. Puddles sat everywhere.

The knight's horses gazed at the barn's surrounding field. *They must be awake*, William thought as he rushed across the road. After leaping over the barnyard's stone wall, he took four strides before a deep growl stopped him. A discomforting knot tied in his stomach. The hound he glimpsed the night before emerged from the barn. Hackles raised along its stooped back. Scars criss-crossed along its snarling muzzle. Blemished skin marked the border of its half-missing left ear. Bold lines along its flank and neck showed many healed cuts.

I've made a big mistake, William thought, he retreated a step. The hound tensed further as his growl boiled over into vicious barks. It presented its jaws with a clear message, 'Move again, and I will attack.' *Get back to the church*, William thought but his legs did not move.

'Argus!' Richard emerged from the barn. The hound's barks simmered to a growl. 'What's wrong with you, lad?' The squire walked around the hound. 'That's William. He's alright.' He stopped, kneeled in front of Argus and stroked his side. They shared a moment before Argus left to inspect the village road. Richard waved William across.

'Don't worry about him, Will,' he explained. 'that's him teasing you. Trust me, if he meant it, you would soon know about it...' Richard lifted his left hand to his mouth and yawned with the whole of his body.

'I woke you up,' William realised. 'I swear, I only wanted to help you with the horses and such.'

Richard finished his yawn by outstretching his arms. 'That's fine.' His voice grew the more he woke. 'I needed an early start anyway. Christopher is visiting an old friend. He intends to hold a feast tonight, so I have lots to prepare.'

'He invited Lord Spearhouse here?' William panicked.

'This feast isn't for the nobility. It's for the village.' The squire's smile widened. 'Christopher grew up here. He understands how much Monroe and his people struggle.' Richard winked. 'Let's just say, they will not struggle so much after our visit.'

The idea of leaving the villages' winter struggles behind almost moved William to tears.

'So...you want to become a squire.' Richard's statement held no questioning, only a casual acknowledgement of the ambition. 'I guess I should make introductions then.' He placed two fingers in his mouth and whistled. A sleek, grey-coated steed emerged from the barn.

'This is Ash, the master's courser. There's a brush inside the barn, on top of the bag closest to the door. If you grab it, you can brush him if you want?'

Brush in hand, William approached the steed's side. *You're nothing but muscle*, he thought.

'Don't go behind his back legs,' Richard warned.

By brushing with one hand and stroking him with the other, William admired the horse's power. 'He's magnificent,' he declared.

'Ash is the best-tempered of all our horses.' Richard said as he ran his hand along the steed's neck. 'Temper is quite important during jousts and mêlées because it allows a rider to keep control.'

'So, Christopher uses Ash for tournaments?'

'Yeah sometimes,' Richard uttered as he stepped away from the horse to look around. A black stallion stood alone at the far side of the barn's field; he nodded at it.

'That is Bucephalus, my master's destrier. His war horse.'

'What's the difference between a courser and a destrier?' William asked.

'Basically, coursers are trained to fight but destriers live to fight,' the squire answered. 'In a race, or for a hunt, I would choose Ash every time. But in a battle, Bucephalus is unsurpassed.'

'He's a warrior then.'

'No, William. He's a bastard,' Richard laughed, 'but he's the master's bastard. The difference is, Ash will do whatever the master orders him to do. Bucephalus will act on his behalf. He kicks, stomps and bites. I swear, he's the only horse I have ever seen head-butt someone.'

William laughed along with the squire. *Is he being serious?* He thought.

'To you, he's just a horse,' Richard continued, 'but to the right person, he's worth more silver than this village can raise in grain, in ten years. A trained destrier can make a knight five times more effective, but only if he is bonded with his steed. That's why Bucephalus doesn't labour like the other horses. His sole purpose is combat. Christopher trains with him daily. If you can, watch them together. You'll notice how well they understand and trust each other.'

Richard read the dream behind William's eyes. 'Do not try to ride him,' he said. 'It takes a knight to ride a destrier. If you insult him by climbing his saddle, he will put you on your arse quicker than you can take his reins.'

'The only mare we have is Shadowless.' Richard pointed out another black horse, close to four others. 'She is the master's palfrey. He rides her when he attends tournaments and such. Her elegance impresses people.'

'What does Christopher care about impressing people?'

'War, jousting, battles, mêlées are a knight's duty,' Richard explained. 'Honour is his reward. A knight cannot hope to have honour if he does not first have respect. Respect is built upon perceptions as much as valour. It is easy for Christopher to show his strength and skill but hard for him to show grace and beauty. That is Shadowless' purpose.'

'You see, most knights inherit some level of respect through their noble titles and family names. Christopher is different. He's built his reputation and honour with his steel, not his blood. What do you know of his origins, William?'

'I have heard stories, but I don't know anything for certain,' William replied.

'After "The Burning"', Richard clarified, 'the church recruited Christopher. In return for the finest training, sword, armour and horses, gold can provide, he pledged himself into the service of the Lord's wrath.

He took his knighted name Christopher in honour of the saint, who he also took as his insignia. As the Lord tasked the saint to carry the weak, so too must my master. His mission is simple; to stand for those who cannot stand for themselves. His pledge is to the church, his devotion is to the poor.

He came from poverty so he will always be one of the people. Now, he is wealthy and wears the finest armour, fights with the finest steel—'

'His sword,' William interrupted.

'He calls his blade Reprobus which is the earthly name of his saint. The blade itself is folded steel. Crafted for the Lord's retribution, it is so sharp the devil himself would fear seeing his reflection in it.'

An education from Father Monroe established a continuous intellectual itch that needed the scratch of information. Unlike scripture, chivalry enthralled William. He intended to ask Richard as many questions as he could. He started with, 'Is Christopher as good as people say he is?'

'Better.' Richard grinned. 'He is the Church's champion. That means he is where he is because of his skill. The noble knights might call him "the bastard knight", but none of them has ever beaten him.'

'What would happen then, if one of them beat Christopher?' William asked.

Richard's lips lost the easy smile that seemed to be his natural expression. 'The church knighted him,' the squire spoke in a slower, more concentrated voice, 'in the belief that he is the warrior chosen by our Lord, God, to pursue his wrath. If he is to be beaten in combat, it can only be through the Will of the Lord, therefore he would have to forfeit his name and his sword.

'If you want to understand anything about my master, William, understand that his sole purpose is to pursue his pledge, to serve the Lord. His victories are the Lord's victories. He doesn't fear death because his life belongs to his Lord. His sole fear is a failure. Now the Lord gave him this quest there is no retreat for him. He will complete the task or die trying.'

Richard changed the subject, and his smile returned. 'The horses over there, near Shadowless, are our rounceys. Like me, they do all the work around here.'

'The two greys, Stormpath and Lunar, are twins. They are fourteen hands tall. The white one is Springly, he's slightly taller. And the brown one is Beck, he's the shortest. All of them are good horses.'

Vocally enjoying rolling around, covering his coat with the various mucks of the village road, Christopher's guard dog drew their attention.

'You must forgive Argus for earlier, Will. He is just passionate about protecting our circle. You can understand that, can't you?'

William nodded as he recognised responsibility for the earlier confrontation. The hound found a post. He scraped his shoulder and side along it.

'He is scratching an old injury,' Richard observed. 'Shall I tell you his story?'

'Yes...please.'

'This town in the south had a problem with dogs running wild on their streets. One of them attacked a child. The villagers recruited a merchant to round up these strays. He starved them, tormented them and then put them in a pit, two at a time.

'In case you're not already aware of this but with blood comes glory, with glory comes gold, and with gold comes greed.'

They strolled across to the barn field's wall, leaned against it and watched the hound.

'The merchant did well from his pit,' Richard continued. 'So when it dried up, he started to steal people's dogs. When they came to take Argus, his master tried to stop them. For that, they gave him their boots and their fists. Caged, Argus could do nothing as the bastards beat his master to death. That same day, they put him into the pit. He did well enough at first. He stayed alive.

'Now, you must understand Will, to survive in that bowel of civilisation is a miracle of savagery. God only knows what horrors he experienced. "The biting fire", they called him. One man told me that Argus made wolves look tame.

'Well, he became the champion of that hellhole. He didn't just fight other dogs though. Sometimes he got hold of his tormentors and made them pay. But that's the true tragedy of his tale. Every time he wrestled himself free and escaped, he returned to the cottage where they took him from. He remained loyal to his old master. Because of that, the merchant and his men knew where to find him. They caught him and brought him back to the pits.

'Our fourth season on the tournament trail. We travelled in the sunshine for two days when out of nowhere a storm struck, forcing us to seek shelter. We spotted a thatched roof. An old cottage. From a distance, it looked abandoned, but when we reached it, we realised we could not enter because Argus stood guard. He greeted us the same way he greeted you earlier. I think his devotion to his dead master touched Christopher. He threw Argus some meat, and for the first, and only time I have ever seen, he backed down.

'Caught in the storm, wet through, with no fire for warmth...I struggled to sleep that night, but I finally managed. When I awoke, it still rained, but I saw we had company.

'Christopher approached the merchant who came to collect Argus. The merchant appeared to have the advantage. Mounted, leading six men afoot, he faced what appeared to be an unarmed, unmounted peasant. The man misread the situation. He dismissed terms. In fact...he leaned down and spat in Christopher's face.'

Richard cringed as he reflected on what the merchant did.

'What happened next?' William pushed.

'Christopher grabbed the fool's collar and yanked him to the turf. He drew the merchant's sword from his horse's saddle before slapping the mount on the arse to send it into the other men.

'The closest man tried to drive his sword into Christopher's chest. He stepped aside, lifted the merchant's broadsword, under the man's arms, and yanked it across. The next man tried an overhand slash. Christopher deflected the attack, bounced his weapon high enough to gather weight and slashed down through the man's wrists.

'I rushed to my feet to join the fight, but that hound,' he pointed at Argus, 'beat me to it. He charged into the rising merchant, took him to the ground and mauled him. That hound comes with fire, Will. If he wanted to hurt you earlier, he would have. While Argus ripped the merchant's throat open, Christopher killed another man. The rest of them ran away.

'After that, we gathered our things and left. We later sold the merchant's weapons, but we kept his horse, called her Shadowless. She wasn't the only new member of our circle. When we rode away that day, Argus came with us.'

***

Christopher followed a river that cut through the field, into the forest then back out into another field. Smoke rose from the shepherd cottage's chimney, but no light escaped through its doors, nor its shut hatches.

An orchard once sat to the south of the home. Pig sheds and a small cattle byre now occupied the area. Beside the river to the north of the cottage, a sole tree remained. The arrows sticking out of the trunk boasted feathers, provided by the flock of geese roaming close to the pigs.

A rusty pan with a ball-ended bone sitting inside rested on the ground. Christopher beat the bone against the metal. The sound rang across the field. A dog barked inside the cottage.

Christopher recalled Marshall's howls that day, fourteen years ago. From half-a-mile away, the hound recognised something was wrong. Crazed, panicked and desperate barks drove the boys home. Two years older, stronger and faster, Thomas beat him to the cottage. The shepherd's son's deep voice screeched with the weakness of encountering horror as he peered through his family's front door.

Thomas Senior lay on his front. Blood seeped from the gashes on his back and side. Thomas dropped to his knees to help his father.

Christopher followed bloody footprints to the rear room of the cottage. Thomas' mother, Lizzie, lay naked, blood smeared down her inner legs. Crimson injustice flowed from the slit in her throat. Thomas' baby brother sat beside her body, screaming. The two boys left him with his dead mother when they realised Thomas' sister, Little Lizzie, was missing.

From behind the cottage, a boy, thirteen years old, whistled. The sound broke Christopher from his memories. With his longbow held in his right hand, the boy waved with his left. Christopher returned the gesture but otherwise continued to wait. The cottage door opened. A barking wolfhound ran towards him. He saw the heckles along the dog's back. *Thank God Argus is not with me*, he thought. The knight knelt with his hands out. The dog approached and licked his fingers.

The boy walked around the cottage, to join a woman who carried a baby in her right arm. Another child walked behind her.

That's the blacksmith's daughter, Willow. Christopher recognised her. *Thomas will treat her better than her father did.*

Willow whispered something to the young man next to her. 'My brother talks about you often.'

Christopher placed his bow on the ground.

'It is a pleasure to finally meet you. I thank you, my Lord, for everything you did that day.'

Christopher smiled and nodded. He understood that day defined a great deal about this family. 'It is good to see you again, Willow.'

'You too, My Lord,' she said. 'Thomas will want to welcome you, but he is out with the flock. Would you wait for him? Ben will fetch him, won't you Ben?'

'Please don't,' Christopher replied. 'Let me find him.' He pointed at the child in her arms and asked, 'Are these your children?'

'Yes.' The joy in her voice along with the happiness in her smile, spread to the visiting knight. *I am glad I came to visit*, he thought.

'This is Christopher,' Willow said, angling her baby for inspection. 'We named him after you, My Lord.'

'I am honoured, thank you.'

'And this is Elizabeth.' As Willow guided the girl from behind her back, Christopher became unsure whether he looked at a living person or a ghost. Although four or five years younger than her aunt "Little Lizzie" on the day her grandparents died, Elizabeth resembled her aunt enough to have been her twin sister.

'Say hello, Sweetheart,' her mother instructed.

'Hello,' the girl braved the word.

'Hello,' Christopher crouched to look her eye to eye, 'I bet they call you Lizzie, don't they?'

The girl nodded.

'I bet you like to sing.'

The girl nodded again.

Her mother spoke for her, 'Her favourite is skipping.'

The knight leaned in and whispered, 'Don't tell anyone, but skipping is my favourite too.'

She giggled. Christopher smiled to disguise his sadness. *If only me and Thomas had returned home sooner,* he reflected.

'Which way is Thomas?' he inquired. Willow and Ben pointed up the river.

'He should be back shortly,' she said. 'I'll make you some breakfast if you like?'

'I have to go back to the village soon. But thank you.' He looked at Ben, 'You shot the arrows into the tree?'

'Yes.'

'Would you give me a demonstration?'

'Of course, My Lord,' Ben collected his bow and took an arrow from his pack. He walked clear of the others and stood facing an open field. Angling his body back as he pulled his bow, he threw his weight forward and released. The arrow flew high and far before diving into the turf three hundred paces away.

'Well, you're better than I am with a bow, and better than your father was,' Christopher acknowledged.

'Thank you, my Lord.'

'The truth is the truth.'

After retrieving his training sword and dagger, Christopher followed Thomas' family to the path beside the river. 'I would like to visit with him alone,' he requested. 'It was a pleasure meeting you all.' He threw his training sword high into the sky, and added, 'farewell.'

As they replied, he bowed and with his hand outstretched, caught his sword, stood straight, slapped his training weapon under his armpit, twirled and walked away. On hearing the children laugh, he pretended to trip to stretch the happiness for them.

He followed the river against the flow to the base of a hill. In his youth, he and Thomas used to race to the top for fun. *I never did beat you,* he thought. Cold and clean, the river water chilled him as he cupped some in his palms and washed his face.

He tapped the flat of his sword against his thigh whilst scoping the ascending path. He urged to run but set off at a jog. When the peak came into view, he responded to the challenge by pushing his legs high and hard. He rejoiced in the deep, rich breaths he sucked in. At the peak, he stopped, panting, toying with his sword, rolling the handle around his hands, swirling it in the air.

Over seventy sheep scattered over the hill and field. *Thomas must be tending several flocks at once.* Away from the sheep, three children practised with bows and arrows. The shepherd slept at the base of the hill. A small barking dog ran at Thomas, who awoke startled. 'SHEPHERD'S SON,' he called.

'CHURCH BOY!' came the reply. Thomas gathered his staff before striding over to greet Christopher. At thirty years old, the shepherd's short hair glistened grey.

'Your hair is as white as your sheep,' Christopher offered his left hand.

'You left all this behind, but you took your cheek with you.' Thomas leaned his staff into his shoulder to take the hand offered, 'I might only have one hand but be careful because it is the better one.'

'I met your family.' Christopher smiled. 'Willow, the blacksmith's daughter...how did you get so lucky?'

'I always wanted to talk to her. Then one day, I visited the village to find her father beating her in the street. So, I stepped in and pummelled him.'

'One-handed?' Christopher queried.

Thomas lifted his arms to show his left hand and his handless right arm. 'Who needs two, anyway? Are you visiting the priest?'

'Yes.'

'How is he?'

'Old...but keeping well.'

'How are you?'

'Good. Though, it is strange, to be back here.'

'I can understand that,' the shepherd agreed, 'but you are a man who does what needs to be done.'

'Are they your boys?' Christopher nodded at the distant archers.

'Two of them are, the other is their cousin.' Thomas glanced at them, but he met his friend's eye as he changed the subject. 'Did my daughter remind you of her?'

'Yes, she did. How about you?'

'I see Lizzie every time I look at her.'

'I am sorry for that.'

'Don't be. She reminds me of my sister. So, I won't forget her.'

'Then she is a blessing.'

'She is, as are my boys, as is my wife...We are friends...what you have done, who you have become, fills me with pride. But I know you, you're here for something, what is it?'

'I came to give you this.' Christopher took a purse from his belt. As he placed it into the shepherd's hand, he reached across and squeezed his forearm.

'Promise me,' he demanded, 'if ever fire lights the horizon you'll take your family and anyone else you hold dear and run. Use the gold in this purse to get you as far as you can in the opposite direction.'

'You think "The Burning" will return?' the shepherd distractedly scanned the horizon for the threat of fire.

'I fear you will soon smell smoke,' the knight answered, 'then yes, fire and destruction shall come, and all those caught in hell's path will burn.'

***

Christopher followed the river back towards Spearhouse forest. Before turning towards the village, he stopped, stripped and waded into the water. A day of exercise and fasting tightened his skin before the flow of the river massaged his muscles with a cold welcome. He cupped the clear water with his hands, poured half into his mouth, and rubbed the rest into his face. Falling backwards, he sat with his chin above the surface. The chilled sensation of his skin faded as his muscles tightened.

He retrieved his training sword from the bank and returned to the waist-deep centre of the water. To test himself, he started with one strong thrust from arm bent to extended. He repeated the motion twice as fast. After four more increases in speed, he hit his peak, and then he thrust and moved in a blur of precision.

To push his endurance he swayed, raised and lowered his elbow as he worked the blade. When his arm burned, he counted one hundred seconds before flicking his sword into his other hand. He repeated the process, switching hands back and forth. His burning muscles became blazes then infernos.

To obey the thoughts of his weapon, he strode forward as though advancing on an enemy, he slashed and hacked to exhaust the last of his energy.

Whereas his steel sword, Reprobus, manifested his pride and his passion, his training sword focused his habits, dedication and discipline. It allowed him to push his body and skills to their limits. This elevated his blessings of talent and inner confidence.

When the fire spread to his lungs, to the point where he could hardly breathe, he brought his sword's hilt to his lips and whispered, 'I am my Lord's weapon.' A bloodless sacrifice, the fire in his breath represented a physical prayer, his way of expressing his dedication.

Outside the water, he used his sheepskin coat to dry himself with, then as a mat to stand on while he dressed: leather leggings, boots then top. After rolling the coat, he tied it with his belt and strapped it to his back to make a scabbard for his training sword, he started a soft jog.

At the base of the hill, behind the village, Christopher could not resist a final test of his fitness. Stepping from his jog into a stride, he powered his way up the steep ground. Avoiding rocks and dips in the turf, he pushed himself to go faster. He treated each step as a better opportunity than the last.

At the peak, he stopped with his head in the air to catch his breath. The sun, leaning towards mid-afternoon, flickered as a flock of geese crossed his vision. Though he intended to view the whole of the valley below, his attention shot beyond the church and its surrounding village to a newly erected tent. Its sheets sported the Spearhouse colours of deep red and rich green. Twelve horses grazed around it. Further still, a horse rode across his view from right to left. *That's a fast courser,* Christopher judged.

At the base of the hill, near the village, Richard rode Ash beside Bucephalus.

If my squire is warming up my Destrier, Christopher thought, *then I'm going to joust.*

A crowd around the church, near to a hundred people, cheered when they spotted Christopher descending the hill. Someone ran from the village towards the Spearhouse tent. Twelve nobles emerged. A messenger rode from the tent. The horse approached the villagers at pace, forcing them to move aside. Richard met the rider.

Excited to spot Christopher, Bucephalus pulled clear of Richard and trotted towards his master. The knight measured what his steed's movements indicated. *Mud is splattered up the horse's legs, so surely the ground is soft from the storms.* He held up his hand. Bucephalus slowed to a walk and pushed his neck against the open palm. The horse stopped when Christopher's fingers began to bend back and forth.

'My Lord,' William said as he ran across to him, 'another knight has challenged you.'

'He already knows,' Richard interjected as he rode past him at a canter. The squire wore a creased silver surcoat with his master's Saint Christopher insignia in the centre, over his leathers.

'Lord Spearhouse has no male heir,' Christopher said without looking away from his horse, 'so who is he?'

'No one from the tournaments,' the squire said. 'William informed me this knight, Sir Oakhill, is a suitor of Spearhouse's daughter, Lady Annabelle.'

'Is my armour ready?' Christopher directed the incoming information to relevance.

'It's in the stable, ready for fitting,' Richard replied. 'Oakhill sent a man to inspect our horses.'

'He wants to make a bet?'

'He's riding a courser—'

'A fast courser,' Christopher overtook Richard's sentence. 'A horse he brought for hunting in Spearhouse's forest, but which he could use if an opportunity for a joust came along.'

Richard laughed as he replied, 'What's the betting he has no idea who you are?'

'Who either of us is, is of little matter to me.' Christopher shrugged. 'Come, let's get ready.'

Walking beside Bucephalus, he waved William closer.

'What do you know about this knight, William?' Christopher measured his horse's imprints in the turf. After a silent moment, he realised the young man waited for permission to speak. The knight gave it with a nod of his head and a lift of his eyebrows.

'He is the second son of house Oakhill.' Christopher did not know the name. 'They are said to have vast wealth and lands. Lord Spearhouse is happy with the match for his daughter.'

Christopher focussed the conversation. 'How long has Oakhill been a guest of Lord Spearhouse?'

'They celebrated his arrival with a mid-summer feast, two months past,' William replied. 'People say Oakhill is waiting for a shipment that contains an extravagant wedding gift for Lord Spearhouse before he weds Lady Annabelle.' Licking his lips, William anticipated further questions.

The younger man's nervous excitement reminded Christopher of the time he and Thomas returned to the shepherd's cottage to find two boys waiting for them. Thomas recognised trouble. He tied his hound, Marshall, to a tree. Christopher felt then how William looked now.

The two pairs of boys met each other one on one. When, without a word, one of the boys smacked him in the face, Christopher lunged forward, driving his head into his opponent's. The boy grabbed his collar. He grabbed the boy's collar. Toe to toe, like stags, they punched it out. Older and stronger, the boy threw harder punches. Christopher held on and punched.

Afterwards, uncertain what happened, who won, who lost, he laughed at his bruised and bleeding face. A week later, the boys returned. The ones who hadn't fought each other the week before sparred off. Thomas and Christopher never fought each other. But the following week, the other two did. He never saw them after that.

'Why do you think Sir Oakhill has challenged me?' Christopher tested William as they approached the village. The crowd parted to let them through.

'He wants to impress Lord Spearhouse by putting on a show.'

The knight's attention shifted. Ahead of him, a clear view opened along the path. Behind the tourney line, Sir Oakhill waited on his chestnut mount. His polished, black armour reflected light from the heat it collected. White streaks slashed across his chest plate, like lightning in the night. Despite the distance, and the helmet hiding Oakhill's face, Christopher met the heat coming from Sir Oakhill's stare, with a fiery glare of his own.

***

Richard showed William how to strap Christopher's steel plates onto his quilted padding. A single, six-inch wide golden Saint Christopher engraved into the centre of the breastplate made the completed armour's sole decoration.

While Christopher tested his manoeuvrability, the squire highlighted the uniqueness of Bucephalus' saddle.

'Destrier saddles are designed for fighting more than riding. See the higher pommel and stabilising bar across its front?' he pointed. 'You need one of them if you're riding at speed into a wooden fist and you want to stay seated.'

'Let's go then,' Christopher prompted his squire.

Richard took Bucephalus by the reins and guided him out of the barn towards the crowd. He lifted his arm and goaded them to cheer. They erupted. Christopher enjoyed their reaction and laughed to himself. *A home crowd for a change*, he thought.

His horse responded positively to the noise; lifted his legs higher and strutted as he walked. Once they passed through the cheers they came to Father Monroe, who smiled nervously.

'A quick prayer, Father.' Christopher winked.

When the knight kneeled, Father Monroe slapped his hand onto the knight's head and shouted, 'GOD-BLESS THIS MAN.' The crowd laughed and roared again. When he rose, the priest winked and then patted him on his back.

Bucephalus stamped his feet and waved his head. *You're excited aren't you*, his rider thought.

'There's no need for you to herald me,' Christopher said. Richard nodded. The two paused. Puzzled, the squire made a show of searching for something.

'What's that sound?' he asked. Christopher twisted his ear towards the wind, as though listening to something approaching on the horizon.

Richard recognised the noise. 'It sounds like battle,' he said.

'Like what?' Christopher quipped.

'LIKE BATTLE.'

'What's it saying?'

'It's calling your name. CHRISTOPHER, CHRISTOPHER...it shouts.'

Christopher lifted himself onto his saddle, 'Then I must not keep it waiting.' He loosely gripped reins to direct his steed into a trot. In the privacy of his cross to the tourney line, Christopher recognised his horse's excitement, its energy waiting for the whisper of release. *Bucephalus*, he thought, *you are a beast with a purpose and the will to pursue it.*

The knight ignored what the destrier told him and examined what he showed him. The mud on his legs and the delay in his steps indicated the ground was too soft for jousting.

He straightened and rode beside the tourney line for the last ten of its hundred paces. At Sir Oakhill's starting point a boy, around twelve years old, stood ceremoniously with his elbows planked into his side. He gripped his master's joust with one hand and rested its shaft on his shoulder. White lines ran along Oakhill's black-stained, fourteen-foot-long lance.

A snarling wolf's head decorated the squire's surcoat. Over the original stitching, a white scar cut from the wolf's lip to its upper cheek. Like the name Oakhill, this insignia meant nothing to Christopher.

Sir Oakhill stood between him and the Lord's open-sided tent. Lord Spearhouse and his family, a wife and four daughters, and two other noble families sat inside. Sir Oakhill flicked his hand. His herald approached Christopher. They met within earshot of the nobles.

Oakhill sported new armour, likely fashioned for his visit with Lord Spearhouse. Water used to cool the wearer, ran off its sleek, untested surface. The lower half of his helmet sat open. Clouds of hot air dispersed around his mouth. A white scar ran from a triangular rip in the right side of his upper lip through his trimmed, jet-black beard. The gap in his lip highlighted his upper canine.

'Sir Knight, my master, Sir Oakhill invites you to a gentleman's game,' the herald pronounced in a clear, southern accent. 'He asks only that you are of the brotherhood of honour. If that is so, do you accept his challenge to a jousting contest?'

The knight's insignia and name meant nothing to Christopher; his scar, however, did. At tournaments, between jousts and during delays, bards entertained the crowds. Though each bard told them differently, they all recited the same stories. Christopher knew each one. Oakhill's scar reminded him of the tale of Blacktooth, "the scarred and barred".

A promising, handsome young knight, Blacktooth fell in love with a lady whose husband warred overseas. The two courted in secret. When the husband returned and discovered them, he challenged Blacktooth to a duel. After bettering him, Blacktooth became mad with passion and beat the husband to death.

Ashamed of her part, Blacktooth's lover attacked him with her husband's sword. After scarring the lips which seduced her, she threw herself upon the weapon, preferring to die for guilt than to live with shame. For his part in the affair, Blacktooth was banished from the tournaments and branded with the name "the scarred and barred".

Each bard embellished the story in their way. Some said Blacktooth wandered in the wild wearing a cloak made from the fur of lone wolves. Others portrayed him as an outlaw who stole newly-wed maids on their wedding nights. One bard, Christopher remembered, swore to have been at the duel itself. He described Blacktooth's scar as a triangular cut to his upper lip, a slash that ran through his short-cut, jet-black beard. Every story highlighted the knight's black armour.

I hope you are Blacktooth, Christopher thought, *and I hope you are as skilled a challenger as the bards promised.* He lifted his hand to save the waiting herald from repeating his question.

'I am of the brotherhood,' he shouted for Lord Spearhouse and the other nobles' benefit, 'and shall accept your master's challenge, providing he offers satisfactory terms.'

The herald echoed his volume. 'My master wishes for you to wager your black palfrey.'

Surprised to hear the bet being offered before battle rules, the knight thought, *you ignored a destrier and courser of higher value. I see your purpose. You wish to win Shadowless as a trophy for your betrothed. I bet you already promised her the horse. Then you have put yourself at my mercy, I may ask what I will of you.*

'Would your master stake the steed he is now riding against it?'

'My master generously proposes two fine rounceys as a counter-wager.'

Christopher lowered his negotiating hand. *Oakhill cannot refuse me. It would make him appear weak before the other nobles.* He directed himself at Oakhill. 'Either we deal on that horse, or I shall refuse your challenge on the grounds of an uneven wager.'

Oakhill conceded with a nod.

'Then it is a deal,' the herald said. *Still, no rules have been negotiated,* Christopher thought about raising the fact but decided against having rules in this engagement. *If the fighting gets dirty, then you will fall even further into my hands.*

He rode twelve paces forwards to stop beside his rival. Both faced the nobility. Lord Spearhouse might have recognised him had he not been admiring his horse.

'My Lords, my Ladies,' Oakhill's herald called, 'thank you for your attendance and your patience. It is Sir Oakhill's pleasure for you to bear witness to his war skills. He dedicates his upcoming triumph to his host, Lord Spearhouse's daughter, Lady Annabelle.' A red-haired maiden's cheeks flushed with embarrassment.

'It is your beauty,' the herald continued, 'that inspires my Lord. He declares that you are fairer than a summer's sky filled with clouds of rose petals. For you, his lady, he shall win his opponent's black mare.'

Christopher made his declaration brief. 'The steed Sir Oakhill now rides shall be won for the glory of our Lord, God.' Without as much as a peek at their reactions, he turned and rode away.

He took to the left of the jousting line, the side Bucephalus would charge in a moment, and he took his time. He wanted his steed to feel familiar with the soft turf. Wanted to check the ground for bumps or weaknesses.

Halfway along the line, he peered back at his opponent. Oakhill's steed paced back and forth, one instruction away from explosion. The show of frustration pleased Christopher.

Richard waited at his end of the tourney line. He held his master's lance in the same manner as Sir Oakhill's squire but the knight's helmet sat hooked over its tip. Christopher placed the helmet over his head, facing between his neck and left shoulder. With a twist, its locking pins gripped in. While his mount moved in position, he connected the two sections of his helmet into one. A hollow, golden-rimmed crucifix created a looking hole. Inside, steel wire guarded his eyes.

Christopher gripped his lance. He considered his half of the tourney and mentally marked out his actions in ten pace sections. Beneath him, Bucephalus shivered with anticipation. Christopher took a deep breath as he switched his attention across the rope to his challenger. He raised his lance into the air. Oakhill mirrored the motion in reply. The black knight lowered his lance horizontally as he spurred his horse into a full gallop. Christopher demanded calm from Bucephalus whose muscles tensed as he wished to charge. He started his steed at a walk.

By ten paces, Oakhill's horse hit full speed, his lance's tip aimed at its target. Bucephalus stepped up from a walk to a trot and built towards a steady canter. By the time he reached ten paces, Oakhill approached thirty. Unlike his destrier, the Church knight felt no desire to prove a point and outmatch his opponent's speed. Almost lazily, he dropped his joust horizontally and assumed a crouched position.

By twenty paces, Bucephalus reached the calculated speed of two-thirds slower than Oakhill's courser, which now powered past the halfway mark. Too fast to slow down, the horse's hooves hardly touched the soft ground. The destriers hardly left it.

With only ten paces between them, the barred and scarred knight roared, leant forward, his visor, like his joust, pointed at the centre of Christopher's helmet.

At five paces distance between them, the courser's hooves thundered above all other noises.

At two paces, Christopher's lance tilted from his opponent's head to the centre of his body.

With only a breath before impact, Christopher recognised his horse's feet stood firm, in the correct position. He dipped his head inwards. Before the tip of his enemy's weapon could follow, the waiting power of a lance collided with Oakhill's chest plate. His swift horse sprung sideways. A cheer came from the village.

Rather than check his success, Christopher concentrated on using the remaining ground to steady his steed into a trot, then a walk. As he neared the end of the tourney line, Lord Spearhouse and the other nobles approached.

'The ground is too soft,' a nobleman protested.

'This was an unsporting contest,' a woman challenged.

I beat your man, Christopher stopped himself from boasting, turned and headed along Oakhill's line of charge.

'IT WAS POORLY DONE,' one called after him.

Christopher took his time to reach his fallen foe. To his relief, the horse he wagered for regained its feet and stood near its rider. Oakhill, turned over, onto his knees, and tried to regain his breath. Richard approached, knelt beside the fallen knight and offered help,

'Would you like me to loosen your plates, my Lord?'

Oakhill lifted his hand and shook it to reject the offer. The nobles, who pursued Christopher, appeared more interested in challenging him than helping Oakhill.

'Lords, ladies...' distorted by a snarl as much as his helmet's added bass, Christopher's voice silenced the crowd. 'You are correct. This contest was poorly made. Sir Oakhill rode bravely but the ground was unsuitable. The wager no longer stands.'

He ushered Bucephalus away from the nobles. The cheers he heard at the crashing of his lance came from the villagers. *The victory for these people, my people, is reward enough.*

'You did well good friend.' He talked to the horse as he stroked its neck.

Before leaving the battlefield, he checked the fallen knight. Oakhill's betrothed, Lady Annabelle, knelt in the mud beside him, matching his pain with her tearful emotions.

Christopher closed his eyes, bowed his head, and laid his palms against the golden Saint Christopher engraved into his chest plate.

'I am my Lord's weapon,' he prayed, 'My victories are his. There is no glory but the Lord's glory. My life is my Lord's life. My soul is my Lord's soul. There is no destiny, only God's will, and man's desire to see it done. Amen.'

***

Christopher emerged from the barn wearing his riding leathers and a surcoat stitched with his insignia. Another surcoat rested tucked into his belt. The crowd clapped and cheered. Richard passed him a cup. Christopher climbed onto the barn field's wall.

'I've been away for a long time,' his announcement silenced the crowd, 'I nearly forgot my good fortune to be raised here amongst you all. May I have a drink to that?' The knight led the crowd by taking a swig of the mead, which Father Monroe provided. 'Now, I understand that the church is reasonable with its taxes.'

'THAT IT IS, MY LORD.' Michael Jacob, who lived on a church farm a mile to the west of the village, called. Two of his brothers stood beside him, nodding. In his youth, Christopher worked with these men in the fields.

'I must inform you all of an important change.' Whispers spread amongst the crowd. 'A knight recently purchased the land you live on. Unfortunately, due to his commitments, he won't be able to govern the land himself, so the church authorities assigned a bishop to the task of collecting and managing your taxes.'

Christopher allowed the crowd to confer.

'It is my honour,' he began again, 'to introduce you to that bishop.'

Father Monroe looked behind the wall, then both entrances to the village.

'Bishop Monroe,' Christopher smiled and pointed at the old man as he proclaimed, 'serves this community with the utmost—' An eruption of cheers interrupted his speech as half of the newly commissioned Bishop's mead sprayed into the air. The old man's congregation massed around him, like children around a returning parent. Christopher abandoned the speech he planned as the emotions within the village expressed more than his words could.

Monroe stretched his neck, tried to lift his head from the excitement and say something, but his emotions affected the flow of his words. As a priest, Monroe always helped his people. As a Bishop, he possessed the ability to improve their lives. *This is a glimpse of heaven*, his adopted father's joy warmed Christopher's soul.

Christopher noticed Sir Oakhill waiting with his courser at the peak of a hill on the horizon.

'Let's have some food, some drink and a good time,' he said. 'Here's to homecomings, and Monroe, our father and BISHOP.'

Like the amen at the end of a prayer, the crowd echoed his last words. 'To Monroe, our father and our Bishop.' They shouted then drained the remaining mead from their cups.

When the knight dropped from the wall, the crowd swarmed him. Women and children wrestled with each other to get close to him. Men grabbed and shook his hand. Others called his name. He smiled, gave polite bows and promised each person an audience later. While he waded through the crowd someone rustled his hair.

'You got big,' said Shaun, the man who taught him how to fish.

'I know,' he replied as he reached across to grab and shake his hand. 'I have some business to attend to, but I will find you afterwards.'

'I will be near the ale.'

'That would've been the first place I looked.' They laughed. Christopher continued through the villagers.

William waited for him with Shadowless at the barn's wall. The mare approached her master. Before collecting her reins, the knight stroked her neck and inspected her face. Though he showed no sadness, it burnt in his heart as he led the mare to the hill.

A man of dark features, Oakhill's eyebrows made two thick, bushy lines above his eyes only one shade lighter than black. His shoulder-length hair sat untidy from sweat. The white speck of his exposed tooth shone from inside his black beard.

'This talk about the unfair ground is embarrassing,' Oakhill grimaced. 'You won the horse fairly, he is yours.'

'I only keep seven mounts,' Christopher retorted. 'Since you have proven your honour, give me your word you shall take care of this mare, and she will be yours.'

'I give you my word.' The two knights approached, arms reached, three paces before they met. 'I did not lose through bad technique,' Oakhill said, 'but poor strategy.'

All nobles are the same, Christopher thought, *they blame themselves, rather than credit someone else*. He nodded. After gripping each other's forearms, they exchanged reins.

'If you ever want to win your horse back,' Christopher said, 'we will wager on that mare.'

Leading the courser away, he presented a rein to William. When the youth tried to take it, he held it tight. 'I talked to Father Monroe about you last night. He thinks you would be happier in my service than in his?'

'I love Father Monroe, but...'

'Nobody's questioning your devotion to him, William,' the knight interrupted. 'Remember, I once left him too, I know how hard it is. But he'd be the first to remind you of the responsibility you have to yourself. You must seek out your path. That's why he's asked me to take you. He knows I am heading into danger, but he believes in you. Now, what do you want to do?'

'I would like to join your service, my Lord.'

'Very well.' Christopher passed him the spare surcoat from his belt. 'Now...I'll give you a trial because of my love for Monroe. You'll start as a page, but if you want to be a squire, you need to work hard and impress me. If you don't, I won't hesitate to send you back. Do you understand?'

'Yes, my lord.'

Christopher's eyes tightened as he examined the sincerity of the answer.

'Then we have a deal.' They walked ten more paces before the Page said,

'My lord...'

'Yes?'

'How come you gave Sir Oakhill your horse?'

'Shadowless served me well. She deserves better than what lies ahead. I believe Sir Oakhill's betrothed will treat her kindly. Anyway, while we're talking about horses, how do you ride?'

'Well,' William declared with a convincing confidence.

'Then I'm going to give this horse to you.' Tears sat over William's eyes as he struggled to control his gratitude. 'It is my gift to welcome you into my service. As you'll be riding him every day, I'll expect your skills to improve. Treat him with respect. Learn to listen to him, but above all, make sure you take charge of him.'

'I will.'

Richard, Christopher's squire, was ready to move on and become a knight. If William, already too old to be a page, wanted his position, he needed to learn fast, otherwise, Christopher would be forced to recruit someone else.

Taking charge of the horse would be a good start. The courser possessed pace and ability. He symbolised the standard his rider should aspire to. The responsibility sat twofold. Christopher placed an equal amount of trust in the courser. *Should we encounter danger in Barbarous,* he thought as he caught the horse's eye, *it is your responsibility to protect your rider, to use your pace and outrun any harm.*

Chapter Three.

The boy's teeth rattled. His body shook. Tears followed frozen trails down his cheeks. Tiredness, hunger and emptiness attacked from inside his body, like birds trying to escape the prison of his bones.

CRUNCH...CRUNCH, his feet shouted every time he stepped into the snow. The boy feared the sounds. They disturbed the stillness of the forest.

Greedy, thick light ahead burned orange and bright. A stranger's thoughts circled the boy's mind. They tried to talk to him, to warn him, but they could not form words.

CRUNCH...CRUNCH. He continued. A village of enflamed cottages disintegrated into masses of ash. Black streams of smoke faded to grey as they ascended into the snow clouds. Thatch roofs crackled. Timbers snapped and hissed. Walls bellowed and collapsed.

Scared, and on the verge of panic, he remembered his father telling him to always be a brave boy. Brave boys do not panic. The stranger's thoughts circled his head: formless, voiceless, unable to help, they added confusion to the child's fears.

'Mum...!' he called with the desperation of a lost fox cub calling for its mother 'Mum...'

The sounds of the fires stopped. The boy tried to ignore the rattle of his teeth. The flames appeared to scrutinize him. 'Mum...Mum!' he called in a challenge to the silence. A scream came from a cottage. His home. Stones blocked its doorway. The scream came again, this time it called a name... 'William!'His mother's voice seemed stretched by desperation, agony and terror.

'Mum...' He wept, 'Mum...!'*I have to be brave for her.* The words within the boy's mind aggravated the stranger's thoughts, which circled his head. They wanted his voice.

CRUNCH...the boy's legs found bravery and began to walk, CRUNCH.

The boy's feet grew heavier with each step. CRUNCH...CRUNCH.

He sank deeper and deeper into the snow. His heels descended then his calves, then his knees until he waded forward. The ground became flat. The circling thoughts grew more aggravated, more alarmed. The boy forced his left leg ahead. When he placed his weight forward, something snapped. A flow began to rise around his heel, up to his calf and towards his thigh. The boy looked down. The snow brightened into pink then red. Released from their cage, the stranger's thoughts screamed a word: 'NO!'

Panic seized the boy. As he tried to scamper back, the sheet of ice he stood on collapsed. CRUNCH—the boy's upper body smacked against the snow. Screaming, he plunged into the icy blood. Red slush gushed into his mouth. He choked. When air left his body, none returned. The boy tried to struggle. He tried to escape. The more he kicked, the more his numb feet dragged him down, to the deepest, darkest red.

Breathe, I have to breathe. Breathe. Breathe.

The hand of death covered William's mouth. When he opened his lips, the hand worked its way down his throat. He gasped for air but the hand squeezed tighter. It let go as sharp coughs brought him out of the pit of blood and into a dark room. He looked around, searching for help. Red embers burned within a cage, outside the door. They meant something to him.

I fell asleep, he scolded himself, *why did I do that? No wonder the dream came. It's my fault. Breathe...I can breathe.* Another surge of air into his lungs made him choke. Not wanting to wake the knight nor the squire, he rushed from his covers, outside into the barnyard, and coughed.

William focused on the bright stars as he breathed in the fresh air with a thirst for oxygen only his nightmare could induce. After emptying his bladder, he fetched some logs from the barn to revive the embers and make the fire into a beacon, to see him through the night. The day would not start for hours. He sat watching the fire, trying to let its brief, fierce life take away his thoughts.

The death song of the logs, their crackle and pops, attracted Christopher's guard dog. He entered the light, his eyes fixed on William.

He's been waiting to get me alone, William feared, *and now he's going to kill me.*

Argus' head dipped then swung up. William lurched back and raised his forearm. A wet bone dropped on his lap. Argus lifted his head and stamped his feet, once, twice and a third time with a soft growl. William picked up the bone and held it out. The hound chewed on it. William's nerves settled. Growing brave, he placed his palm on the dog's side. The continued chewing encouraged him to lift his hand to Argus' shoulder. He stroked down his flank, over tuffs where hair gave way to scars.

To the hound, the boy was someone to hold his bone. But to the boy, the hound was a much-needed companion in a dark hour. The feelings of loneliness and vulnerability that marked William's waking moments slipped away easier than usual, as though the guard dog scared them off. Letting go of the bone, William embraced Argus. When the hound's head jerked, the page realised his mistake.

He's going to rip my face off. He closed his eyes and grimaced. The hound's tongue scraped up his chin and cheek in a moment of mutual affection that thawed some of the red snow from William's soul.

***

The cockerel's first call stirred William from staring into the fire. Richard walked out of the barn as the bird bellowed a second time. Facing away from him, breaking the body's first need, that of the bladder, the squire said over his shoulder, 'From now on, you're going to learn to do things our way. When you've mastered your duties, we'll start your training. So, work hard, and learn fast. Okay?' Richard belted his leather leggings. 'Let's get started.'

Returning to the barn, he collected the horses one at a time. While he led them outside, William followed, carrying their saddles. They brushed each horse before preparing them for the road. Once set, the mounts received feed bags. Richard and William joined Christopher, who prepared a breakfast of mutton, mushrooms, buttered toast and hard-boiled eggs.

They walked their horses east towards a dawning sun that bridged the horizon.

'Morning,' the miller, lively despite the previous night's drunkenness, called from beside his cottage. Richard raised his hand and nodded.

The church door opened at a push. Flour footprints led back and forth from the rectory attached to the church hall. This mess, and that around the bread oven attached to the flour trail, would have been cleaned away if William stayed here last night. *After everything Monroe's done for me, I'm going to abandon him,* he thought. *I should stay and look after him.*

Bishop Monroe sat on the front pew, praying.

'We came to say goodbye,' Christopher said. Used to hearing Monroe expressing his mind, William found his silence much more meaningful.

'I'm sorry we can't stay any longer,' Christopher continued.

'Not until midday at least?' Monroe requested.

'We can't spare the time, Father. It's a two-day ride to Ullumber. We must find this man, Ellrick, and get to sea before the season changes. I am sorry to be leaving so soon, but it has been good to see you.'

'And you.' Monroe glanced at William. This tested the page's emotions. He caught them in a breath and held them down. 'I waited so long for this visit. It went by too fast. I thanked you for a thousand things in the past few days, but I never said thank you for visiting. It means everything to me. God gave me the best sons anyone could ask for.' Monroe embraced Christopher. 'Please, let me give you all a blessing?' he asked as he let his son go.

When Christopher kneeled, his squire and page joined him. William did not look at Father Monroe. He knew, if he did, he would break. *I cannot let them see me cry*, he told himself.

'You know my Lord,' Monroe held his hands together, 'how I question the ruthlessness of this world. How I questioned the suffering of man. How I do not understand why some have plenty, and some have little. I pray that the men before me are your answer to my questions.'

'I pray for this because their strength is humble, and it is pure.

'I pray my Lord, that my belief, that what I see in these men, is your will; vested in flesh, is true. Bless them my Lord and thereby bless the people and the earth that lies outside of your light. Let them deliver your justice. Be the strength in their soul. Be with them, when they step out of your kingdom. For you are the power, the glory and the one truth. Amen.'

The blessing reminded William of a conversation he held with Father Monroe when he decided that he did not want to become a priest.

'There are many paths you can walk, William,' Monroe told him. 'Only one will make you happy. That is the path of your heart. It is no one else's place to tell you what that is. You must discover that path. It is your responsibility to pursue it, no matter where it takes you.'

As Christopher stood to leave, William realised, *this is the start of my path.* The thought provoked a confusion of emotions; excitement but also guilt and sadness.

Bishop Monroe escorted Christopher outside, along the graveyard path, through the archway and along the village road to the white rouncey, Springly. A line tied Bucephalus to his master's saddle. Father and son talked privately. Both displayed happiness for having their reunion. After another embrace, Monroe approached Richard. Stood beside Stormpath, the squire held a line attaching Ash to his saddle. Finally, the priest approached his last adopted son. While William embraced the man at the centre of his world for as long as he could remember, the other horses started to walk away.

'Your path is waiting,' Monroe said. Tears threatened. William nodded and climbed onto his horse.

'Thank you, Father, for everything.' The words released the tears from William's eyes.

'Listen to me.' Monroe's words freed his tears too but he focused his strength on his voice. 'I have absolute faith in you. You are strong enough for anything the world can throw at you. Listen to Christopher and Richard, they will make sure you stay on a true path. But promise me, man to man, if there comes a time when you have to fight, you will do everything you must to survive.'

William's horse began to follow the others. He turned his head to keep his father's eyes. 'I will,' he promised.

'You better,' the bishop replied. 'Now wipe your tears before you catch up with the others.'

Before he wiped his eyes, William ensured the old man understood how much he meant to him. 'I love you, Father.'

'I know you do,' Monroe's wet eyes winced. 'I love you too.'

No one told the villagers about the early departure. Those already going about their morning routines stopped to watch the departing horses. Some children ran behind them. William's horse followed the others. This freed him to peer over his shoulder at the only world he ever knew. When the church and Bishop Monroe disappeared, he turned around to take in the path ahead.

***

Beyond the wheat fields, the soft soil toughened and dried as the path changed to match the new surroundings. The passage led into a forest defined by deepening green leaves on the cusp of fading into autumn brown. The near silence of the wind rushing over fields became the soft charms of birdsong captured by dense trees.

William rode at the rear of Christopher's trail. The steady ride extended for hours. The day began to take a physical toll. His backside and thighs numbed.

In the mid-afternoon, the trail cut into a larger, thicker track. Here a crack cut through the tree canopy overhead and more light shone below. Richard steered his horse aside to wait for him, and said, 'This road connects the dock town, Ullumber, to the east, and the market town, Golby, to the west. Keep an eye on the road behind you. If you see anyone, let me know. Yes?'

William's nod satisfied the squire. Richard rode ahead. An hour later, the horses in front stopped. Richard approached on foot.

'There's no need for a fire tonight, William.'

When the page dropped from his horse, the squire passed him two breadcakes stuffed with lamb and a beaker topped with mead.

'After this,' Richard continued, 'we'll tend the horses. How have you found your first day?'

'Tiring.'

'You'll get used to that.' Richard both ate and elaborated with his hands. 'Tomorrow, ride upfront with me and Chris. Ask questions, pay attention, learn. Have you thought of a name for your horse yet?'

No, but I've tried to, William thought, *I sound like a child,' I* talk to him and stroke him, but he doesn't respond.' The horse needed little guidance and reacted to every command efficiently. Though William admired the steed, he did not feel any emotional connection.

'Don't worry about that for now,' Richard reassured. 'You'll learn his name when he decides to tell you it.'

The mead made a stronger impression on William than the food and a dizziness distracted him as he helped Richard to unsaddle and brush down the horses.

Christopher took Bucephalus for a run along the road. While they waited for him to return, William helped Richard dress in chain mail. Though excited to watch his masters' sparring session, the toll of the day weighed heavy on the page. He sat down, and without any of his usually vigorous resistance, fell asleep.

***

Breathe, I have to breathe. Breathe. Breathe... William rolled onto his side and tried to cough the fluid from his chest. *I'm drowning; I need to spit it out.*

Still tired when he sat up, his body wanted sleep, but his racing mind threatened further punishment if he did. He stood hoping for a chill to assist his waking. Steam evaporated from his chest, but no chill came. He walked to a tree and measured a full moon. He urinated with one hand while he rubbed his eyes with the other.

A day's ride is a dangerous thing, he reflected. The desire to return to his quilt tempted him. *It will still be warm. I can just lay still and not go to sleep.* A brief vision of red snow breaking below his feet convinced him otherwise.

His fellow travellers lay, hidden, under a tree. Also awake, Argus, who lay beside Christopher, lifted his head to follow William's movements. The page knelt beside the other sleeper.

'Richard,' he whispered, shaking the squire.

'What do you want, William?'

'Can I start a fire?'

'There's a pouch with flints and kindling on Springly's saddle. It's fat and soft.'

'Thanks.'

'Wake me at dawn.'

'I will.'

'With breakfast.'

'Yes.'

'Hot oats.'

'I will.'

'Good, now let me sleep.'

After creating a triangle with sticks foraged from the forest border, William searched amongst the saddles for the pouch and then used the contents to start a fire. Argus walked across and lay beside the flames.

When the dark faded, William made a start on saddling the horses. He prepared Bucephalus and Ash to ride before he started the breakfast Richard requested.

'You've done a good job of the horses.' Richard's voice startled him.

'I want to master my duties,' William said, 'so I can learn how to fight.'

'While we're at sea will be a good opportunity for that.'

After breakfast, they saddled the other horses. Yesterday, Richard showed William how to do things. Today, he allowed the page to display what he learned. Though the squire made comments, he seemed satisfied with the progress.

While Christopher ate his breakfast, William tampered down the fire. Smoke smouldered from the dirt as they set out eastward, towards Ullumber and the coast. William started with the deficit of soreness from the previous day. He shuffled in the harness, but his lower back soon throbbed.

The road continued unchanged for hours until they came to a fallen tree which blocked the path.

'Wait here,' Christopher instructed, 'stay in your saddle.'

Both knight and squire dismounted to escort the horses over the obstacle one by one.

'Do you want me to help?' the page asked.

'No,' Richard grinned. 'Wait there.'

Leaving all the horses on the other side of the obstacle, Christopher jumped the tree, approached and gripped William's courser's rein. He said, smiling, 'Do you remember how you told me you can ride?'

'Yes?' William sensed something amiss.

'Well now is the time to prove it,' Christopher slapped the steed on its hide. The horse bucked before setting into a charge. Thrust backwards, William forced himself into a riding squat as his stallion found its speed. With the trunk fast approaching, he adjusted his reins so as not to interrupt his mount.

The horse leapt. In clearing the log, they reached a height William believed impossible. *I'm going to be thrown from the saddle,* he thought. The horse's landing became the first steps of a more aggressive gallop. The tension of holding his position returned to his legs. William found his balance. A surge of courage arose through him.

'GO ON THEN BOY!' he shouted, 'GO ON!' Each step up in speed increased the flow of wind which brushed past his face. The road transformed into an angry stream of irrelevant dangers as his horse's thunderously pounding hooves became wings. *We are flying together.* Speed prioritised illusion over truth.

Uncontrollable, loud and reckless laughter escaped him. Life reached a new territory. His soul escaped his body, freeing him of all its memories and torments. He discovered adventure, finding it to be wild, freeing and fast.

He allowed himself ten deep breaths of sucked-in intoxication before he started to control his horse's reins.

'CALM NOW,' he instructed, 'Calm now!' The horse slowed into a canter. William sat back down and regained full control with his stirrups. Stopping the horse on the right-hand side of the road, he leaned forward. 'Thank you for taking me with you.' The words came from his heart, not his mind. 'It is an honour to share your speed.'

When Christopher and Richard caught up to him, they both smiled.

'Startling the horse is a joke played on every new page, William,' Richard called out. 'But you did well. We thought you would have fallen off.'

'He didn't, though,' Christopher noted.

'Thunderwind,' William said.

'What's that?' Christopher asked.

'The name of my horse,' William replied. 'It is Thunderwind.'

'The name suits him,' Richard admired the page and his mount.

'That it does,' Christopher added before riding ahead.

William smiled and giggled. His happiness spread to the world around him. He found joy in the birds singing and wondered what other adventures would be waiting further along the road. A temptation to kick his stirrups and start his steed again sat in his gut like the thirst for one last cup of wine.

At midday, Richard twisted to say something but instead showed amusement.

'He's still smiling,' he said to Christopher. The announcement pleased the knight.

His lingering happiness surprised William, who had never before experienced this elevation of emotions. Throughout the hours of riding, he tried to define the sensation. He failed. He became convinced, his horse, *Thunderwind,* mirrored his feelings. For in the leaping of the tree, and the ride that followed, they flew together, and in doing so, became the same bird.

***

Dusk came. The sun set but still they rode. The darker the road became the closer distances between the horses narrowed. Half-asleep in his saddle, William rode into a bog of rotting fish. He lifted his riding top over his nose to try to block the odour. It did not work. The stench strengthened until it tickled his throat.

The light ahead brightened until the flames of a torch-lit the path below and above them. Two lines of stone buildings flanked the five-metre-wide road. Christopher steered his trail to the left. A woman crossed the road to talk to him. William missed the question she asked his master, but caught the firm 'NO,' she received back.

Argus, having trailed behind them all day, ran ahead. The hound startled a gathering of black rats and killed two before chasing others into an alley.

So, this is what Ullumber looks like. William, who never visited a town before, presumed them to be like a big village. *Villages are homes and land,* he surmised, *this place is a human hole on top of another human hole.*

As they rode further from the border with the forest, the torch dimmed creating a sensation of descending. The deeper the shadows grew the more trouble loomed.

After four hundred paces, they came to a four-way crossroad. Opposite them, a tavern offloaded its rowdy noise outside. The men massed around the door and did not notice them ride past. Some sang, some shouted, some groped women.

That place is dangerous. William thought. *Those men are menacing.* His physical confidence, earned through threshing wheat and hauling sacks of grain to the mill, seemed left behind in his village. When they turned left, he tried to shake the sense of intimidation.

'Stay calm boy,' he said to Thunderwind. Shrieking laughter tore his attention. A group of men walked past. One of them glared at him and bared his rotten teeth in a snarl. William switched his attention back to his horse.

The deeper they descended into Ullumber, the more the stench of fish increased. They stopped where the road curved to the right.

Another torch drew them to a building detached from the others. He overheard Richard say,

'This is the church.' Father Monroe's love for churches, "Gardens of faith", he called them, taught William to think of them as the centres of human life. The building shattered his expectations. Perhaps once completely stone, only four feet of its original foundations remained. Decayed timbers served as replacement walls. Its open oak door leant on the ground.

Within its unkempt graveyard, four freshly carpentered grave markers underscored the deterioration around them. *One of them must be the marker for this church's spirit*, judged the former trainee deacon. When Christopher dismounted and Richard did not, William hoped this meant he would not have to enter the crumbling church.

***

Christopher slipped by a broken church door that rested against the ground in an open position. Within a slice of intruding streetlight, he knelt to make the shape of the cross. A breeze circulated dampness from the rattling timber walls. The scent added another texture to the stench of fish.

A barrier of darkness divided him from the weak candlelight on a three-foot-tall holder at the end of the room. The light, which shone mostly on a stone altar, silhouetted six people perched on pews. He suspected more people sat in the dark.

Each floorboard *en route* to the candle creaked. A woman twisted to glance at him as he came out of the dark. She wiped away tears. At the end of the pews, to his right, rapid tapping mixed with the movements of one-stepping foot and another foot dragging behind it.

'Light comes in search of light.'

Spoken words seemed out of place in this church, like an aggressive gust that pushed through the breeze.

'Who goes there?' Christopher challenged.

'Who goes there?' came the reply.

'A traveller, who seeks a religious man...Mullens.'

'You are the champion who seeks Ellrick?' A waving stick entered the boundary of visibility. The old man who followed, leaned forward, crippled by old age. The rags he wore made his poverty unquestionable. A metallic blue of blindness tinted his dead eyes. *Poor Bastard,* Christopher thought. 'Are you not the Church's Sword?'

'I am.'

'Ellrick waits for you in the Red Horse Tavern.'

This must be Father Mullens, Christopher realised as the man continued his slow approach.

'Continue along the road you have been following and you will find it. Good luck, Christopher.'

'How did you know my name?' Christopher tensed to stop himself from stepping aside to evade the man's reaching hands.

'I have witnessed your destiny in my dreams. You will champion the light in the kingdom of darkness.'

'If I am a champion,' the knight thumbed the Saint Christopher medallion on his sword's hilt, as though evoking the saint's spiritual protection in this supernatural matter. 'Who am I to challenge?'

The blind man dropped his tapping stick as he grabbed Christopher's forearm. The knight leaned forward to better listen.

'...Tis called the Azz-ta. Tis a demon. Tis man-flesh, cursed and twisted by pain, purged of purity, and refilled with hate. Tis the dark which curses the light.'

When the priest released his grip, Christopher knelt to collect Mullen's tapping stick. Before standing he took three silver coins from a purse in his boot. 'You wish to warn me, thank you, but I must confess, I made no sense of your words.' He put the stick into one hand and placed the coins into the other. 'Pray for me, Father, and I will pray for you.'

The priest's smile possessed more life than his eyes. 'Thank you.'

Back outside, Christopher appreciated the truth of illumination, which granted dimensions to the world. The distant sounds of the tavern they passed sounded more frantic now. The breeze flowed stronger through the street. Richard brought Springly forward.

'He's at the Red Horse, down the road,' Christopher pointed. As he mounted, a thud came from the church door as a woman knocked into it in her rush to get outside.

'Thank you, Me Lord,' weeping, she hooked one arm around his heel and kissed his boot. The knight noticed her hand squeezed tight and understood that the priest had given her one of his coins.

Five more women came outside. All of them cried. The hardness of life in Ullumber struck the knight, whose understanding of poverty came from experience. *Life is hard when such windfalls as a silver coin, even three shared amongst six, overwhelm every expectation. Poverty,* he reflected *is an increasing strangulation. When it loses its grip, a person experiences a moment of freedom, of fresh air.*

His mind visited the earliest memory of his life. A time before Monroe, when his experience of life pivoted between hunger and hardship. He remembered holding his mother's hand. She carried his baby brother. She smiled at him. 'Everything's going to be alright,' she said.

He remembered walking behind a trail of people, struggling to catch up. A horse rode by. It may have been an accident, or the rider could have felt pity for the fatherless family, but a small sack of food fell from the mount and landed at his mother's feet.

Every time he prayed before a meal, Christopher thought of the bread and apples inside the rider's bag. He saw his mother's tears being cried from the eyes of the women kissing his boots.

'Thank you, M'Lord.' They talked over each other. 'Thank you, M'Lord!...Thank you, my lord.' Each woman feared their gratitude would not be recognised. He slid from the saddle and embraced each woman in turn.

'Everything's going to be alright,' he reassured them as he opened his purse and made sure every woman possessed a coin of their own. *For you Mum,* he thought.

'Thank you, M'Lord...' the multiple voices continued. 'Thank you!' 'Thank you.'

The blind priest stood in the doorway, smiling as though he watched the women.

'Return in the morrow,' Father Mullens stood at the threshold of the church. 'Allow me to bless you before you leave.'

Is this priest implying I will set sail tomorrow? Christopher expected it to take at least a day, perhaps two, to prepare the ship.

'Just as long,' Christopher answered, 'as there's not a crowd of people expecting coins from me.'

'I will be alone.'

'Very well,' Christopher conceded. He remounted Springly. The women stood back. The horses continued.

***

The deeper they rode into Ullumber, the more the clap of horseshoes on cobbles filled the silence. Buildings beside the road became darkening mysteries. Faint, solitary outlines of people lingered in gloomy alleyways.

A small torch ahead expressed no powers of illumination over the streets but acted as a beacon that drew them close. Its weak light shone on a red horse painted on the stone wall.

Christopher stopped and dismounted. He took a boar-hide cloak from Springly's saddle. Richard stopped beside the horse and collected his reins.

'Go to the blacksmith we used the last time we visited this town,' the knight instructed his squire. 'Use his barn for the night. In the morning, have him shoe the horses. If I don't return, wait for me there.'

'Will do,' Richard said, before turning to William to say, 'The fresher the shoe, the better the horse.'

The knight draped the cloak over his shoulders before he entered the tavern. After he ducked under a door frame, he met an atmosphere of warmth and stale ale. At one side of the room, two drinking men talked. On the other side, a man rested his head inside his arm on a table. *He mustn't have anything worth stealing,* Christopher perceived.

The knight claimed the empty corner. He scraped a table across the floor as he made space to sit facing the room. The talking men turned their attention his way. Intoxication hazed their eyes. The other man woke up, sat back and scratched the inside of his beard. A flustered, plump, red-haired serving girl emerged from a back room. She wiped gravy on her apron as she rushed across to him.

'What do you want, Lovie?' She asked. 'I have ale, cider, good beef stew served with bread, and there are rooms free.' One of the drunks huffed mockingly at her words. She ignored him, placed her hands on her hips, tilted her head and smiled.

'I'll take all three if you can tell me the whereabouts of a sailor called Ellrick.'

Her eyes went from his to the man sitting by himself.

'I don't believe I owe you money, friend.' Ellrick's tied-back, unbrushed hair matched his grey-tinged black beard. His accent came from further north.

'Would you like something to eat? To drink?' Christopher offered.

Ellrick shook his head to answer no. Christopher passed the girl a silver coin. Without glancing at it, she shoved it into her pocket.

'Cider or ale, me Lord?' she asked.

'Both.'

'Will anyone be joining you?' Now quiet, the drinking men listened to him.

'I travel alone.' He walked across to Ellrick and lifted the side of his cloak to show his sword. 'My name is Christopher. I've come on Gaston's request.'

Ellrick stood, dropped the stabbing knife hidden underneath the table and offered Christopher his hand.

'I doubted you would ever come.'

The sailor's face transformed. The tone of his voice softened. After grasping each other's forearms, Christopher sat with his back against the wall.

'My ship,' Ellrick continued, 'the *Thetis* is at your disposal.'

'She's your ship? You own her?' All Christopher knew about Ellrick came from a line in Gaston's letter; 'My man is capable.'

'I will when I deliver you to Saint Constantines.' He explained. 'One ship for one champion.' *I can understand Monroe's and Theodus' needs, but why are monks exchanging a ship for me?*

'I have been using the *Thetis* for fishing, but I can have her ready to sail on the next favourable tide if you so like.'

'When's that?'

'Noon.'

The serving maid returned. She put two beakers onto the table and placed the bowl resting on her forearm beside them. Next to a wooden spoon, a crust of bread rested half in, half out, of the stew. She rushed away to the backroom.

'Tell me about your ship?' Christopher said.

'She breaks the tide fair enough, but her crew is the best thing about her. Each man was born for the waves.' Though listening, Christopher started on the stew. His teeth struggled against the salted beef, which being old, had been boiled again and again in an attempt to soften it. *The tavern would have bought it cheap from the docks. This is most likely the remains of rations from a ship's voyage.* The bread tasted better without the gravy.

'How about an inspection?' Christopher suggested. He sipped both drinks before choosing the cider to wash away the aftertaste in his mouth.

'Now is as good a time as any.' Ellrick offered.

'Then lead the way.'

Before leaving, Ellrick stooped beside the door, picked up a lantern and lit it. Outside, he lifted it to indicate which way to go.

'The docks are meant to be closed during the night,' Ellrick explained, 'but I have friends on the gate.' They walked sixty paces, beyond the Red Horse's beacon light, when a mass of noises approached behind them. A crowd marched their way.

'This is trouble,' Ellrick said. 'Let's go before they catch up to us.' As the sailor made to blow out his light, the knight stopped him.

'Leave the lantern on the ground,' Christopher instructed, 'and step back from sight.' The crowd that massed around the Red Horse's beacon consisted mostly of men and women, but children scurried amongst them. Before they could storm the tavern, the Knight garnered their attention, 'You're looking for me.'

A group of men acted as the crowd's head. When they moved towards him, the others reshuffled behind them like a flock of birds adjusting to the whims of their leader. The crowd spread out to fill the width of the street four times over.

Men shoved a woman, whom Christopher recognised from kissing his boots earlier, to the front. A tare split her top around the collar. Her swollen cheek showed the early shine of bruising. Ashamed, she looked at Christopher and nodded.

The man leading the crowd strode from the beacon's light into the lanterns. His strut and smile seemed full of alcohol-induced confidence. After glancing at Christopher, he looked at the ground and put his hands behind his back.

'I beg an audience with you, Me Lord.'

Two other men made slow progress towards them.

Christopher remained silent, allowing the man to come two steps in front of him before he nodded and said, 'Please speak.'

'The town's folk chose me to talk to you, Me Lord.' He stood straight, placed one hand over his heart and pointed behind him with the other hand. *This man is performing,* the knight measured, *enjoying himself.* 'Fannie told us of your generosity. Well, it's been a harsh season. Floods forced us off the land, and our children starve. We are poor and in need of charity. If you would only spare a little more of your silver, we...they, our starving children, could know what a godly pleasure it is to have a full stomach.'

Christopher measured two men who stopped behind their leader. Their over-focused eyes indicated their intentions. More men inched closer.

'I'm a proud man, Me Lord. I wouldn't ask this of you, if not for the children.'

Christopher knew the man's tactics; lie behind a truth. He empathised with the poverty of the crowd. He wanted to help them.

But he would not deal with the frontman, who, despite his plea for charity, hid a smithy's hammer tucked into his sleeve.

'I can see the people here struggle,' Christopher announced to the crowd. 'I will do something about it.'

'What will you do about it Me Lord?' The man countered. His hands slid behind his back.

'FOOD!' Christopher directed his answer beyond the man. 'Come here tomorrow, at noon, and you, your people, shall be fed.'

'Damn your food,' the man scowled. *Don't try intimidating me,* Christopher thought, looking into the man's eyes. 'We want silver, Me Lord.'

Christopher shrugged the cloak from his shoulders and held his hands up, open and beside his chest. He appeared compromising, but he spoke in a low growl. 'You've had your answer. Now get.'

His words caused the response he expected. The man swung his smithy's hammer from beside his hip. Christopher, primed to counter, caught the attacking forearm with his left hand and used it as a lever to yank the man's momentum forward into his right elbow. The man's head jerked. With one hand, Christopher pushed him into the men behind him. With his other hand, he drew his dagger.

A knife thrust at his stomach. The knight stepped aside and turned away from the weapon. He drove his dagger upward into the attacker's armpit.

The second supporting attacker leapt forward. Christopher drew Reprobus right-handed. His left palm caught the sword's flat steel and shot it into a reinforced punch. The man's nose crumbled in the collision of steel and flesh; his lower body upturned as his upper body dropped.

A scattered line of men charged. Christopher sprinted into a counterattack. Making his steel the closest man's attention, he faked a thrust. The man flinched. Christopher grabbed the homemade spear his enemy thrust at him. After pulling it past his side, he switched his sword from the false thrust into a downward hack. Sharpened steel was carved through the spear first then the wrist of the man holding it.

Reprobus' pommel snapped up and crashed against the chin of a man who came at him with a knife. Christopher swayed backwards to evade an axe head that slashed inches from his face. A counter-slash opened the attacker's upper arms and chest. An axe sparked as it pinged off the cobbled street.

Christopher's ears flooded with an influx of sounds. The screams and cries of the injured. The roars and war cries from the men charging at him. The encouraging calls from the crowd. Above all of them, his mind paid attention to the noise it recognised; the excited barking his hound made when running which grew louder each second, to warn of Argus' approach.

Witnesses to the blood and screams, the five men who charged at him, now reconsidered their attack. Three men were too close to turn away. They came at him side by side.

Christopher manoeuvred to keep himself on the outside of the man to his right. The man swung his club. The knight stepped back and cut at the space his foe's arm moved into. Reprobus carved through the limb and in the same motion redirected to the thigh of the man standing beside the attacker. One man fell forward, clutching his leg. The other backed away, stirring at his maimed arm.

'I'M GONNA KILL YOU,' the remaining man roared. He came at Christopher with a reconstructed hay rake.

Like a coiled snake, Reprobus snapped forward, dipped two inches into the attacker's shoulder then returned to a poised position. The man stumbled back, his mouth opened to scream, but shock suppressed the sound.

'BASTARD,' another man ran at Christopher, a clump of sharpened metal in his hand. Two others chased him.

'NO, Jud...Don't!' they tried to call him back.

Emotionally charged, tears of rage gleamed from Jud's eyes. *Don't do it,* Christopher thought.

Excited barking drew Jud's attention, and his expression changed. Fear froze the surface of his face. He dropped his weapon and turned to flee.

Argus passed Christopher at full speed, leapt at the man, snapped onto his triceps, tore into the flesh and forced him to the ground. Snarls entwined with shrieks. The knight ran to support the hound. He got to him first. The second man to arrive stopped five paces away and held his empty hands out wide. He seemed as scared for himself as for the man screaming on the ground.

'Please, he's my brother me lord...Please...Mercy...Please...'

Christopher noted the shared horror of the crowd. Men, who pulled out of their charge, stared unbelievingly.

'BASTARD!' the next man to arrive said.

'Argus, back.' The knight shoved the hound with his boot to get his attention. 'Argus, back...' he repeated. The hound snarled at the man he let free from his teeth. Jud scuttled back to his brother and collapsed at his feet.

'You can collect the rest of your men,' Christopher allowed, 'after I've gone.'

'As you say, M'Lord.'

The knight backed away with Argus at his heels. The hound snarled and growled at the wounded as they passed. Warm blood trickled from Reprobus' fuller, the groove in the middle of his sword, the thirsty throat of his weapon.

Christopher stopped to measure the man who approached him asking for charity, who tried to intimidate him, who forced his hand. Though stunned, he would have witnessed the majority of the fighting.

'Here,' lifted his knee, the knight picked the purse from his boot and tossed it to the man, 'Your blood silver.' *The rest of them will kill you for this,* he thought, *you should at least have your prize.*

A cobble flew through the air towards him. It missed. Christopher pointed his sword at the youth who threw it. Reminded of his cowardice, the boy ran back to the crowd. After gathering his cloak, he kicked Ellrick's lantern over, dispelled its light and walked away from the screaming street.

***

'I thought a ship is always worth more than a man, but a man who can do what you just did, is...is priceless. Well...' having given undiluted admiration, Ellrick seemed embarrassed. 'You're worth at least two ships.'

'How long do you stay at sea?' Christopher inquired.

'We do four nights away, then four at home. We got back three days ago, so we're lucky you came when you did.'

'Where did that hound come from?' Argus hit the man on the street with ferocity and weight, his ripping jaws manipulated his victim's body into defenceless jerks. The captain seemed unnerved from witnessing the animal attack.

'Argus took his education from the fighting pits. They taught him to attack, kill then mutilate. He is a hound from Hell,' Christopher answered. 'He will be travelling with us.'

'He may need tying up, friend.'

'He can tell the difference between friend and foe. He will do neither you nor your men harm, so long as you leave him be.'

'Well...I'll take your word for it.'

The path continued for a quarter mile. When the surrounding buildings stopped, another street cut across, dividing the town from a dock. Lanterns hung from an opposing, seven-foot wall. A horse and cart, attended by two men with shovels, made progress towards them.

'Come on,' Christopher commanded Argus, who rolled in one of the piles of dung heaped on the town side of the road. Ellrick led them across the street. When they entered a gate's light, a guard said,

'My wife loved that fish!' Ellrick smiled, held his palms outward and shrugged in an expression that disregarded gratitude. A doorway disguised in the gate opened.

'Whose dog's that?' the guard flinched as Argus ran past. The hound gave silent chase to something which scurried away.

'He belongs to my friend, here,' Ellrick lifted a directing palm in Christopher's direction.

'Oh...' the guard, measuring the knight, recognised him as a fighting man. 'He finally came then.'

'Matthew, this is Christopher,' Ellrick gestured. 'Christopher, this is Matthew. He runs the gate.'

They nodded acquaintance.

'Good evening,' a younger guard added welcome.

'Good evening,' the knight replied, before strolling out of earshot of the three friends. A moment later, Ellrick said something as he walked away. All three men laughed.

'There're four gates along the wall,' Ellrick explained as he caught up with Christopher. 'The guards who run them control the dock. Treat them to a few fish from every catch, give them some fresh rations every time you store ship, give them things for their wives, and they will look after you.'

'They ensure your haul is the first out of the gate. They introduce you to merchants. They take care of your men when they return drunk. Cross the guards though, and you will find yourself waiting outside longer than you should, or perhaps some of your goods will go missing.'

This is where the stench of fish comes from, Christopher noted as Argus took in breaths so strong they could be bites of the air.

A half-moon provided a sheet of illumination to a street equal in size to the one on the other side of the wall. Berthed boats rocked against the thick timbers of the dock's edge. Large boats and ships sat secured to a wooden jetty that extended two hundred paces into the river. Compared to the other ships, the *Thetis* stood out because of her size.

'My crew carved her while I visited Monroe,' Ellrick pointed out a newly added figurehead dominated as her most distinct feature. Depicted as emerging from the water, the mythological maiden's lifelike face expressed potential movement, like she might smile or wink at him. 'Anyone who goes to sea needs fortune on their side. Trust me, I made the mistake of going out on the waves without a blessing, and that did not fare well for me.'

'Now,' Ellrick's voice stretched as he walked over to a wooden plank bridge, 'this gangway will not take the weight of your horses, so we will run out the thicker one.'

Christopher followed the sailor onto the ship. *This is highly maintained*, he thought. Ropes and lines hoisted out of the way near the main sails' beams. Tools, knives, boat hooks, snaffling hooks, all hung up ready to be used. Thick mooring lines sat coiled up, two aft and two forward. At the rear, a fishing net waited to roll from the ship. Coiled next to it, two attached lines measured as tall as him.

Ellrick led him aft, opened a hatch and descended into a hot and stuffy hold. The five-foot high ceiling forced him to stoop.

'Captain,' one of the men acknowledged them as they entered.

'Nemak,' Ellrick answered.

Two uneven lines of hammocks, some occupied, stretched along the twenty paces of the hold. At the far corner, ration barrels acted as tables.

'Is there a level below this?' Christopher asked.

'Two,' Ellrick informed him. 'We use one for storing fish and the other for salt.'

'How many men crew your ship?'

'Twelve of my crew sleep on board. Six others have families in town. They will stay in Ullumber when we leave. Depending on how many men you have, you could use their hammocks.'

'I have two men, seven horses and one hound,' Christopher looked around. 'I would prefer to stay with my horses. Or at least be close to them.'

'Okay,' Ellrick considered the request. 'Follow me.' Back on the upper deck, the captain opened a trapdoor midships, to show a tunnel that went to the bottom of the ship.

'The bottom level is waist high. That level runs the length of the Thetis,' the sailor explained. 'To the aft, are two other levels above, the mess and salt cellar. Forward, is one big room, which we use for prepping our catch. Right now, this room homes working tables and such things. By tomorrow, all of that will be cleared. The room will be scrubbed down and ready for your horses. Three hammocks will be placed inside for you and your men.'

'You know your ship well. Are you confident you can store my lances, armour, saddles and equipment, and still have enough room for supplies?'

'Easily,' Ellrick nodded as he answered.

'Thank you for being so accommodating,' his confidence pleased Christopher. 'I want my horses rested, not stiff. Will I be able to walk them on the upper deck?'

'Course you can. The ramp from the forward hold runs the length of the ship. It is not steep. They will be able to walk that. There is not much room up here either,' Ellrick continued, 'but a prince once told me; the sea air makes a mount more sporting.' The sailor looked around as though visualising the horses on the deck.

'I like you, Ellrick,' Christopher smiled. 'You know your business.'

'Thank you.'

'How long will the journey take to reach Saint Constantines?'

'The first two days will be the roughest. The sail north is horrible. On the third day, we will sail through deep water before we arrive at the black rock. Afterwards, we sail east, towards sunrise. How long it takes to find land again depends on the ice. If we can sail through, we should take two days. If we need to go around, we may take as long as four days to a week.

When we reach the cliff walls of the continent, we'll follow them north, to their sharpest point. It is there, at the edge of Christendom, where Saint Constantines stands. After that, my ship will turn back. You, your men, your horses, your hound, will go in the opposite direction.'

'I have a task to do in the morning,' Christopher said. 'So, I will escort my squire here first. He will oversee the loading of my horses and equipment. He will give you money enough to purchase the food I promised the crowd. Please could you work out a deal with the guards for me, to have them deliver and distribute it?'

'You owe those people nothing.' Ellrick sounded disgusted. 'They deserve nothing.'

'Charity makes a difference,' Christopher stated. 'Trust me, I know this.'

'I will see this done for you because you asked me to.'

'Thank you. I trust you can take care of everything. I shall see you tomorrow.'

''Till tomorrow.'

The sailor escorted him to the gangway and watched him leave. Christopher gave a brief wave at the end of the walkway.

As he stepped onto the jetty, something scuttled from beside his foot. He tracked the black rat's movement onto the rear breast line.

Its smooth sprint up the line and entrance onto the ship gave him the impression of a resident dweller.

A large, bright half-moon took his attention away from the rodent. Directly above the route out of Ullumber, its light created a line through the water, like a barrier guarding the exit. A sensation of being eyeball to eyeball with a foe scratched at his thought. *Stay away from Barbarous*, a warning voice whispered inside his mind. When he turned away, he felt the moon continuing to glare at him. *It is like I have made an enemy of the very night itself.*

Chapter Four.

Ullumber in the morning presented a new environment to William. Accustomed to rural fields and country air, the town walled him in on both sides with buildings of various heights, widths and purposes. Above the chatter of the people pushing past came the calls of women, who shouted across the street to one another.

Mounted men pressed through the crowd, thoughtless of the people their horses forced aside. A fresh, stronger smell of fish welcomed in the morning.

William negotiated his way through the human flow while Christopher walked a straight line. People avoided the knight.

Christopher waited for him outside of Father Mullen's church.

'A strong wind will knock the walls down,' William commented.

'I brought you here, Will,' Christopher replied, 'to remember the church as it looks now.' After a purposeful pause, he added 'This morning, I paid six men who will no longer be sailing with Ellrick, to replace the church's walls and roof.'

'Why?'

'When we return,' William interpreted by Christopher's sharp tone, the puzzlement in his question displeased his master,' this church won't be rotting, it'll be thriving. Why else would we do what we do, if not to make a difference?'

'A man either fights for a cause, or he is fighting for nothing. Barbarous is my cause. People there need help, and I intend to deliver it. Now, I realise revenge is your cause—'

The words created a hole in William's gut which his stomach fell through.

'And I can understand why, but when I succeed in Barbarous, marvellous things will happen.' Looking his page in the eye, the knight forced his focus in the same manner as someone grabbing him by the scruff of his neck.

'What good will come from your revenge?' No sooner had did he asked, he entered the church.

My nightmares, William's mind mustered defensive thoughts, *my nightmares will end.* Nightmares seemed weak things during the day, his attempt to use them to justify himself, felt petty.

The church door remained open from the night before. Inside, a tapping sound came from a person approaching from within the shade, who said,

'As promised, you have returned.' Two ghosts of eyes emerged as milky blue phantoms of the shade. They focussed on William.

'This one dreams of red snow.' The words disjointed William's body from his mind. He forgot how to breathe. His forehead simmered with sweat. *Why...how...how can anyone know that?*

He took a breath, held the air captive inside his lungs then released it through his nose. His paralysis relented into a shaky, chilly, aftershock. Christopher patted his shoulder.

'Alright Will,' the knight reassured him, before lifting his voice, 'Our blessing please, Father.'

'Yes, yes. You wish to set sail.' Speaking to Christopher the man sounded human, not spectre. The knight knelt first, and William duplicated the motion. When his knees hit the ground, his mind's eye transformed it into snow. Red rose through it. He wanted to stand and run from the church but the strength seeped from his legs.

William took in none of the blessings. By the time his nerves softened enough to allow him to breathe Christopher stood to speak.

'Once I set sail, men will bring food for your people. Their instructions are to hand it out only after you eat. So, you must feed yourself for the sake of your followers.'

Do his blind eyes feel their tears? William wondered.

'Tomorrow morning,' Christopher continued, 'other men will come to replace the church roof. I've instructed them to be respectful. If they are not, tell them I shall find out.'

'Do you wish me to tell you the outcome of your meeting with the darkness?' The priest directed his right ear at them as he asked.

'Skill and steel will decide my fortune.' Said Christopher 'God bless you, Father.' He spun on his heel and marched away.

A sensation of fingers hovering over his shoulders, tickled William as he got closer towards the doorway. He visualised the blind eyes that haunted the church. Had Christopher not been in front of him, he would have run outside.

The doorway saved him. In the daylight, nightmares, and fears, became weak things. Thoughts of them seemed petty.

A voice whispered into his ear. 'Do you wish me to tell you what you must do when the red snow comes again?'

William stood, torn between following and going back inside. *Nothing good can come from listening to this man,* he imagined Bishop Monroe advising him. *He talked of the red snow,* William told himself. He nodded before remembering the speaker's blindness. 'Yes,' he answered.

'Death once danced with you in the red snow. She learnt your name and remembers your face. She will take you if she can. To stay Death's hand, you must prove yourself worthy to Life. You must Fight! 'Tis your only chance. Fight, prove yourself worthy to Life, and you will earn a path of glory wielded for you.'

'But be warned William, for though revenge is a strong cause, 'tis not a path, 'tis a river, which sweeps men away.'

'How do you know such things?'

'No one is blind. Some just see different things.' The whisper in his ear ended. The same voice, but now far inside the church, called to him: 'YOU MUST FIGHT, THAT IS YOUR ONLY CHANCE.'

***

Even though William walked with the flow, he struggled to catch up to Christopher. Too many people now populated the streets. Being focused on his master's head, he spotted suspicious people approaching the knight.

'MASTER!' The sounds of the streets swallowed his alarm. He pushed people aside in a struggle to weave through. The understanding that he would be too late, generated sensations of weakness and powerlessness. 'MASTER,' he warned, 'MASTER.'

Oh no, William anticipated a fatal strike into his master's unprotected side as one of the stalkers accelerated. Christopher spun and seemed to collide with him. The others swept forward.

His restricted view of the street's population presented only a vision of the knight's head bobbing up and down.

William arrived to find one attacker left standing. He charged, pushed the man in the back and shouted.

'OY!' His fists lifted in front of him: half-aggressive, half-defensive.

'Don't you dare!' Christopher threatened the man, who after being flung against the crowd, advanced towards William. 'Take your men and piss off.'

A crowd circled the fight. Unwilling to be touched and therefore affiliated with the attackers, people stepped aside for them. The villains faded into the crowd.

'Well done,' the knight patted his page on the back.

'I didn't know what to do,' William confessed.

'Well, you didn't run,' Christopher said. 'And those who don't run, stand tall.'

William only realised how much tension and nerves swirled within him when he exhaled.

'Good news,' The Knight laughed. 'I got my dagger back.' He held it out. Blood covered the blade, his forearms and his hand.

William smiled but he did not feel any better. *What would I have done*, he thought, *if I needed to fight?*'

***

Above the dockyard, stationary seagulls glided against the brisk wind, which followed the tide out to sea. Heads down, their keen eyes scrutinized the *Thetis* and her crew, who made their last pre-sailing preparations.

Laid in a sunspot to the side of the jetty, Argus stood and walked to his master, tail wagging. Christopher squatted to greet the dog and scratched behind his ears.

'Come on then,' he said. Argus ran up the wooden, bridge-like gangway. Criss-crossing the deck, his nose to the timber, he identified a particular scent amongst many.

'Everything's in order,' Richard confirmed as the knight stepped on deck,' all the horses and equipment are onboard.'

'Let's have the gangway stowed, lads.' Ellrick ordered his crew, the moment William stepped onboard.

'Good,' Christopher acknowledged Richard before turning to Ellrick. 'When will we be setting sail?' He asked.

'The *Thetis* is in your service. We await your command.'

'You're the ship's captain. From here to Saint Constantines, it's your rules, your way. Set sail when you please.' Christopher set simple objectives for the sail; oversee the horses. Initiate William's combat training.

Crew pulled long holding pins from the gangway to the deck then hauled the timber structure away. After overseeing its storage, Ellrick rubbed his hands together, and bellowed at his men,

'RIGHT, YOU LAZY BASTARDS! YOU'VE SAID YOUR GOODBYES, SO GET YOUR HEADS OUT OF THE SKIES.

OUR MISTRESS MADAM TIDE IS SINGING TO US. SO, LET'S GO DANCE WITH HER!'

He leaned over the wooden railing.

'SLIP THE BREAST LINES.' At this instruction six dock hands slipped the middle two holding lines from the jetty. The men who hauled them on board then rushed to join the teams who manned the rear and forward lines. Richard took William with him to help with the rear line.

'SLIP THE MAIN LINES!'

'Good Luck!' one of the dock hands shouted.

'Fair Winds,' another called.

The sailors gave enough slack on the holding lines to allow the dockhands to free them from the bollards on the jetty. Seduced by the flow of the tide, the *Thetis* glided away with the river.

'COME ON, HAUL THOSE LINES IN.'

The ship picked up momentum and began to bump as it floated over increasingly larger waves. Men rushed to release the main sail. Caught by the wind, the sail's corners crackled as tension flushed through them. A surge of speed pushed the ship faster.

Ellrick stood beside his pilot, pointing out the path with a straight stiff hand in front of his face. A mass of black and grey, the captain's hair and beard conjoined, flowed then rippled at the end. Richard's inquisitiveness drew him into a conversation with the captain. *He looks like the co-pilot* Christopher noted, *he'll ask to steer the tiller soon.*

William leaned against the port side railing, watching Ullumber shrink. *Just remember*, Christopher told himself as he approached his page, *this is his first time away from the village, now he is at sea.*

'Do you feel sick?'

'No.' William shook his head.

'Sea air has a way of getting to people, that's all,' Christopher explained. 'If it gets you, and you need to be sick, just do it overboard.'

'Yes, master.'

'We haven't been able to start your sword training yet because we needed to travel to Ullumber. Tomorrow, you should finish your duties early. Afterwards, go see Richard. He'll start your schooling.'

'Really?' William expressed with a childish excitement.

'Richard's very knowledgeable,' Christopher said, 'but it's up to you to learn, so give every opportunity he gives you, everything you can offer. Endure the pain. Endure the embarrassments and failures. Grow stronger. Move faster. Do everything you're told. Don't ever, EVER quit, nor leave a lesson knowing you could have done better.'

'Yes, master.'

'Other lads your age are squires,' Christopher continued, 'or knights, already. They'll have years of training over you. Some will have perfected the craft of killing. And your task isn't just to catch them up, Will, your task is to become better than they are. Remember that every time you pick up your training sword. Remember also who you want to be, and how great you want to become.'

'Yes master,' William nodded. *He's trying not to smile.*

The water widened. The river moved faster. The ship rocked. They left the town far behind them. Argus barked. Christopher recognised excitement in the hound's tone. He took a boat hook, which hung on two brackets attached to the side railing and passed it to William,

'C'mon,' he beckoned the page to follow him. With a lunge, the large hound knocked a storage barrel over. The barrel rolled away from his attempts to scratch his way inside. The crew assembled around the scene. All with tools in hand.

'Ready?' A man who used his foot to stop the barrel asked.

'Eye, go on then,' someone answered.

'Be quick,' Christopher advised William, 'because they are.'

The man broke the lid with one swing of his axe. Black rats surged from the barrel, scattering in all directions. The gathered crew reacted like flames spread under their feet. They crashed into each other as they stamped at the rodents.

Argus moved through the living smoke, biting and being bitten in return. When his jaws snapped, a limp body dropped to the deck. Christopher cocked his hand, ready to throw his dagger. William bumped into him. Instead of attacking, he laughed at his page, who lifted his leg while stabbing at the rats. While trying to avoid one, William stepped on another. The rat swung around and snapped at his foot. William's boat hook struck, impaling the shrieking rat to the deck.

The other rats ran from danger, escaped down holes in the deck, hid within fishing nets, hid behind storage barrels and climbed over the railings into the river. Argus pursued the majority towards the open storage level hatch at the centre of the deck.

'I'll check the horses,' Richard said. He went to the forward hold via a long sloping ramp at the rear of the ship.

The sailors boasted and laughed about the rats.

At least four of you are claiming one of Argus' kills as your own Christopher observed.

'You silly pricks,' Ellrick laughed as he came across to inspect the scene, 'screaming like girls about a few rats.'

'Big Rats,' one man replied.

'Huge,' another added.

'The young lad killed the biggest.' Said Ellrick who pointed to the rat pinned to the deck.

'Bigger than you, boy,' a sailor said, then laughed at his own words.

'And prettier than you, Nemak,' the man beside taunted.

'Hey, that's his sister you're talking about,' another joked. Nemak smiled and winked at William.

'The pretty one,' someone else added, 'the pride of the family.'

'And he killed it with your arse-picker,' Nemak retorted.

Christopher tapped William's shoulder and indicated for him to follow. As they walked away, one of the men called after them.

'Ey, Lad. Teach Nemak how to use that boat hook, won't you?' William looked back to show his smile.

'You didn't hurt your chin, did you William?' Christopher asked.

'No, why?'

'I've never seen someone lift their legs so high before. I thought you might have kneed yourself in the face, that's all.' William smiled.

'I've never seen so many rats before!' he said.

'Don't worry about them, Will. Argus will hunt down the rest. You did well to lance that one when you did. It nearly took a toe from you.'

'Or my foot.'

'You've got natural speed though, which is promising. You'll need to work on controlling yourself.' Having meant to only comment, Christopher found himself explaining further as William's face encouraged him with an expression of enthusiasm. 'The more you practice with weapons, the better you will understand how to use them. Through dedication, you will master them as you will master your mind, toughen it against the weakness of pain, and make it astute against possible mistakes. If you can be patient but decisive, fast but measured, you will have what I deem as "control".'

'And control leads to victory?' William asked.

'Control is keeping your mind fixed on victory, no matter the influence on the things going on around you. If you're floored, control will lift you off the ground, put you on your feet and keep you fighting. Control is being your best when you choose to be. When you have it, you will understand it.' Patting William on the back, deciding to leave him with the words, Christopher headed for the under apartment.

Bigger waves bid the *Thetis* entry into the centre current of the Ullumber River. Before descending into the ship, Christopher glanced at the last view of his homeland, at the strip of greens and browns. The view did not interest him. What mattered to him waited beyond the waves, beyond Christendom, in the lands of Barbarous, in a place called "The Abyss of Trees".

***

'Sea duties are different from travelling duties,' Richard explained. 'Before we can take care of the horses, we have to sweep away the mess they've made. Grab a brush. We'll make a start.'

Both men swept the mixture of left-over hay and horse muck into a pile at the bottom of the ramp. Side by side, they worked the waste to the upper deck and over the side of the ship.

'While I fetch the fresh hay, you re-sweep our tracks,' Richard instructed.

William went to the bottom of the ramp. This time, he brushed towards himself as he ascended backwards. Christopher patted William's shoulder as he passed. The knight went to the leeward side of the ship, the port side, to urinate out to sea.

'We'll do a bit before breakfast,' he said over his shoulder to Richard.

'Okay,' the squire replied. 'Will,' Richard called across while he approached, 'after sweeping up, carry on with the horses. Brush them, saddle them, take them for a walk around the upper deck, twenty or so times each. The sea might spook them, so make sure you keep a firm hold of their reins. Afterwards, give them their feed bags. When you've finished, come find me.'

For sword schooling, William wanted to say. 'Will do,' he said. He returned to his task. *They'll laugh at my excitement,* he thought. Still, he smiled.

Apart from the dirt in the gaps between the decking, he left the trail in acceptable order. Inside the hold, there was already fresh manure and puddles of piss. He enjoyed his duties with the horses, but the promise of combat training made the responsibilities a task to be completed as quickly as possible.

He took Bucephalus aside and brushed him from neck to tail before saddling him. On the upper deck, the horse did not demand his usual attraction. The crew, scattered around the ship, paused their tasks to concentrate on the knight and squire sparring.

Armed with a wooden sword and shield each, Christopher and Richard, matched each other with constant movement. Their speed shamed William's eyes. He could not watch them both at once. They used the whole span of their height. Attacks, which ranged from ankles to head, snapped against a quick defence.

To attempt to latch onto a rhythm meant to be misled. Taps of wood on wood portrayed phantom movements. *If I cannot even follow this with my eyes,* William realised, *what chance do I have to join the dance?*

William, who concentrated more on the sparring than his duties, allowed the horse to take the lead. Closer than he should be, Bucephalus pulled to Christopher. 'No. No,' William muttered while trying to pull him back.

Forced to stop his sparring, Richard said, 'If he's walking you, William, he's not going to listen when you speak. If you want him, or anyone else to follow you, you must lead them.' The attention paid to the sparring now focussed on him. He flushed with embarrassment.

'Sorry,' William said leading Bucephalus away, 'I shall.'

He tried to pay no attention to the sparring while he walked the horse around the upper deck. He failed in that but succeeded in controlling the destrier. He returned Bucephalus to the lower deck, attached his feed bag then moved on to the next horse, Ash.

He walked the courser around the upper deck while Christopher and Richard shared breakfast. The squire brought William a bowl of plain pottage. He patted him on the back as he handed it to him. The gesture encouraged him to stop thinking about the mistake he made of letting the horse lead him. He hooked Ash's reins around his arm and ate the pottage on his route.

Christopher, having donned his armour, practised defending and counter striking while William walked Stormpath around the deck.

On Lunar's route around the ship, Richard wore the armour and practised the same drills of his master. The knight and his squire measured identical in height and size. The armour fit each one perfectly.

'The older one is just that bit quicker,' he overheard one sailor comment to another as he passed.

By the time he brought Springly and Beck to the upper deck, his superiors' training ended. Christopher and Richard leaned over a railing and talked.

He returned with Thunderwind. Sailors stopped to admire the horse. William wanted to tell them about how wonderful the mount rode at full charge but felt like he could not describe something so meaningful to him.

Thunderwind is a force of nature, and I ride him, he thought. In his mind, he lived through the moment of magic again; Thunderwind charged at the fallen tree and floated over it before flying across the track with speed enough to enter a higher existence.

The second he attached Thunderwind's feed bag, he forgot his pride. He marched to the upper deck, sensations of excitement mixed with nerves, and his fingers tingled.

Richard stood in the area he and Christopher used for sparring, waiting for him with a smile wide enough to convey he understood the younger man's emotions and motivations. He tossed a wooden sword across the ship, over the top of men who, on their knees, cleaned the upper deck.

***

The ship's company, Christopher and Ellrick included, eyed the spiralling sword which dropped towards William. He missed it with his grip but managed to clamp it against his chest with his arms. *I nearly dropped it,* he berated himself, *come on, do better.*

'You've worked hard for Monroe, as you have for our master,' Richard said as the page approached. 'That earned you today's opportunity. Now, you must earn the right to come back tomorrow.'

Sailors, gathered around to listen to Richard's instructions. Their presence distracted William. He glanced at them. His teacher's sword smacked his hand. He grimaced, grabbed the source of pain as he looked at Richard open-mouthed and surprised.

'Hurts, doesn't it?'

'Yes.' He tried to shake the pain out of his hand.

'It'll hurt more the next time I tell you something and you don't listen.' Genuinely angry, Richard intimidated him. 'This is sword training, not daisy picking, so pull your head out of your arse. Listen. Concentrate.'

'I'm sorry.'

'In sword schooling we are never sorry. We listen...we concentrate...we are punished if we do not learn fast enough, understand?'

'Yes.' William believed it best to speak loudly.

'Let's hope for your hands' sake, you do. That training sword is yours, so take care of it. Learn from it. Instead of playing with your prick, play with that.'

To his left, a sailor laughed. William, who instinctively turned to look at him, recognised his mistake. He flinched. Richard's sword smacked his hand.

'Hurt more that time, didn't it?' Richard smirked as his pupil winced and nodded. 'The more you hurt, the more you learn. Take it from someone who's learned a lot. Save your thinking for your schooling. Choose this time to be at your best.' William nodded as he followed. 'Skill is something which will develop over time. So, for now, we are going to improve your speed and stamina. Your task is to block me. If you're feeling brave, by all means, try to attack,' the squire scoffed, 'but be warned...that will cost you.'

William lifted his sword to block Richards.

'Okay,' Richard tucked his sword underneath his armpit. 'Grip your weapon like this.' He pushed William's hands closer together and interlocked his right hand's little finger with his left hand's index finger. 'Okay, again.'

Slowly, Richard swung his sword across his body, from left to right, right to left. As wood tapped he said, 'Good...Good.' Afterwards, he cut down from his left shoulder then from his right shoulder, 'Good...Good.'

Next, the sword came up from his left heel then up from his right heel.

'Okay,' Richard tucked his sword underneath his armpit. 'Do you know what endurance means, William?'

'To keep going when things are hard.'

'Excellent. Do you know what persistence means?'

William thought about the question. 'The same thing,' he suggested.

'Persistence means to never give in. So, tell me what they both mean?'

'Endurance means to keep going. Persistence means to never give in.'

'Every time you defend yourself,' Richard said, 'I want you to shout *endurance*, then the next time shout *persistence*.'

'Okay.'

'You understand why I want you to do it, don't you?'

'So, I remember them when I'm fighting.'

Richard's sword snapped out of his armpit and smacked his hand, 'So their meaning is engraved onto your soul,' He said 'The way ahead of us is hell, and there's no turning back, so you best get tough boy.' Richard's sword swung at him. William defended himself.

'Endurance,' he yelped.

'Louder.'

Delivered at the same speed, the second attack came with more power.

'PERSISTENCE,' he bellowed. 'ENDURANCE,' He screamed. PERSISTENCE...ENDURANCE... PERSISTENCE...ENDURANCE...PERSISTENCE...ENDURANCE..."

For half-an-hour he called and defended himself.

'Right, the point is made now, Will,' the squire said. 'You can stop shouting. It's time to see what you've got.' Richard swung his sword with no intermission, no communicational tap and pause. He went from one strike smoothly to the next. Though William anticipated the direction of each strike, he struggled to intercept it. He stepped back. After each set of movements, the speed increased. Set by set by set. Every time the sword caught him; he winced but continued.

Please don't go faster. He prayed but dare not request. The increased speed came. *I will have to stop soon. I cannot continue like this.* One more mistake, one more strike of pain, and he would drop the sword. When he made the mistake and the pain came, his grip tightened. *You haven't earned the right to come back tomorrow,* he thought. *Christopher won't want you for a squire.*

As Richard's sword attacked, someone from the crowd yelled, 'ENDURANCE.' It sounded like Christopher. 'PERSISTENCE.'

*KEEP   GOING...*His   body   weakened...*DON'T   GIVE IN*...William growled as though to scare away the pain.

'ENDURANCE.' The voice gained the support of the sailors. Who picked up the chorus, PERSISTENCE, ENDURANCE, PERSISTENCE, ENDURANCE.

'GO ON LAD,' one of them shouted.

Keep going, William thought. *KEEP GOING AND DON'T GIVE IN*, he became to tired to waste energy on thinking. The speed stepped up again. His sword moved in a constant defensive pattern. His arms burned. The muscles of the arms he lifted to block Richard's sword faded. Not thoughts, but commands, ordered his arms to keep moving, *Endurance, Persistence.*

Richard finally battered the sword from his hands. In exchange for a grip on his weapon, he grabbed onto the fear of failure. A wave of dread flushed through him. William dived to grab his sword before it hit the deck.

'No, William,' Richard said above the crews clapping, 'you've done enough, lad.'

William stretched out and regathered his sword's handle before letting his head rest on the deck. His body burned. His chest beat hot air.

Breath by breath, as the tiredness left him, he realised *the words made a difference. Endurance means to keep going. Persistence means to never give in. No matter what lies ahead,* he promised himself, *I will embody both meanings.*

***

The daily mixture of sea air, duties and sword schooling pushed William to the edge of his energy. By nightfall, tiredness swayed him to sleep without resistance. Initially, exhaustion prevented his recurring nightmare.

Later, during the loneliest, darkest hours, weeds of emotion scratched, tore and reopened the unhealed scabs on his soul. Rooted in his stomach, they twisted their way up his spine and beyond his neck. Spiral on top of spiral, they wrapped themselves around his skull until they found a route through to his mind. Along the corridors of his memory, the weeds of emotion stretched. Past thousands of bright, colourful experiences, they persisted in straight lines. From the new, they reached towards the old. The corridors of memory dimmed.

The surrounding experiences became smaller, their light weaker. The weeds persevered. The sides of the shrinking corridors became tight. The weeds pushed through crumbling channels. They burrowed into the dark of forgetfulness until they broke through the wall of a chamber. They found an old but well-preserved, glowing experience and plunged into its surface. Sparks filled the chamber. The experience cindered, smoked then ignited. The nightmare began.

William became the boy who took his last breath, plummeted through red snow, and struggled not to drown.

On his third night at sea, William awoke to the pain of failing lungs. *Breathe* he told himself, *just breathe.* With each breath, he mitigated panic into calmness. Above his thoughts, came the sound of voices moving above him. His routine thus far when waking, was to lay in his hammock thinking, through the day's sword training, mentally reliving his mistakes and fixing them.

What is going on? He thought as more voices above awoke more curiosity within.

Blind inside the dark, by touch alone, he dressed in the leathers he used as a pillow. He slipped on his boots and shoved his arms through the sleeves of the sheepskin coat Richard handed down to him.

Once dressed, he swept a foot to navigate his route across to the ramp. He pressed his hand against the side of the ship while ascending. At the top, he opened the hatch, slipped outside and closed it with as little sound as possible.

The moonlit world gifted his vision. The clarity of the voices increased.

Ellrick and two men stood mid-ships, facing starboard, watching an island pass by. Ten times the length of the ship and four times its height, the island's steep, cliff-like edges reflected moonlight in their jagged cuts the same way as the waves below did.

'Is that land or rock?' William asked as he approached.

'Neither,' Ellrick replied.

'It's a hill of ice,' a sailor added.

'Most of it is underwater.' William recognised Nemak's voice.

'From now on,' Ellrick said, 'we'll have to keep an extra eye on the horizon.'

While William tracked the strange island drifting into the dark horizon, he thought about Monroe. *Does he know such things exist?* he wondered. For the first time he understood, he now lived outside of the world of his childhood. In seeing something outside of Monroe's knowledge, he took steps into his manhood.

***

The hope of seeing an ice hill during the day nagged at William every time he went onto the upper deck. The *Thetis* sailed towards the open horizon. Nothing disturbed the view.

A day passed before someone spied a faint line of smoke lifting far ahead. The captain changed his ship's course, to head straight towards it.

From the mist of distance, a black mound appeared at the base of the upward trail. The island revealed itself only when they got close. From the mound at its centre, ash surged high, became a passenger of the wind and created dense clouds that dominated the horizon. *What's burning?* William thought. *What could create so much smoke?*

The originality of the wildness they encountered here, at the end of the world, drew the crew's attention. Even Argus rested from hunting rats, to lift his fore paws onto the side railing to check the view. Ellrick alone paid no excitement to their destination. From deep and unfathomable, the seawater became a clear turquoise blue until they sailed into a rich red, underwater cloud.

'Krill,' a sailor announced. William spotted a swirl cutting through the swarm. A dog-like face with a muzzle and whiskers broke the surface, peered into William's eyes and snorted.

'What is that?' he asked the closest sailor.

'A seal,' the man informed him. 'Tough fur, fatty meat,' he said as though William considered eating the animal. 'But they're a good sign for fish.'

Long-necked, black, birds, moved within the swarm. They squawked at the ship before returning to their hunt.

'RIGHT THEN,' Ellrick's shout startled his distracted crew. 'THIS IS CLOSE ENOUGH. We'll drop anchor here.' Woven onto the three-foot high, iron anchor, a two hundred-paces long, arm thickness, line ran back and forth along the forecastle. A man on either side, holding opposing grips, dropped the anchor overboard. Getting low and moving fast, they evaded the danger of the whipping overboard. After forty paces, the line slowed. Ten more and the ship drifted with the tide. The crew attached the line to a bollard before stowing away the slack.

'RIGHT THEN.' Ellrick smiled at his crew. 'Let's see who can catch the biggest fish for supper.'

While the crew worked on baiting lines, William scrutinized the island. The smoke came from the highest of its peaks, where red glowed through waves of fresh ash. *What on this rock could burn?* he wondered. Someone touched his shoulder. William turned to find Richard holding out a training sword.

'Fancy it?' he asked.

'Yes,' William replied, reaching for the sword. Richard dropped the weapon. When the page clasped its handle, the practice began.

Fast and powerful, the squire's cross-body sweeps stayed easy to anticipate. William defended one attack, before defending another and another. Defend and retreat, defend and retreat. The pace pushed his body towards the edge of its ability. He tried to step further away, to make blocking a stroke easier. He got caught on the forearm and winced.

Without warning he struggled to defend himself. On the fourth slap of his right hand, he nearly let go of his sword. Rather than step backwards, he dared to push out. He swung for Richard.

The squire laughed. With insulting ease, he hooked his weapon underneath his student's. He clamped one hand over both of William's, squeezed them against the handle, and lifted his student's arms above his shoulders. First, he pretended to head butt him, before demonstrating how, if he wanted to, he could knee him in the groin. In the break, Richard's sword smacked William's little finger. The pain throbbed through his hand.

William returned to the pattern of defending against the cross-body sweep from the left, cross-body from the right, overhead left, overhead right, upwards left, and upward right. Exhaustion developed a gradual, foul taste in his chest. He coughed as he breathed. PERSISTENCE, ENDURANCE, his mind screamed. PERSISTENCE, clash, ENDURANCE, clash...deep breath. PERSISTENCE, clash, ENDURANCE, clash...deep breath. His defence became weak and lethargic.

Richard's sword jerked back and as his student went to intercept a phantom attack, the squire batted the weapon out of his hands.

'Good effort, Will,' he said, indicating the end of the practice.

William walked away, his mouth wide open, head back trying to catch his breath. His forearms and hands tingled, indicating growing bruises. Gently finger-testing them, he grimaced, grinned and giggled at the same time.

'You might get me one day,' Richard said, laughing. The squire understood and expected, that his student wished to return the pain his master handed him. 'Well, maybe you will, maybe you won't...but you're tough, William. I like that about you.'

Crew members set fire to wood held within iron cages brought up from the storage hold. The fierce orange brightened against the dimming sunlight. Richard and William joined Christopher who stood by Argus who sat beside the closest cage to the forward hold.

'You wouldn't think this was a wooden ship, would you?' Richard referred to the danger of the fires.

'Shall I take the horses for another walk around the upper deck?' William asked.

'In a while,' Christopher's answer permitted William to rest. He held his hands over the fire. He did not mind the throbbing from the bruising, but the cold made his finger bones hurt.

'Here you are.' Ellrick presented three beakers, steaming with fresh fish stew.

Christopher took the first, Richard the second, and William the third. 'Thank you,' they all said in turn.

Richard nodded at the black island as he asked, 'How did you find out about this place?'

'I used to sail on another ship,' Ellrick held his hands out to the fire, in a gestural equivalent to breaking bread with them. '*The Straight Wave*, we called her. For twenty years, me and my brothers and cousins scouted shores, found territories and mapped out trading towns.

'People pay good money for routes to settlements that will trade.' He raised his eyebrows at William and added, 'They pay even more for routes to places ripe for plunder.'

'On a venture to the north, we hit a storm, the likes I'd never seen before. The sea made war with the sky, and the Straight Wave got caught in the middle of them. The sea tossed us every which way it could. It smacked us from all sides. Then the wind ripped away the ship's mainsail from its beam. It just lifted straight up.'

'The deck tipped like this.' Ellrick flipped his hand back and forth, horizontal to horizontal to make his point. 'Then came the big wave. Biggest I've ever seen. As we lifted, we tilted. The sea swallowed us.'

'I survived by chance. A line wrapped around my chest and pinned me against a piece of wood, which turned out to be the seat of a boat we used for going ashore. The boat pulled me to the surface. It sat upside down at first. A wave hit and turned me right.'

'After I wriggled myself loose, I bailed water out of the boat with my hands. I should have died in that storm. I don't remember falling asleep, but when I woke up, I found myself here, in the bay of this island.'

'What about your brothers and cousins?' William inquired.

Ellrick shook his head.

'What happened next?' Richard asked, then guessed, 'Did a passing ship pick you up?'

'No.' Ellrick scoffed at the easiness of that suggestion. 'I stayed here for two days. Fixed my boat and built my strength up. I sailed east.'

'Why?' William asked.

'If I didn't, I would've died here,' Ellrick shook his head in a gesture to evade the thought entering his mind. 'What will take this ship two days to sail, took me ten. I spent three days at sea without food or water.

On the third night, I prepared myself for death.

Constant rain hid any night sky to guide me. No stars. No moon. No nothing. I wondered why I survived the storm just to die drifting on the tide.

From the depths of the darkest night, I spotted a speck on the horizon. I knew...by the grace of God, to go to that light.

The light came from Saint Constantines' west tower where the monks keep a fire burning.

I got ashore. In the dark and rain, I climbed the cliff steps that led to the monastery. The next day, they found me. They brought me inside and gave me the rest and food I needed to recover.

The only escape from Saint Constantine is by sea. I waited a long time for a ship. To prevent madness from boredom, I committed the monastery's maps, sailing routes and position of this island to memory.'

'How come this monk Gaston trusted you with his message?' Richard pushed.

'There's nothing like a miracle to make a man believe. He nursed me back to health. He knows I would not disgrace the favour the Lord granted me.'

'I have gotten to know you all during our voyage. I do owe Gaston my loyalty but I also owe you as much information as I can give you.'

'The monks are afraid of the woods,' the captain confessed. 'They keep a two-man guard over their gates. Have you ever known monks to do that?'

'I am in Gaston's service,' Christopher said. 'Nothing you can say will change that. So, tell me, friend, what happened during your stay?'

'Apart from the wind and rain,' Ellrick sighed, 'the monastery is a quiet, peaceful place. One night, banging and screaming awoke me. I followed the sound to the eastward gates. The watchmen tried to keep its entrance closed. Gaston pushed them aside and opened the gates.

'An old man, a traveller who appeared as drained as myself when I arrived, lay on the ground. Though I never met him again, I can see his face as clearly as I can yours. Still, I cannot decide if his expression conveyed relief, fear or some form of demented happiness. The only part I am certain of is the madness caught within his eyes.

'The next day he killed himself. That night Gaston told me a ship would soon arrive. He told me if I deliver a message to your man Monroe. I wait for a champion to find me. I deliver you to him, then this ship will become mine.'

'What about Barbarous itself?' Christopher asked before he leaned over to whisper in William's ear. 'It is the captain's business to know the land and to understand people. Take note of the things he points out.'

The knight nodded and bade Ellrick continue.

'Saint Constantines is a strange building. Old in some places. New in others. The woodlands surrounding it are called "The Abyss of Trees". The name fits. Those woods are a strange, unnatural place. The trees that grow within are bigger and thicker than any other I have ever seen. Trees shouldn't grow like that. Let alone so far north. Travel two days by sea in every other direction, and you will see smaller, thinner trees with needle-like leaves. No wildlife goes into the abyss. You could listen all day and not hear a bird's song.'

'No civilisation?' Richard pressed.

'Dead civilisation.' Ellrick replied. 'An aqueduct leads into those woods. Whoever built Saint Constantines and that aqueduct invested large sums. They tried to tame the woodlands. To turn it into a forest. These creators were city builders. Ask yourself, 'why would they abandon such an investment?'

'Why tell us this?' Christopher queried, 'What do you think we should know?'

'All walls keep secrets,' Ellrick said. 'Monasteries more than most. Before you go into those woods, ask questions. Get answers.'

***

When dawn broke, the outline of the ramp to the upper deck took shape. William rolled from his hammock and shuddered as chills spread from the floor up his feet and legs. The ship's venture into the increasing coldness, taught him improved efficiency. He lay with the underlayer of thick cloth closest to his body, and therefore the warmest, then his leathers and furs.

As he raced up the ramp, the rocking of the ship caused him to reach out and steady his steps. Usually, when he went on deck, he went straight to the side and urinated. The *Thetis* rocked and bounced. Sea spray whipped his left side. He gripped a beam to stop himself from slipping.

The upper deck transferred from dark blue tones to developing dimensions and details. Sounds came from something passing by above him. *Birds*, he thought. One swooped passed the main sail.

'Seagulls.' Nemak called the bird and informed him, 'They're a good sign of land.'

'Oy...toughnuts!' Ellrick always called people what he wanted to, rather than by their name, therefore when he spoke, his entire crew checked if he talked to them. This time, the captain referred to William. He pointed at something beyond the ship's helm.

Land, William thought. *Civilisation* he corrected himself. *This is the end of the horizon.* A cliff wall, like the barrier between two realms, separated sea and land. A deep shadowy scar cut down its centre. Silhouetted, human-made shapes crowned the cliff. The light at the top of a sea-facing tower caught his eye. Seagulls, specks at this distance, swooped around the torch room like bees surrounding a hive.

'Behold Saint Constantines monastery,' Ellrick confirmed their location. 'Here ends Christendom. Here begins Barbarous.'

PROLOGUE
Part two

Too weak to speak, Lucius' screams remained trapped within his mind. One regret materialised into thought. *If only I had died in the cave.*

Vines bound his hands and wrists over the back of his head. Though numb, they agonised if he tried to move. Dug into his skin, the vine's thorns became teeth that bit down to punish any movements.

Trapped by the weight on his arms, his shoulders cramped.

He hung in an area guarded against breezes and exposed to the midday sun. His mouth dried. His head throbbed.

He realised the sun scolded the front of his body because when a movement occurred, despite his best efforts for stillness, the scolding pain added to the other insults he suffered.

The sun parched time. The day stretched into the longest experience of Lucius' life, longer than all the days before his hanging combined.

The madness of relentless pain caused him to forget himself. His identity disappeared. The desire to understand how he became this creature, evolved from torture, pushed him to open his eyes.

A bead of sweat dropped from his nose. Fell through the brightness onto the crucifix on his chest. A desire to lick the liquid pushed him to stretch out with his tongue. The pain he unleashed caused him to faint.

'You should finish it yourself, Padre.' The dream stirred his consciousness, so despite not knowing his own identity, he recognised the talker as Barfant. They stood within the cave where everyone else died. The big man threw wood into a fire.

'How?' Lucius begged for the knowledge.

'Use your legs.' Barfant laughed at him.

Lucius followed a piece of the wood. It landed on a large pyre. Within the heap bodies mixed with burning foliage. The dead faces of the men peered pitilessly at him. Scipio, his throat torn open, his neck flesh folded by slashes, laid in such a fashion his hand reached for him.

'Hurry up, Padre.' Barfant urged. 'They'll be back for you soon.'

Aware of his failing opportunity to end his suffering, Lucius mustered the courage to move. Heavy-legged and weak-bodied, he struggled to lift his knees into his waist. He slung them down. Thorns bit into his arms. Their scratches scraped away scolded skin.

I have to finish it. Though he tried to lift his legs again they did not move. He wriggled and struggled until he lacked the strength to do anything but sway in the sun. His screams of desperation, screams of defiance of his situation, emitted only a crackle in his throat. A single thought, *If only I had died in the cave,* bounced through his mind.

***

Exhaustion stretched the link between Lucius' senses and understanding. When the surrounding environment transformed, he perceived the changes as illusions. He mistook being lowered as the trees grew. His descent into the deep woods became darkness thinning into a fog.

Voices, their language and the whispered way they muttered words sparked recognition and brought to life vivid memories.

He faced his reflection in a dead man's eyes. Behind him, a creature of shadow stood in the firelight. Scipio's body slumped over the beast's long, black, human-like arm. Another claw plunged through the centurion's chain mail, pried open his chest and peeled back his ribcage. Bones snapped like twigs.

The man fell from the monster's grip. His heart remained in a claw.

The beast's black eyes looked into the same dead eyes as Lucius. In the dead mirrors their attentions became fixed on one another. The beast ate its prize while holding eye contact. Lucius understood the fear, which made his heart pound, skin shiver and bladder empty, increased the creature's pleasure.

Once finished, the shadow leaned over the hole it arose from, grasped the inner wall and descended into its lair.

Over a long silence, the light from the torch faded leaving him in darkness.

Later, whispers of a strange language neared. Scraping and sliding sounds came from the bodies being dragged out of the cave. A hand grabbed Lucius' leg and pulled. He sprung to life and kicked himself free. His resistance scared whoever tried to take him.

More hands returned. They grasped him by arms and legs. He tried to fight them off, but too many strong fingers grasped his skin. They took hold of him and dragged him away as their prize amongst the dead.

In the skylight outside the cave, a crowd of men gathered around him. Shame, for being reduced to a soul captured within a useless body, gripped his heart. Panic brought tears to his eyes. 'Jesus Christ!' he prayed.

When the men did not deliver death, his breath thinned to gasps. He realised; *they're planning something worse for me.*

***

The vane slacked. Weight went onto Lucius' weak legs which folded beneath him. He fell, face first, into the ground. Arms hooked underneath his armpits and hoisted him up. Waves of tension surged throughout his shoulder. Harsh tugs freed the thorns from his wrists.

Just kill me, he tried to plead but only moans escaped him. His captors hauled him through rotten leaves and soggy branches. They came into a clear area. Primitive dwellings, leafed branches bound together, more like animal nests than homes, reflected the barely human people who witnessed the rough handling of their captive.

Men lifted Lucius and pushed his back against a tree.

The grunts around him stopped. Someone approached. Spotlights from a small fire highlighted bones woven into the nearing figure's rags. *It's the witch,* Lucius recognised the halfway eyes, one living, one dead of the woman he encountered during the battle with the savages.

The witch talked spiritedly, making a distorted mixture of slurs, clicks, whistles and growls. Whether a surreal song or the casting of some curse, she directed her sounds at him. Stopping when her nose touched his, she forced her menace and madness into his eyes. *I have not yet descended into the depths of depravity you intended for me, have I?*

In mustering a growl, he matched her lunacy with the last of his defiance. This provoked her anger. She lashed out. Grabbed his hair and tore handfuls from his head. After scratching burnt flesh from his face, she grabbed his crucifix. Grafted into his skin by sunburn, it tore flesh when she pulled it free. She rubbed the iron into his face to aggravate his burnt skin.

Confused by her attack, unable to understand the words she screamed, he understood only that his cross instigated her vendetta. When she stopped, a girl brought her a Roman-made, wooden jug. *That came from one of the work parties that disappeared in the woods* he realised. The liquid dried onto its surface and gleamed black.

The witch lifted a hand to her mouth and said a word, 'Azz-ta.'

She caught the word in her hand, as though it were a bird fleeing her mouth, and placed it into the jug. The word excited the gathered savages.

'Azz-ta, Azz-ta, Azz-ta,' they chanted.

The child brought the jug to Lucius. Hands slid across his face and thrust his jaw open.

'Azz-ta...Azz-ta,' the men holding him chanted into his ear. Something wet rushed passed his lips, tongue and down his throat. He swallowed, trying not to choke.

The barbarians' excitement increased. The beat got louder and faster.

'AZZ-TA...AZZ-TA...AZZ-TA...'

His body tried to reject the fluid. He choked. One of the barbarians pressed their hand over his lips. He swallowed to fight the horrible sensation of drowning. He wanted to die, but his body, his prison, refused his desire.

His chokes faded. The hand on his lips and those supporting his body, let go. Lucius slumped to the ground. The witch knelt. She closed her dead eye first and measured him. Then closed her living eye and measured him again. She smiled in the manner of a dog showing teeth as a warning. A savagery satisfaction.

They left him unrestrained. Too weak to move, too hurt to care. He stared up at the moon. *If the moon is in the sky,* he comforted himself, *that means the sun cannot hurt me.*

They woke him at dawn.

Oh no, oh no, oh no... The moon, his idol of the sanctuary, no longer looked over him. Men returned him to the same tree from the day before.

'No, no, no, no,' he pleaded. When his captors slung him to the ground, one of them stamped on his nose. He stopped pleading. The foot hovered over his face but did not drop again. The fire returned to his shoulder as they spun him onto his front and moved his arms into a hauling position.

'Please no...' he mumbled. Thorns entrenched into his skin as the vines gripped his wrists. The men hauled the line. Lucius's arms swung above his head. The men hauled again. The teeth bit into his wrist. His feet lifted from the ground. The fire in his shoulder flashed over into an inferno of pain.

Each haul took him a step higher, into the sunspot of hell above. Lucius nodded his head as a means of trying to cope with the pain. He blinked in and out of consciousness.

The dawn light showed the savages' settlement. A clear area of ground, devoid of buildings.

Another haul, he forced himself to continue his observation, because he spotted something in the trees, which required further investigation.

Movement increased the pain but improved his view. Dead mercenaries, the men he marched into barbarous with, hung from branches, by their legs. Dried crimson painted their faces.

The tension and pain elevated again, as his body moved further up. Though a barrier of pain held him back, Lucius leaned forward until he recognised the wooden, Roman jugs on the ground below the bodies. The same as the jug he drank from the night before. Enough dawn light landed on the jugs to transform the black gleam of the liquid inside into red.

Lucius regurgitated down himself. The red liquid which came out of him tasted of blood. *What have I done* Lucius used the strength, gained from the night's rest, to curse his self-damnation with a lung-scraping shriek.

Another haul up and the sunlight welcomed him back to another day of torture.

Chapter Five.

The *Thetis* anchored in front of a channel that cut between two cliffs. Beyond the stone pier, a trail ascended to Saint Constantines.

'Usually, ships anchor here and use smaller boats to row ashore,' Ellrick explained. 'But that won't work because your horses are too big. So, we're going to feed the ship into the tide, and let it take us to the pier. Once we're secured, we'll get your horses ashore. Top priority.'

'They'll be ready to go,' Christopher said.

'Once they're ashore, should my ship need to pull out, we can use a boat to transfer your cargo. To get out, we'll lower the mainsail and use the wind to pull ourselves clear.'

A returning wind met the tide guiding the sea into the channel. Catching the cusp of the waves, it turned it into fine spray. Swirls rotated around boulders. Waves crashed against the cliff sides.

'The sea's angry,' Christopher said sizing up the harshness of the waterway.

'Mistress Tide doesn't like to be squeezed,' the captain replied. 'And she's already in a bad mood. There's a storm coming. When the wind from the sea meets the wind coming from the land, the sea and sky will clash.'

'Then I'm glad we'll be on land,' Richard added.

'I would take a storm at sea over a trek into "The Abyss of Trees" any day,' Ellrick confessed with a sympathetic smile at the squire. *The fact that the captain lost a ship in a storm emphasises his unease about Barbarous' woods.* Christopher thought.

In preparation for entering the channel, the crew hung rolled-up nets over the side as makeshift fenders, that would cushion any collision with a boulder.

To prevent the tide from controlling the ship, the crew looped the line attached to the embedded anchor around the main sail mast and then crisscrossed around two forward bollards. Six crew members fed the slack. Should they lose control of the line, it would tighten on itself and hold the ship still.

The anchor line became taut.

'Prep the horses,' Christopher instructed Richard. 'Saddle them and line them up, ready to ascend the ramp.'

Ellrick walked alongside the anchor line until he stood next to his pilot at the tiller. Should the ship spin, or anchor line snap, he would likely be killed. *Don't ask your men to do something you wouldn't do yourself*, the leader in Christopher acknowledged.

By overviewing the line, talking to his pilot and hand signalling the anchor crew, the captain managed his ship's entry into the channel. The anchor line became too tight. The ship tugged and resisted the pull of the tide. The *Thetis* cut through a returning wave, the wind became wet. A heavy, sideways rain whipped across the deck.

'PAY THE LINE OUT!' Ellrick commanded. Two sailors hooked a wooden beam between the crosses on the bollard, jumped and held onto its end. Their weight, combined with a bounce of the ship, loosened the tension in the line. The ship moved. The anchor crew kept speed with the movement.

This is like guiding an untrained horse through thick woods, Christopher observed. To him, the ship acted as an animal that wanted to follow its feet, rather than listen to instructions.

At the helm of the ship, Nemak shouted, 'HOLD IT!' as they approached the pier. High-pitched, half-panicked, half-excited, the sailor's voice matched the tone heard in the heart of a mêlée when some lord thought he could control the havoc.

He rested weight on the front of his feet and bobbed up and down in a preparation position. When the ship dipped, he leapt overboard, dropped onto the pier and stepped away from the edge. A thin line looped over his shoulder attached to a thicker holding line. Hand over hand, he hauled it towards a bollard.

Four crew members adjusted the makeshift fenders to the pier's level. Sailors aft swung out the looped head of the rear holding line to Nemak, who coiled it over another bollard. It took ten men, hauling on the rear holding line, to bring the ship horizontally to the pier. They then tightened the forward line and secured the ship.

'Sort that gangway.' Ellrick clapped his hands while he spoke and raced his men to the side railing. After a quick look over the pier, his head continued to turn until his eyes connected with Christopher's. The knight stood at the head of the ramp. Ellrick held out his palm, as though to say, 'be ready.'

'Leave that, Will. Come here,' Christopher said to his page, who swept the forward hold. William ran up the ramp. 'You're coming ashore with me. I want you to take control of the horses.'

'Do you want me to take one ashore?'

'No, I'll do that.'

Ellrick waved. Christopher raced down the ramp, took Bucephalus' reins and led the steed, up the ramp, across the deck and down the gangway to the start of the track ten paces away. There, he handed over the reins before collecting each horse in turn.

With his horses ashore, Christopher left Richard to organise the cargo Ellrick's men deposited on the jetty. He returned to the base of the gangway and whistled; low pitch at first but ending with a sharp rise. Crew members paused to admire Argus as he cantered passed them.

Argus enjoyed the voyage more than the rest of the team. The second morning, the crew lowered him into the bottom deck. They left him hunting all day. When night came, a man went to retrieve him. He took a bucket to cart away the anticipated dead rats. He filled it five times. Industrious during the night, sailors changed their morning routine to clear the upper deck of any rat corpses before work.

The hound ran from the gangway to Richard, who greeted him by shoving his muzzle before stroking his flank.

After the sailors finished delivering their cargo, they paused to exchange farewells with Richard and William. They only nodded as they passed Christopher to return to the ship. His lethal skills created distance between himself and others.

'Wait there, friend,' Ellrick said. He strode down the gangway and held out his hand. Christopher reached up and grabbed him by the forearm.

'I'm heading south,' the captain explained, 'to a town called Norsestone. If, after your mission, you wish to return to Ullumber, have the brothers send for me.'

'I shall.'

'You're a good man, Knight.'

'So are you, Captain. You have a strong ship and an outstanding crew. Thank you for your hospitality.'

'Give Gaston my regards.' Christopher smiled and nodded to indicate he said everything he wanted to.

'May the Lord be with you,' Ellrick said.

'And with you.' Turning away from each other, the two men faced different worlds.

***

The human contribution to the landscape interested Christopher more than the living horizon of the sea and the fortitude of the cliffs. He looked over the path to Saint Constantines while Richard and William prepared the horses.

Through the camouflaging effects of time and neglect, he identified the purpose behind the monastery's design. Eroded rock walls, now inhabited by seagulls, would have once shown the trademark of human design; straight edges. As wide as the pier, twenty-five, interconnected ramps made an inclining corridor through the cliff.

Maximise the advantage of height. Christopher understood the tactics. *Make them do what you want them to do.* Should anyone try to take the fortification, they would need to storm the cliff path. Longer than necessary, this pathway would slow down, if not exhaust, any attackers. Arrows and boulders would gain velocity from the wind and the fall.

'What are you thinking?' Richard said.

'I'm thinking they built that fortress, by cutting stone from these cliffs. They lied when they told us Saint Constantines is a monastery.'

'Didn't Ellrick say there is an aqueduct that leads into the abyss...the barbarian woods? I will wager that's made of cliff stone as well.'

'A fortification only approachable by the sea,' Christopher remarked. 'Foundations made with stone, designed to last forever. Powerful, ambitious people wanted these woods. The cliff path is a statement of their determination. Its makers built intelligently and with vast, vast manpower, yet they gave in...Why? Why would someone with so much strength surrender such an investment?'

The question simmered in the knight's mind as he continued to measure the path. Crashing waves drew him back from his distant thinking. Richard gave him a lead attached to Argus' leather harness.

'Go on,' the knight pointed at the path. Argus trotted ahead until his lead became tight. Each ramp measured ten paces deep. Sea spray dampened the broken stone ground of the bottom level making it slippery. Christopher walked at the front of his horses. Each tied to another, they made an interconnected line towards Thunderwind. William and Richard walked beside each other at the rear.

On his route upwards, walking from left to right, right to left, Christopher reviewed the wind. A constant force, it became more variable the higher he hiked. *This climb would be difficult at a charge, with arrows flying down and boulders falling.*

On the tenth level, seagulls landed in front of Argus. His lead snapped tight as he tried to catch one. Escaping seagulls aggravated the horses when they flew off.

On the fifteenth level, Christopher glanced down. William, still on the fourteenth level, happened to be looking up. Their eyes met for a second. *What a way to become a fighting man*, he contemplated, *being dragged to the end of the world, to an unknown abyss.*

But that is how boys become men, his mind countered itself. *The boy is sword-shy, but he will not stay that way for long.*

Twenty levels up, the wind lightened and became thinner and less hostile.

At the top, the crossing between the cliff top and Saint Constantines' formidable walls resembled the scalp of a balding man, with constant grass but visible stone ground. Christopher encountered a building designed and constructed as a fortress. *They have tamed a predator,* he thought.

Moss and weeds covered its weathered walls. Outlines of killing holes hid behind reeds. The gate opposite the path displayed signs of neglect, with rotten timber and rusting hinges. The knight identified multiple weaknesses with a casual glance. *Invaders would not need a battering ram,* he decided, *they could burn the gates down.* A square build tower measured twice the size of the walls. A renovated roof stood in contrast to its surroundings.

'It's the oldest castle I've ever seen,' Richard pointed out as he brought up the last of the horses.

'Castles are soldiers, swords and stone. These are only the forgotten foundations. They sent for us, but the gate isn't opening.'

No one is watching the sea. The tower invites trouble. They're either strange, stupid or both.'

'Here,' Richard passed him the sleeve that held Gaston's letter.

'Stay with the horses,' Christopher instructed. 'Keep them saddled. We might have to find another entrance. While I'm gone, explain to William the strengths and weaknesses of this position.'

The knight's knocks broke the tranquillity of the monastery's deserted shade. He glimpsed movement in the lowest of the tower's killing holes. Moments later, Argus sniffed at the base of the gate. A peephole opened. Christopher stepped back to display his docility, held up the sleeve, and said, 'Gaston.'

The response came in a rapid, unfamiliar language.

Holding the sleeve out, Christopher approached the hole. 'Gaston,' he repeated, sliding it through. The hole shut.

He returned to the horses and he tied Argus' lead to Bucephalus' saddle. His squire and page sparred. He walked to the edge of the cliff path, the rock wall.

The view from above is better than at the pier. How would an archer approach this, he thought while reviewing everything within range. A skilled bowman could choose a target for anywhere along the path, but a line of archers on either side of the passage could kill hundreds with each volley.

From here, waves that rocked the *Thetis* appeared to be insignificant white twists. The blue tone of the sea deepened into black as a storm dominated the horizon. Horns of boiling white spread outwards like smoke caught beneath an invisible roof. Explosions from the angry clouds guts attacked a defence of horrendous waves. *Eternal forces going to war,* Ellrick described such weather.

'Master!' Richard said. The squire held Bucephalus' reins. William held Argus' lead. They waited halfway between him and Saint Constantines' open gate. An envoy of six monks approached.

'Gaston?' Christopher met the brother at their head, who measured him more intently than the others.

'Yes,' the monk confirmed. *He's stocky for a religious man,* Christopher noted. Plump and muscular, Gaston looked compressed. Thick, dark eyebrows matched a line of grey hair over his lip, but the rest of his head displayed natural baldness.

'Welcome to Saint Constantines,' he raised his left hand, as though preparing to grasp his guest's name.

'On his knighthood,' Richard declared, 'My lord received the name Christopher.'

'Christopher,' Gaston grasped the knight's hand with both his own and vibrated it with affection. 'The guardian of travellers, a fitting omen for our journey, no?'

The closer the storm came, the bigger it grew, the damper the air turned. Thunder ricocheted off the cliffs and the monastery. The storm distracted Gaston enough for his expression to show a moment of fear.

'Shall we go inside?' the knight suggested.

'My Brothers' shall take your horses to our stables,' Gaston said. 'Please follow me.'

Before entering Saint Constantines, Christopher checked on the development of the storm. The sea defended itself with high, crashing waves, against being swallowed by the sky. Aware of its enemy, the land strengthened its defences, and the wind made a whistling war song as it pushed past him to face the coming threat. *Eternal forces*, Christopher mused, *or are these omens?*

***

Once through the passageway leading to the gate, William discovered a world of colour. Boxed in by twenty-foot-high walls, the ache-sized, roofless space teemed with more tones than a tapestry. Its vegetation ranged from row upon row of vegetables and crops to an assortment of fruit trees, berry bushes and meadow area.

The moment heavy rain arrived, two monks ran outside to cover a bee hive with sheets. With the perfumes of the garden dampened down by the rain, the odour of livestock filled the air.

Argus's lead, which pulled in William's hand, alerted the page to his party's movements.

Gaston led them around the garden, through a tall corridor. Each door on the outer wall sat open. The small rooms housed a simple bed, table and stool. The garden light stopped these rooms from being dark.

They entered another corridor. This time, instead of a garden, the open area housed livestock, pigs, sheep, chickens, geese and a pair of milking cows.

Distracted, William paid no attention as loop after loop of the dog lead slipped out of his hand. It whipped free. The hound avoided the livestock and sprinted towards a large heap of manure. He scattered the horde of seagulls that picked at it, climbed his way to the summit, dived onto his side and slid downwards. William, having given chase, could almost see the smile on the hound's face.

'Come on,' he said searching around the ground for the lead, 'get out of there.'

Halfway through his second climb of the manure, Argus caught his master's whistle. After one last roll, he ran toward the call, his filthy leash trailing behind him. Again, giving chase, William almost slipped on the soft mud.

Back inside the corridor, he pursued the hound's trail of dirt. He rounded a corner at speed and slipped as he tried to avoid colliding with an elderly monk. William fell forwards. His head only missed the bottom step of a stairway by a hair's breadth. Someone on the stairs rushed to help him but stopped, as though taking control of themselves. He glanced in their direction, met their eyes and realised; *You're a woman*. From shock grew attraction. *A beautiful woman*.

The moment slowed. The lust which surged through him created a confused excitement of both fear and wonder.

She took another step closer. *Did she do this to allow me to view her better?* Cut short, her brown hair highlighted the elegance of her neck and shoulders. Her brown eyes expressed a thousand things, but in his disorientation he could not define one of them.

The monk, who William nearly ran into, knelt and offered his hand. He spoke fast and in a language the page did not understand. William stood and tried to apologise by using hand gestures. Twice he checked the empty staircase for her.

The monk pointed to where he should go. William walked away. His head down, he strode over the muddy paw prints. Soon he gravitated towards voices.

'This is William,' Christopher announced him. 'Before becoming my page, he acted as Bishop Monroe's senior deacon. If he speaks to you, I trust you to grant him my authority.' Gaston acknowledged him with a smile as Christopher's introduction elevated his status.

'As I said, winter seems to have arrived as we have,' the knight continued. 'How long will it be before the rain is replaced by snow?'

'Always listen to our master,' Richard once advised. William tried to concentrate on the questions asked rather than the answers given. *What is she doing here?* thoughts about the woman distracted him.

'It tends to happen within the same month,' Gaston said. Christopher controlled conversations with his eyes. When he looked at you, it meant talk. When he turned away, it indicated to pause while he considered something.

'Well, we should be grateful for any advantage over the snow,' he said. 'You shall require suitable robes for the wet and the cold. I trust you can provide my men with the things we will need for the trek?'

'Of course.' Gaston nodded and smiled in an effort to establish a friendly rapport. William liked him.

'I trust you can ride a horse?'

'It has been a while. But one does not forget. We can provide two donkeys for the journey.'

'Thank you, but no. Our horses will carry our supplies. You can ride the first one that becomes available.

In your letter you referred to a guide. I presume he is busy, and that is why we have not already met him?'

'I'm afraid we have a matter to discuss about our guide.'

Footsteps at the door drew the attention of the room. William found himself ambushed by feelings he did not know existed inside of him. Hot flushes and nervousness radiated with tingles up from his stomach to the tips of his limbs. Though beautiful in half-light, her sense of distance created safety then but now, in the open air, up close, the realness of the woman created a power over him.

'Sir Christopher,' Gaston said. 'Allow me to introduce you to our guide, Lady Eve.'

Shocked, William gauged his master's reaction. Christopher's face tensed with anger.

***

The storm raging outside mirrored the one trapped inside Christopher. He lay on a wooden bed unable to sleep.

I do not want the monk travelling with me, he directed frustrated thoughts at Gaston, *but I need him. The language problems are one example of that. I do not trust Gaston. His motives for bringing me to the monastery seem selfish. Theodus' request for help gave the monk an opportunity of some kind. I will help those in need, but I will not be manipulated.*

He rose out of bed, his bare feet nudged past Argus to find the cold, stone floor.

Even in the dark, he could tell the difference between the two figures in the opposing beds. Richard lay still, resting like a leaf with no wind beneath it. William moved as he wrestled against his dreams.

Accompanied by Argus, he left the room. Rain in the garden glistened in the glow from the seaward tower that lit up the allotment. The lanterns, which illuminated the inside corridors, had expired.

Christopher returned to the room Gaston took them to earlier. He led Argus to the monk's stool. The hound wagged his tail while he sniffed, before trotting out of the room, his nose to the ground. He headed in a straight line, before turning onto some stairs. At the top, he turned again onto a corridor. He stopped at a door. Light seeped underneath its seal.

From inside came a sound like someone struggling to breathe. He pushed the door open. The room, similar to the ones below; small and simple with a bed, a table and a stool, boasted one exception; a window. Nails held its shutters closed. On his knees praying, Gaston turned away from the fading lantern which illuminated the room.

'Christopher,' he said. 'How can I help you?'

I misinterpreted the breathing sound. Christopher realised...*the sound was his weeping.*

'The girl doesn't come with us.'

'Please, come inside and be seated.' The knight sat on the bed, the monk on the stool.

'I can assure you,' Gaston continued, 'Eve understands the woods better than anyone. She will be a vital addition to our team.'

'There is a safety within these walls which I cannot provide for her in the woods.' Despite hating being rude to a man of God, Christopher decided it best to be blunt. 'Of all the horrors men meet at the hands of other men, none are so bad as the things men are capable of doing to women...'

Gaston interrupted. 'You think she is safe from such things here?'

'I have a squire and a page to consider,' Christopher countered. 'It is not fair to ask them all the things I am asking of them and then test them with temptation as well.'

'But she knows the way.'

'Then she can give us directions.'

'Things are not as simple as you think,' the monk's voice broke. 'By God, she earned the right to go...'

'She isn't coming, and if you feel so strongly about it, then don't come either.'

'STOP!' Gaston pleaded. 'Stop.'

The monk looked away for a second, towards the window, then met Christopher's eyes with a new resolve. 'After all this time, I finally have to bare my soul. And, if in the telling, I shall lose it again, then so be it.'

The Monk paused to muster courage. 'I have a trade for you, Sir. In exchange for Eve's place on your mission, I will give *you* my confession. Let me assure you, the truth I will tell you is very valuable, for no one knows it, except the Lord and I.'

***

William pulled himself out of the pool of blood, from the vivid nightmare and back into consciousness. His right hand pressed against his chest and rubbed his numb skin. Gasping for breath, he focused on the door, which caught in a draft, tapped open and shut. He synchronised his chest with the movement. Damp, cold air rushed into his lungs. He coughed.

The sound of rainfall, flowing through the monastery's drains, gave William a strong need to urinate. He rushed out of bed, got to the side of the allotment and groaned as he relieved himself.

A pale orange, from the sea tower's beacon, filtered through thick rain onto the allotment's meadow, orchard and rows of crops. William flinched as someone appeared.

'Can't sleep?' Richard asked as he stood next to him.

'I never can.' Both men faced forward while they talked and urinated.

'Well, if you can't sleep,' said Richard, 'I won't sleep either. When Gaston showed us around earlier, did you notice the other tower?'

'No, I needed to chase Argus, and...'

'Well, I did,' the squire interrupted him. 'It's directly across from the beacon tower. If that one faces the sea, then the other one must face the woods. Let's go there, wait for sunrise and have a look at this abyss of trees.'

Richard fetched a stool from his room. He stamped on each leg, breaking them loose. Next, he fetched a pillow and flints. He ripped the pillowcase open, shook the feathers out into the allotment, then rubbed the cloth in the oil of a nearby expired lantern. After he stripped the pillowcase into strips, he wrapped cloth around the end of each stool leg. He used a flint to light the first torch. A pocket of light stressed the corridor's size.

This place is huge, William thought. The squire went into the room a third time and returned with his clothes in a heap.

'Get dressed Will,' he instructed. 'It will be wet and windy up there, so borrow Christopher's hooded cloak.'

Richard led them to a staircase wider than any of the inter-floor staircases. Water flowed down it into a gutter placed between the corridor and the livestock field to stop it from flooding.

'Let's go up.'

Richard lit another torch and handed it to William.

Rain ran over William's feet as they climbed the stairs. After turning four times, they came to two closed doors on either side of the corridor. *They must open onto the roof of the monastery*, he thought as they passed.

The strength of the storm's breath increased as they ascended the stairs above the main building. The torch thinned and ran horizontally as though pointing down the stairs, asking them to turn back.

Richard handed William his torch before he pried loose the boards which restricted most of the access to the tower room. Wind and rain came in through holes in the roof. A decrepit, three-foot-high barrier restricted the view towards the woods. From the deep darkness came a constant wet whipping rain.

Both men hid behind a pillar, their backs against the stone, their feet freezing, while they waited for the sunrise.

***

'One month after I arrived here to start my training,' Gastion confessed. 'Theodus' mission arrived. They came to deliver the Lord's word to the wilderness beyond these walls. I never knew courage, nor honour, like it. I wanted to join them, but I feared disobeying my Holy Orders. After Theodus left, I thought of nothing but joining the mission.'

'All men dream of greatness, Christopher. Monks are no different. When I turned twenty, I decided to join the mission. One day, while the other monks ate, I dropped from the upper wall into the aqueduct. I followed the flow of water day after day.

Since I promised to tell you the truth, I must admit that in those few days of freedom, I lived with more passion in my spirit than any day before or since. When the water road ended, I should have turned back. I understood this at the time, but, youth, arrogance, faith...'

'When I left the aqueduct, I took to sleeping in the trees. I found a trail I thought would lead me to the mission. Instead of stopping one night when I should have, I pushed on, determined to reach my new home.'

A girl appeared on the track. Remembering her fear breaks my heart. She ran straight into my arms and squeezed as though to never let go.

Behind her, a boy ran along the same path. He too turned his scared eyes upon me and perceived me to be his salvation. Before reaching me, something grabbed him. Confused at first, I did not understand how the boy rose into the air. Then I saw the black, clawed hand which held him.'

'Rather than help the boy,' Gaston hesitated. His hands shook. Tears flowed down his cheek to drip off his chin. 'I threw myself to the ground. I landed on top of the girl. She made no sound. I thought I killed her, but I didn't care. I wanted to save myself.'

'Did you look at it?' Christopher asked

'The demon stood in the moonlight,' Gaston answered. 'It looked like the shadow of a man manifested into flesh. The lips of its muzzle peeled back because its teeth were too long, like nail-edged fingers.

Something metallic contrasted its black skin and protruded from its chest. The demon held the boy in the object's way, preventing me from identifying its shape.' Gaston paused for a breath. The wind at the window blew harder as though objecting to the confession.

'Since that moment then, to this one now, I wonder how the demon did not see me,' he said. 'My only answer is the Lord even grants cowards favours. The boy saw me, though. Before they disappeared, he looked into my eyes. He recognised the kind of man I am that I would not help him. In a blink, both beast and boy faded into the night.'

'Sometimes somethings become instantly clear,' the monk explained. 'I knew, at that moment, that a greater power tested me. I also understood I failed my Lord, myself, everything I ever stood for.'

Gaston's eyes drifted back to memory. 'When the morning came, I took the girl and ran.'

'What more could you have done?' The knight squeezed the man's knee to entice him to look at the empathy in his expression. 'Perhaps the Lord's purpose for you was to save Eve.' He understood the girl he talked of must be Eve. 'If it not been for you, she would have died.'

'Try as one may,' Gaston replied, 'you cannot hide the truth from your own heart. I acted cowardly. I failed.' Though the storm beat at the window, the stillness inside the room indicated Gaston no longer wanted to talk.

Christopher grasped the need to encourage the man who would soon be his responsibility. 'So you brought me here to help her?' He said.

'When I first brought her here,' Gaston said, 'the brothers saw the child, not her sex. They granted her stay, but they also named her Eve, so we would not forget the woman she would become. As a child, she provided laughter and joy in these halls. We treated her as a gift.'

'Yet as Eve grew into a woman, the brothers who accepted her began to be replaced by younger men, with youthful lusts. Look and you will detect the ungodly desires in some of their eyes. For now, the old order maintains discipline, but it will not last forever. Change is coming to the monastery, and when that happens, I am certain something terrible will happen to Eve.'

'In truth, it is for my brothers' sake as much as hers that she should leave Saint Constantines. She must return but also live safely in the mission, that's why I helped bring you here.'

'She may come with us,' Christopher said, 'so long as you promise me to find peace with what happened.'

'For a long time, I tried to forget what happened in the abyss. I cannot. So, I tried to live with the memories. I cannot. For years, I've waited to die. Then one night, six months ago, a man came out of the woods. When I listened to his story, listened to the purpose of his journey, I thanked the Lord for offering me the chance to redeem myself.

Yes, my Lord may have forgiven me, but I have not forgiven myself. If I can get her home, however, then maybe I can find redemption.'

Having come to understand Gaston, the storm inside Christopher stopped. He now wanted to take the monk, and the girl, to the mission. He stood and walked to the doorway.

'It took courage for you to confess all that you did,' he said. 'You have done Eve proud.'

'When I ran,' Gaston said, 'I feared the demon, but it was the boy who followed me here. It is his face, the fear in his eyes, the disappointment and loss of hope, which survives in my memories. I see him in my prayers. His gaze haunts me, he is still looking into my eyes.'

***

William tried to shield himself from the thickening rain. Wind from the strengthening storm blew around the pillar he hid behind and stung his face. His torch, long expired, lay discarded on the floor.

Torchlight grew into the room. Richard held a silencing finger over his lips. The person who approached froze when they encountered two men inside.

'We mean you no harm, Eve,' Richard said.

Initially too heavily wrapped up for William to recognise her, when he met her eyes, his skin tingled, and he sweated despite the consistent cold of the night.

'I'm sorry,' she replied. 'I didn't expect anyone to be here.'

'We're waiting for the sunrise. We want to see Barbarous.'

'That is why I came,' she glanced from one to the other. 'I have no place in the monastery. My place is out there.' She pointed a finger into the storm.

'You talk as though Saint Constantines and "The Abyss of Trees" are the only two places that exist.' Richard huffed, 'You do understand the world is much bigger?'

'I have never known anything other than the monastery.'

'Please, tell us about it.'

'How is your history? are you aware of the Romans?'

'I went to Rome,' Richard retorted, 'met Romans, ate their food, drank their wine and beheld the wonders of their city.' Eve's eyes widened. *She's impressed* William realised, *I wish I impressed her.*

'Well, when the Romans discovered Barbarous, they wanted to forest its trees and mine its mountains. They built Saint Constantines, not as a monastery but as the centre of a northern trading city.'

'What went wrong?' William asked. 'Why did they abandon it?'

'They wanted an aqueduct and a road to stretch from here to the mountains. While they built them, unexpected things happened. A workforce disappeared into the woods.

A legion went after them, to discover their fate. They found bodies, mutilated, riddled with forearm-sized bite marks. Each night a legionnaire disappeared. Those who made it back to the monastery gave the woods its name, "The Abyss of Trees". A quote from one man labelled it; "the dark place, where men slip into the screams, where a man's soul falls from his hands." The legionnaires arrived on eight ships. They left on only one.'

'That's when Rome abandoned th...'

'No,' Eve interrupted. 'First, they brought in their best centurion, Scipio, a beast hunter of acclaim. Everything I told you came from the records of one of the monasteries' first priests, Lucius. He went with Scipio and his men, "the tusk takers", into the abyss.' *And they never returned*, thought William.

'One more workforce went into the abyss,' Eve said.

'Disappeared?' Richard guessed.

'Not just them,' Eve continued. 'A supply boat came to Saint Constantines after an extraordinarily harsh winter. They found the monastery's halls empty, save for the streaks of blood leading into the woods.'

'So how did this place become a monastery?' Richard enquired.

'The first brothers to come here, years after its abandonment, did so as an act of faith; to show they trusted God to protect them. They've been here ever since. Praying, tending their gardens, committing themselves to scriptures.'

'How come you're here?' William said. 'A lone woman amongst so many men?'

'I was born in the mission, which is why Gaston believes I will be able to find the way.'

'Find the way?' Richard said. 'You're meant to be our guide?'

'Gaston told your master that, so he would take me back. Please understand. My mother came here to seek help. She died of exhaustion, so it became my responsibility to find help for the...'

Unwanted memories swept forward from the silent rear of William's mind. A child again, he walked the path beaten nightly through his dreams. The white world became a burning world, ash, not snow, fell. His mother screamed his name. Something broke beneath his foot. Red came through the white. The plunging feeling rushed through his stomach. He choked and tasted blood.

'Are you alright, Will?' Richard asked as the Page coughed. He caught his lost breath and asked Eve, 'Your mother died?'

'I don't remember her. Gaston manned the gate the night she arrived, she told him she came from Theodus' mission, seeking help. Which means I may have family still waiting for aid.

I've always wanted to go back, but Gaston made me promise not to go until help came. It never did. The mission became another one of the workforces that disappeared. Then the old man came out of the woods, and we sent for help again. There have been other requests, but this time your master answered the call and you,' she looked from Richard to William, 'you came as well.'

A thrill of nerves flushed up his arms, tingling the cold sweat on his back as she acknowledged he existed.

'If you are going to help Theodus' mission,' Eve declared. 'I will do everything I can to help you. And if we fail, then no one else will come. Hope will die and the mission will disappear into the "Abyss of Trees".'

***

Argus sniffed at the freshly strung chickens and geese, the shanks of lamb, pork, beef, and sacks of oats, fresh herbs, vegetables and fruits that hung from Ash's saddle. Thunderwind carried the same rations. Though bred for better burdens, the coursers carried three days' worth of rations each.

The four rounceys: Stormpath, Lunar, Springly and Beck, carried five days of rations each.

'We're going to need plenty of fire, for warmth, cooking our food and drying our clothes.' On Richard's suggestion a leather pouch full of the oil, which the brothers used in their lanterns, hung from each saddle. 'We should assume all the wood we can collect will be wet, so let us make making fire as easy as possible.'

Awake since his visit to Gaston, Christopher brought their departure forward to noon that day. *There is no benefit in waiting.* He decided.

At first, Gaston contributed to the collective effort to prepare the horses, but as news spread of his early departure, his brothers distracted him as they came to say farewell.

These people, who clearly cared for each other, shared a rushed moment in a damp, windy corridor to say goodbye. Many men cried. *You understand how they feel, don't you,* he thought upon seeing William's eyes glaze with tears.

'Are you thinking of Monroe?' He asked the page.

'Yes Master.'

'Then remember everything you see, return to visit him and tell him about it all, that will make him happy.'

Many monks came to wish Gaston farewell. None visited Eve.

Gaston embraced an older, senior one of his brothers when Christopher approached.

'I am sorry to be taking so much from you,' Christopher said to the monk. 'You will have to fast to compensate for the food we are taking. For that I am grateful. Please understand that the decision to leave early was not an easy one.'

'I understand,' the monk replied. 'Please accept these offerings with love and hope.' To Gaston, he said, 'May you find what you are looking for out there, brother.'

'Peace be with you.'

'And you. And to you Christopher.'

'And you.' The knight stayed still. 'May I have a word with you Gaston?'

'Of course.'

'Richard and William know already, and I've just said this to Eve. If you're coming with me, it is your own choice. As soon as we step out of those gates, you do as you're told. The stronger we stay, the better our chance for success.

I've made decisions on how to best reach the mission. Because I need horses more than I need people, they got the better of the compromise.

The further we go, the more our rations will be divided amongst them. For now, we all walk. No one rides, until everyone can ride.

'You and Eve will lead the way when the aqueduct ends. Until then, I lead, you two will follow me, and my two will follow you. If anything happens, Richard and William will protect you.

We'll stop and rest well before sunset. At night, we all keep watches. Fall asleep on a watch and I'll send you back.

Is everything I just said understood?'

'Yes, of course...Thank you again for doing this...For me...For her.'

'Listen to me, to my men, and you'll get her home, Gaston.' Could Christopher take the monk's worries, he would have. Still, the words seemed to soothe the fear of failure sitting within Gaston's eyes.

As more monks came to see Gaston off, Richard supervised William as he fitted Christopher's armour. Placed over a layer of padding, the steel plates worked as insulation, keeping heat in.

Argus, who anticipated their departure, walked by the horses lined along the corridor, stopped at the front and wagged his tail.

'Do you hear that, Brother?' Christopher asked.

'I did,' Richard confirmed.

'It's calling William's name. Do you hear it?'

'I heard it too...It called his name.'

'Can you hear it, William?'

'Hear what?' the page leaned with his ear, listening for the sound.

'Battle, little brother,' Richard said. 'Battle is calling your name. William...William...William.' The page laughed.

'It's not funny, William...This is serious.'

'No. I know. But...' Christopher and Richard both smirked, waiting for his attempt at an impossible answer.

'Don't worry,' Richard patted his back. 'Just remember, when the time comes, if you fight, you have a chance.' William's eyes widened. Richard's words shook his nerves.

Though the door built into the gate opened occasionally, the last time most likely for the man from the woods, the actual main gate had been stationary for a long time. A mixture of older and younger monks worked on opening it that morning. They stood to the side of the corridor leading to the gate. All but one of them approached Gaston as he came around the corner.

An old monk held his hands out to Eve. He smiled at her with a toothless grin that conveyed the memory of lots of innocent laughter. Christopher thought, *at least someone loved her.*

Rain gushed down the hole created by the open gate. Christopher put on his cloak, lifted his hood and led Bucephalus out of Saint Constantines. The war horse carried minimal extra weight, only his master's shield and a stripped-down saddle. Even with the added requirements of the situation, it would be folly to restrict his most lethal weapon. A knight mounted on a destrier became seven times deadlier. *I might need that advantage,* he judged.

He led them diagonally before straightening up next to the twenty-foot-high, moss-ridden aqueduct wall. It wept from cracks. Water overflowed, ran down its stone bricks, and then through fractures in the path.

Six horses and four escorts followed Christopher. *Eve lacks confidence with the horses,* he recognised.

Earlier, while Richard and William fitted fleece-lined leather coats to the horses, she stood back, reluctant to touch and engage. She later rushed to help Gaston gather things from the gardens.

When Christopher told her she would be walking for a long while, she looked relieved.

At some point she needs to learn how to ride, he decided. *At the end of each day, Richard shall give her a lesson. If anything happens the horses will give her a better chance of escape.*

In front, Argus' tail splashed through the rain. Ahead further, the outline of the giant trees acted as a barrier against the storm.

What's waiting inside you? Christopher thought. *Storms? Darkness? Demons? Death?*

Dwarfed by the trunks of the surrounding trees, the aqueduct stretched into the woods, a looming tunnel, it marked man's previous failed attempts to tame "The Abyss of Trees". The wildness that grew over the top cancelled out the notion of claimed land.

This will be Richard's last ride. Christopher thought. In his last correspondence with his Administrator, he nominated Richard for the trials of the Sacred Fires.

Forty days and forty nights of examinations, the trials tested mental and physical strengths. When Richard succeeded, after a commissioning ceremony Christopher hoped to attend, the new knight would be presented with armour, a shield and a sword, forged from the finest blacksmiths within the Christian Empire's reach.

His brother would be baptised as a champion of the holy mission. He would be renamed after a saint of his choosing, both to represent and to be guided by.

I believe in you Richard, Christopher intended to say at the moment of their parting, *you will surpass my achievements. One day I will be looking up at you from the horse you knocked me off. I thank you for your service.* His parting gift would be the squire's favourite horse, Ash.

For now, he needed Richard. Not just for his sword, but to get William to an appropriate standard to replace him. With Richard gone, the page would have to be ready to step up, or the knight would have to find someone else. He could ill afford weaknesses.

With Richard's assessment to come after Barbarous, William's evaluation started now. He needed to prove his potential.

Tall, with a good reach and starting to broaden to the requirements of his training, he presented a good physical prospect. Christopher liked him. Richard liked him. Inquisitive and enthusiastic about his new trade, William loved working with the horses. He showed up for sword training with the key ingredient, enthusiasm. Usually, he only needed to be shown things once before he understood them, and he was either smart enough or tough enough, to not complain, ever.

Christopher possessed one concern; the nightmares, *is that the chink in his armour? Or a part of the mental toughness he displayed during his sword training?*

Ahead, Argus faded into the dark. Feeling himself enter into the shadow of the woods, Christopher thought, *Now, let us find out what is awaiting us inside?*

Chapter Six.

Inside the woods, light concentrated around the aqueduct. Long ago replacing the ancient trees, the stone construction created a crack in the canopy above where wind and rain weaved through.

Though bogged with soggy foliage, the path beside the aqueduct allowed for good progress but offered little shelter against the weather. They walked through constant rain.

The long day of marching distanced the monastery, and sea voyage before that, from William's memory. Tiredness, hunger and the chill of being soaked grounded the page in the moment.

'Everywhere you go,' Richard suggested that morning, 'improve your basics. Talk to your horse, learn to hear how he speaks to you. Practice with your training sword.'

Thunderwind followed the horse in front, which allowed William to experiment with his weapon.

At first, he duplicated Richard's warm-ups, he thrust and slashed. The Squire, who walked in front of him, then put combinations together that the page could not manage. He returned to the basics.

When the squire moved onto skills with his sword; moving his body at the same time as thrusting, almost dancing with the training weapon, William did not even try to duplicate the motions. He stuck to passing the sword around his hands.

Later, he challenged himself to catch the spinning handle or manoeuvre the weapon with his eyes closed. He often dropped the sword.

Regardless of success, or improvement, he enjoyed the game. A sense of self-growth came from investigating the weapon and teaching himself its tendencies.

'Halt,' Richard said. 'Guard the rear.' The squire went to the front and conferred with the knight. They lit torches before they walked into the woods. Their flames dimmed like embers dissolving into water.

At the rear, by himself, William recognised his vulnerability. He clenched his training sword as though to make it a weapon.

'Dusk is drawing light from the air.' He said to Thunderwind. The horse seemed relaxed. He turned to face the way back. His vision stretched a stone's throw along the aqueduct. The haze beyond, with its sense of mystery in a world requiring clarity, unsettled him.

Christopher remerged, took Bucephalus' reins and led him into the woods. Richard returned to the rear.

'When we've sorted the horses,' the squire said while approaching, 'I've got something for you to do.'

The stable aqueduct path gave way to soft ground which crunched with broken, rotting branches. Tree roots rose out of the earth. They grew over and around each other and ranged in width from a few feet to half-as-wide as a tree themselves.

Confronted with a tree, thicker, wider and taller than anything he ever encountered before, he thought, *how can I describe this to Father Monroe?* More a product of the sky than the earth, towering above smaller trees, its head resembled a brown and green cloud.

Entwined roots, grown into each other, made pools for rainwater, but also acted as borders around raised mud beds.

'We'll camp here tonight.' Christopher indicated towards a flat area. His voice contrasted with the massive silence. 'Gaston, Eve, prepare a fire and some food. Eve, you can take the first watch. Gaston, you can take the second. Before any of you go to sleep, dry yourself by the fire first.'

Rather than being told what to do, William copied Richard. He took his horse aside, unpacked the things on top of the saddle first and laid them the furthest away. When he re-saddled, he would reverse this order. Next, he brushed down Thunderwind and gave him a feed bag. Upon completion of his horse duties, Richard approached him with a single-sided, three-foot axe. He said,

'Follow me.' He walked back towards the aqueduct, but he stopped by a tree within sight of the camp.

'The axe weighs more than a sword,' the squire rotated the handle in his hand while he explained. 'So, by the time you come to use steel, you'll find it easy to handle. You're going to use this to develop controlled strength. Observe me.'

Richard held the axe beside his shoulder, his legs firmly planted. Its blade swept in a blur, taking a bite from the trunk, then returned to its original position. He repeated the process, the only difference being the axe head sunk further into the trunk. Quicker than the first two, it bit again. Quicker still, it bit again. Each time it targeted the same spot.

Richard paused with the axe in the starting position.

'Ahhh, that feels good,' he breathed deep. 'Your turn.' He kept the axe frozen in the air and stepped back while extending his arm. William took the tool. *This isn't as heavy as I thought.*

In an attempt to imitate Richard, he twisted his body into the sweep. The hit landed higher and further around the tree than the established crater. He pushed the axe from side to side to pry it loose.

'Forget about my cut, Will,' Richard said, lifting the page's elbow upwards. 'Pick your spot. Somewhere between your waist and your shoulder would be best.'

William threw himself into the swing, his hands jarred on impact, and the thump tingled his ear. He pried the axe loose. Before he could try for the same cut, Richard stopped him.

'Take a deep breath first,' the squire advised and demonstrated. 'With it, acknowledge your strength. You're a big, powerful bastard. Remember that. Then when you're ready, breathe out and command your weapon.'

William nodded but never took his concentration away from his target. He built his chest up with a deep breath and held the oxygen in his lungs for a moment, before releasing it and the axe. As the metal sliced through the air, it diverted his attention. He glanced away from the target. His hands slid together. He missed by three inches.

'Rather than try to find your target with your weapon, use your eyes to tell the axe where to hit,' Richard said. 'Focus on a spot. Think about what you're going to do. Then do it. And don't try to place all your weight onto the top. Spread the weight throughout the axe.' With empty hands, Richard demonstrated what he meant. 'Just remember, you're in charge, not the axe. Try again.'

'RICHARD,' Christopher called. The squire patted his apprentice on the back, 'Keep going,' he instructed before leaving.

William repeated the pattern of breathing, targeting and thinking through his actions. He practised again and again. Frustration grew at being unable to hit the target consecutively.

After every successful hit, he missed more the next time. *I'm getting lucky when I hit the target* he acknowledged. *I'm not hitting it by ability. Richard displayed his power and skill with gracefulness and purpose. I'm just swinging the axe and hoping for the best.* After pushing himself to his limit, he rested with the axe in the starting position.

Laughter drew his attention to Richard who guided Ash, mounted by Eve, towards the aqueduct. Nervous to be riding, she displayed a dependency on Richard. *Why him, why not me? This small, close moment should be mine.* More interested in his horse, Richard paid Eve no more attention than making sure she would not fall. *I would have talked to her,* William thought, *I would have made the most of the opportunity.*

He tried to return his attention to the tree. Though tired, he swung the axe to cover up his interest.

She laughed again from further away.

He swung the axe. The tool's tooth found its natural target. He swung again, his worst miss yet.

Seeing Richard and Eve together mixed his emotions. They swirled in his stomach. Now, as his emotions settled, he became angry. Angry at Eve for not looking at him the way she looked at Richard. Angry for not being able to control himself and for caring too much.

He swung his axe again and again, his body guided it into the target. Focussing on this action, forgetting about the axe itself, he found a rhythm. Each hit edged closer to the last until he landed one perfectly.

When his strength gave way, while he stared and panted, he realised what Richard tried to tell him earlier. *The weapon doesn't hold the power, I do.* His means of grasping the knowledge tickled him. He laughed, coughed, and inhaled. *Why did I allow myself to feel so angry?* He wondered. *Why did I direct my anger towards Richard? Why did I...*

'MUM...' A child screamed.

The axe dropped from his hand. He searched the woods, the light areas and the unseen parts of the abyss. Nothing appeared out of place. Richard walked Ash and Eve. Gaston stood beside a fire, tending a boiling pot. Christopher cleaned his armour.

The horrible tingling inside him seemed to have no justification. But it did. *I know what I heard.* He recognised the scream, because every night, in his nightmares, he screamed that same way.

***

The second day duplicated the first, with the addition of a morning hike. A landscape above them, the canopy grew like hills. Each new titanic tree contributed to a valley of treetops. The rain seeped through. The wind blew down. The more they hiked, the deeper an obsession developed within William. Yes, he aimed to become a knight. For now, the thought of becoming a squire excited him more.

He wanted to be like Richard: practical but intelligent; confident; well-travelled; battle-hardened and skilled in swordsmanship and horsemanship.

I want to be able to manipulate my sword as well as he can. A step behind the squire, his concentration often led him into a trance of admiration focussed on the movements of the training sword.

For all his attributes, Richard is modest as well. Able to talk to anyone, on any level; peasants and knights, sailors and ship captains, monks and women.

During his daydreams, William remembered the sparring sessions between knight and squire on the Thetis. *I hope one day that will be me sparring with Christopher.* Though he could imagine lots of things, this dream seemed too far a stretch for his mind's eye.

Though he spent lots of time thinking, he still spent time practising. After two days, he mastered the art of sword training while keeping pace.

As the day wore on, his thoughts centred more and more on axe training. The act of firing an axe into a tree, being physically harder, felt more rewarding, like each swing became a step towards his goal.

Christopher created their routine with the night watchmen's hourglass. A day's march lasted eleven turns, with three breaks included. Each night split into four duties, each of which, lasted three turns.

One turn went into other duties: cooking, riding and axe training. After setting up the camp, Christopher untied his armour and polished it before drying himself by the fire. He prayed by himself, with his sword in his hand then practised with the weapon.

Richard, having worked out the team's dietary needs before the departure, did not want to have to hunt or rely on the woods for anything. He briefed Gaston on which rations to use for each evening's stews; chickens first, and the geese second before progressing onto the lamb. The pork would be next before moving onto the salted previsions, salted pork first and then salted beef.

Christopher did extra watch hours to help the monk, the oldest member of his team, cope with the extensive marching.

William's fantasy of becoming a squire belonged to his daytime dreams. During the long and lonely night watch, with only a fire to maintain and a small area to patrol, he thought backwards rather than forwards.

He anticipated hearing the boy cry "Mum" again. It did not come, but memories did.

He replayed his earliest memory; of a sunset that lasted an entire day, and a wind which smelt of smoke. He remembered "The Burning" coming close until one day it arrived in his village. With the first light of morning, he imagined himself as a squire or a knight, equipped with armour and on horseback, ready to revenge the wrongs done to him.

The sounds of the weather became constant along with the shallow flow of water over the road, otherwise, the woods remained silent and deceptive.

On the third day, they crossed an area of path eroded by the water which bulged over the top and then washed away into the woods. The team sunk to their knees in mud while crossing it.

Once, while urinating next to a tree, William sighted a beam of light cutting through the canopy, which—being so vast—resembled an overcast sky. Streams, collected above the treeline, fell through the opening, mixed with the wind and rain, and made a captivating descent. William watched the water disappear into the shade and stillness. *A person could disappear into the abyss just as easily* he realised.

On the fourth day, they came to the mound of stones which marked the aqueduct's end. Tree roots bulged through the ten-foot stone pebbles of the clearing ahead. Natural light, accompanied by waning rain and wind, descended through an opening above.

'I'm going up to take a look,' Christopher announced before he climbed up the mound. Richard followed, then Eve.

'I'll stay with the horses,' Gaston said to William.

The page followed. At the top, two wall tops stretched along the sides of the endless stream. Waves blew away from them. *There's no going back now,* William appreciated the distance they travelled. They stayed for a moment, admiring a view forgotten by civilisation. When Christopher walked away, the others followed.

'If we go east,' Gaston said, 'we will either see the mountains or come across running water. Either one will lead us to a lake. That is where the mission is.'

'How do you know this?' Richard said.

'The man who came out of the woods told me.'

'Then you'll lead the way,' Christopher said. 'Richard, you walk with those two. William, you will walk with me.'

***

The company continued east. Silence and shade took them. Bogs of water, some as large as ponds, sat in borders of tree roots that grew into each other. A large space opened above a pool of boiling water. Bubbles burst on the surface, releasing a foul-smelling steam. Defusing the potential glimpse at the sky above as the vapour made a beam of upward drifting mist.

Midway through the eleventh turn of the hourglass, they found a rocky clearing surrounded by smaller trees, where they set up camp.

Eve collected branches throughout the day. Some she tied to Springly's saddle, others she carried. This gave her a head start on making a fire. With the extra time, she helped to unsaddle and brush down the horses.

'I enjoy the lessons,' she explained, 'I want to start them early.'

The night before, when William awoke from his nightmare, he discovered Eve walking Springly around the camp. She stroked his neck and hummed. Instead of coughing himself awake, and rushing to his feet, William lay with his eyes closed and listened. Her voice soothed his tension.

Being close to her now disordered him. His skin flushed. Nervousness sent tingles through his stomach. *I should not feel so strongly about anything other than becoming a squire*, the thought inspired him to seek time to himself. He collected a torch and his training axe before walking away from the camp.

Out of sight, he stabbed his torch into the ground, lifted his axe and flung himself into the first strike. *Sloppy,* he rated the effort. *Think, breathe, act.* The next swing hit better. THUMP, THUMP. His muscles woke up. As he guided his weapon, life became the breath he took in preparation, the blur of motion and beat of connection. Powerful, and liberating, the rhythm created concentration, from that focus came a succession of strong, swift strikes.

A branch snapped within the abyss. Something within the darkness approached. A wave of discomfort fluttered up William, making his stomach uncomfortable, his heart race and his breath catch within his lungs.

Another branch snapped.

I'm too far from the camp.

Another snapped.

Don't look, he tried to command his eyes which turned towards a small boy, who walked out the abyss. A stone's throw away, he smiled with an innocence that brought tears to William's eyes. The page laughed because for a moment all of the demons within him died.

The boy turned his ears towards a noise within the abyss. 'MUM!' he called.

No! William's heart thundered as he recognised the child's fate. A woman screamed. *No,* he would not let his nightmare repeat itself. He strode towards the boy. The boy walked back towards the abyss. William ran. Twigs scratched his face. He ducked under a branch. The boy stopped. Hurt, pain and desperation transformed his features, his eyes streamed and his mouth quivered.

No! William dived forward, reaching for his hand. His fingers touched cold skin as the phantom dropped from his grasp. He lay still, defeated and sick inside as his emotions simmered. Far harder than forcing himself awake after a nightmare, he carried a cold in his stomach as he got up and wiped the mud and tears from his cheek. Exhaustion numbed him. He stared into the distance at something that stood out amongst the dull greens and browns above him.

Is that a large eye? he wondered. *No, it's a bird. Those are unique colours.* The black-beaked, brown-headed, and pure white-bodied, crow dropped to a closer perch.

'How long have you been watching me?' William asked. *What did you see? the boy? the torture and anguish trapped inside of me?*

This bird witnessed everything an instinct within him answered *and understood what happened.*

With another jump, the bird took to flight. He followed its line of flight over his head.

Eve stood behind him, holding his axe.

'Richard sent me to fetch you,' she said. 'That bird was watching you?' As she expected an explanation, he said,

'It must have been attracted to my axe...'

'The axe I picked up from beside that tree? No...he bird jumped closer to you.'

She saw the bird but not the boy, William realised.

'It is just a bird.'

'Do you not know the myths about white birds?' she said. 'They are the eyes of the woods and the keepers of its secrets. They are said to escort the dead to judgement. Legend tells us that when a white bird deems a soul worthy, its feathers will turn black with the knowledge of its deeds. If the bird then tells these deeds to the gods of the woods, they may grant such men favours. That is not a bird, William, it is an omen.'

As though giving a command, Eve's words made the distant winds scream in a chilling tone. The woods changed. In place of stillness came a tension. Then the noise cut through them again.

'What is that?' Eve asked. William recognised it from stories Father Monroe told of the woods.

'It's the noise wolves make.' He explained. 'It is howling.'

***

Stood by the fire, watching the cooking pot, Christopher heard the howl. He turned to the east, where the baseless tone came from, and listened to the second and the third call. *The sounds are travelling far because lots of voices are merging to create them.* He decided.

'Shall I put the fire out?' Gaston asked.

'Don't worry,' the knight shook his head and smiled. 'They won't know we're here yet. They're at least a day away, so don't be scared.'

Below the bubbling pot, flames concentrated on destroying wood. No wind made the fire dance and the smoke rose straight up.

When the next howl started, the knight measured Gaston. A flinch of fear contorted his face, but in the eyes which met Christopher's, there appeared hope. *Perhaps we will avoid them,* he judged the monk to be thinking.

In Christopher's mind, if the wolves could detect your scent, then they would detect your scent. *I have no option other than to carry on as planned.* To slow down or divert their course meant increasing the risk of facing the winter snow, which in turn would be a greater threat to their progress than wolves. Weather ate away a team's strength. Between the wolves and the winter, he chose to fight the wolves.

Eve and William returned to camp as a howl came from the east. Eve flinched. William squeezed and half-lifted his axe as though expecting an attack.

Between applying himself with his training sword and axe drills, Christopher considered. *William must be spending a lot of time daydreaming about using his weapon. No amount of preparation can counter the doubt created by inexperience.*

He will have a clear idea of what he wants to do, and how to do it, but until that moment comes, he will be unsure if he is capable of achieving it.

But you are a fighter, boy, I knew that the first time I met you, struggling for life in the red snow. In time, you will prove yourself.

Another howl reminded Christopher of seeing lightning in a storm. Everyone looked towards it, waiting for the sound of thunder.

'Nothing is coming this way,' Richard assured the others. 'These woods just make sounds seem closer.'

'Thank you,' said Gaston.

Richard nodded, but when the monk bent to the cooking pot, he caught Christopher's eye. With a casual gesture, the squire directed him towards the horses. Their ears were drawn back, their bodies tense and they all shuffled around as though preparing to run.

Christopher presented himself ten paces to the side of Bucephalus. When the horse stopped moving, he approached one careful step at a time.

Stood five paces away, he made soothing sounds, 'Shh, shh, shh.' By the time Christopher laid his hand on his neck, Bucephalus calmed down. He stroked while whispering to the destrier.

'You're not afraid, you're just unfamiliar with these noises. Share my fearlessness, Brother, as I have often shared yours.' The horse's head swung towards him. He ran his fingers along his neck. 'They'll have to take me before they can take you.'

With Richard's help, he relaxed each horse. Two of the rounceys, Stormpath and Lunar, took comfort in each other's company. The spell cast by the howling created no effect on them. Thunderwind walked over to William and placed his head into the boy's hand. *They'll enjoy learning to joust together*, Christopher reflected.

'Supper is ready lord,' Gaston said.

Argus stood alone at the edge of the camp closest to the howls. Christopher whistled. The hound did not react. He whistled again louder, but still, the hound paid him no attention.

'Argus,' Christopher called. As he approached, he observed the hound's strong stance. Having spent so long taming, then training Argus, he remembered his dominant battle features; the scars on the loose skin around his neck, the rips on his ears, the size of his muzzle.

His mind flashed back to the night he met the hound at the abandoned cottage, guarding the threshold. It took one glance to see the savagery the hound experienced. He understood that should he aggravate the dog into a fight, he'd need to kill it. It would not back down.

Another howl came. Argus whined and barked. Christopher understood; *To him, the howls are not the cries of distant wolves. To Argus, they are the echoes of a past, where one animal would inflict the harshest cruelties it could on another. These howls are the sound of hungry death. They are the looms of ripping and tearing teeth. They are the killing pits calling him back.*

***

'As of last night,' Christopher said as his team breakfasted on warmed-up stew, 'things have changed. The howls came from the east. We're marching east, which means there's going to be trouble. Does anyone want to turn back?'

He inspected his team for an indication of compliance. The question surprised his squire, page, monk and Eve. Each of them took guard duty last night, which gave them time alone with their thoughts, and allowed doubts to grow.

'We can spare a horse and enough rations for someone to return to Saint Constantines.' He pressed.

'You are happy to continue?' He pointed first at Gaston.

'Yes,' the monk answered.

'Yes,' Eve said. *Good*, Christopher thought. *Those are the two I worried about.*

'Yes,' William said.

'Which horse can I have?' Richard asked.

'Take Bucephalus if you want.' The knight reminded his squire of the one time he tried to ride Bucephalus. The horse threw him from his saddle. He did this to stress his seriousness. Otherwise, Richard would persist with stupid comments until he won a smile, or worse, a laugh.

'I've changed my mind,' Richard said. 'I will come after all.'

Before the start of the day's march, Christopher gave Eve and Gaston spears he made during his watch.

'If anything happens, drop the rations from the saddle. The wolves should be happy with them. If not, mount your horse and use the spear to create distance. If you can, jab them with the tip.

Most importantly, if anything does happen, stick together, and stay close to my lads. These woods belong to the wolves. They will try to split you up. Try to make you panic and run. If you do that, if you run, then you'll never escape the abyss. Do you understand?'

'Yes.'

'Stay together, stay strong.'

Gaston and Eve looked at one another, each grateful to be sharing the stress of the situation.

Argus waited for the team to set off. The day before, he escorted Richard to the rear. Now he stood at the front, eager to encounter any enemies.

Despite the encouragement of the morning's talk, the team struggled to maintain the pace of the previous days. The roots of the titanic trees grew over each other, creating banks where rainwater became bogs. Each one needed to be walked around.

Boulders obstructed walkways. At a large, open gravel pit, they entered a warm mist which sprayed out of the bubbling water and restricted their vision for an hour.

They came into a suitable camp on the eighth turn of his hourglass. Christopher, having picked up on his team's fatigue, conceded to an early finish.

'William, no axe practice this evening,' he instructed. 'Eve, no riding either. Gaston, you will not take a guard duty, I want you all to have a full night's rest.'

The howls started at the same time as the night before and lasted just as long. In the abyss, the sounds created a brief autumn. They changed everything for as long as they lasted. They became alive when everything else appeared dead. Though the howls themselves stayed still, they sounded louder because Christopher's group moved closer to them.

His guts told him; *that tomorrow these wolves will learn that we are in their woods.*

The following morning, he instructed Gaston to put extra rations into a breakfast pottage.

'Today, everyone rides,' he told them. 'We cannot afford to lose time, like yesterday.'

Eve and Gaston rode Stormpath and Lunar, he trusted the horses, not the riders, to keep close together during an attack. Because William rode Thunderwind, Richard rode Ash. *The squire cannot be expected to ride a lesser horse than the page he is instructing,* the knight rationalised.

Christopher rode the tallest of his rounceys; Springly. Bucephalus rode behind him. In an attack, he would swap saddles.

Today Christopher left the pathfinding to the others and rode at the rear. This left him free to overview his group and focus on the terrain. He spotted the streak of light, which appeared far away on their right. *So, we are through the thickest part of the abyss.* He thought.

'LIGHT,' Eve's hand shot up as she called. The others looked.

'We have to investigate where the light comes from.' Gaston's tone suggested uncertainty. Eve took advantage of the monk's hesitation, touched heels to hide and pushed Stormpath onwards.

The ground took a downward slope. A natural road of broken rock created a hole in the canopy overhead. Being so deep inside the woods, they only now realised the rain had stopped. Not warm, but bright, the afternoon sunlight infused life and purity into the surrounding trees. Chilled, fresh air blew down.

The trickling of running water came from somewhere close by. Argus, who pulled tight on his lead, led them to a stream that seeped out of loose pebbles.

'The water will lead us to the lake, and the mission.' Eve said.

'We must follow it,' Gaston agreed.

'Let the horses drink from the water first,' Christopher added. The knight slid from his saddle, kneeled next to a rock pool and plunged his head into the water. The refreshing chill on his face cleared his mind.

May God guide me, he thought, reminding himself why he came to these woods.

Eve and Gaston led them alongside the flow of the stream. Pebbles merged with rocks to create a path at ground level which resulted in a slit to the canopy above.

Streams of rainwater emerged from the abyss and joined the water they followed to build its width and strengthen its flow. The water's voice, which began as whispering motions, grew into a tune of crashing water.

Eve stated periodically, 'This will lead us to the mission.'

Gaston whistled hymns to himself. Richard and William shared a joke. *That is good to hear,* the knight thought when he heard them laugh.

Christopher stayed back observing. *Nothing could survive for long in the deep of these woods,* he thought, *but here, at the border of the abyss, life could exist.*

The ride continued through the afternoon, towards dusk. The stream grew wider.

Christopher turned his hourglass for the tenth time of the day. *We are in danger of being caught out in the dark. We need to set up camp.* He decided.

Argus, who stayed at the lead all day, dropped his nose to the ground. He criss-crossed until he caught a scent then tracked it. Excitement spread through the team. Richard overtook the others to lead the chase.

Careful not to miss anything interesting around the stream, Christopher kept to a steady trot. He caught up at a passageway between two trees. Argus' fresh paw prints contrasted with more established markings in the mud.

'Are those footprints what I think they are?' Christopher addressed Richard.

'Man-made,' Richard answered. 'Yes...Yes, they are.'

'Where is Argus?'

'He ran ahead.'

'Well, we better catch him up. I'll ride at the front.'

A path trampled into the earth from consistent footfall ran for forty paces. The mud surface showed evidence of users, barefooted people, but no wolves.

The path opened into a wide space. Once cultivated, but now shady, reed ridden. The canopy stretched overhead. Smaller, younger trees surrounded the area. Diagonal to the opening, the pathway picked up again. Argus waited amongst the looming shadows of the passage.

The others came into the opening and focussed on the hound and the path.

'Over there.' Eve led Gaston and William in the path's direction.

'We'll take the trail in the morning.' Christopher stopped them. 'Now we have to make camp—'

'What?' Gaston interrupted. 'Why? If we rush, we could make the mission before nightfall.'

'That's not an option, Gaston.' Christopher kept a matter-of-fact tone, 'The day is dying, we won't make it...'

'If we rushed, we could,' the knight locked eyes with the monk.

'If we rush,' he explained, 'we risk everything on an unproven path. Before long, we'll be exposed, spread in a single file and in the dark.

'Even if we did manage to find the mission, why would they welcome anyone travelling at night? These woods belong to the wolves. Our best bet is to claim a territory and defend it. We've plenty of strength. We just need to use it effectively.

'Right now, this area's too big. It needs halving. We'll use branches to create a border. Richard, take charge while I unstrap my armour. No one starts their duties until the border is finished. It's going to be a long night. But tomorrow, we shall find the mission.'

When the knight dropped from his saddle, he looked at the second trail, which cut into the woods. If they made it to morning, this pathway promised to lead them to the mission.

The howls will start again soon. He thought. *How close would they be tonight? Or will there even be howls? Will the wolves just attack?* Still looking at the path, he realised it mirrored tomorrow; hidden from view, and a dangerous night away.

***

Rather than halting their work, nightfall increased their urgency. The absence of howls created a sense of expectation, within which, the pressure mounted.

Before completion of the border, the start of duties or any food could be cooked, Christopher took William aside and ordered him to sleep. As the third watchman, he needed to be sharp and focused.

Forced to lie down, William felt left out, like he wasted his work by not seeing the task through to completion.

I'm falling asleep, he thought. Blinking became difficult. His eyelids fell and refused to lift.

The rest passed too swiftly for it to class as sleep. Hands shook him awake rather than his nightmare. The hourglass, sand mounded at the bottom, rested beside his head. He reset it before standing.

The completed border fenced them in on three sides. The centre barrier, running from one treeline to another, divided the opening into the camp, and then unwanted space beyond.

A heap of firewood sat beside the horses.

The fire, the largest of their travels so far, became prey to a wind coming from the stream as its core spiralled upwards into a disintegrating trail of sparks, ash and smoke.

Christopher sat in armour, on an upturned pan, with Bucephalus' reins in one hand. His sword lay over his lap and his shield rested against his knees. Though asleep, he appeared ready for danger.

Richard threw wood onto the fire. William yawned as he approached.

'You know this,' the squire said, 'but I'm going to tell you again anyway.' He passed William a beaker. The hot water inside scorched his tongue and helped him to wake up. 'While you're on watch, your duty is to keep everyone safe. If anything happens, shout out and give an alarm. If you're attacked, defend yourself. If not, fetch the master his horse and me mine.

'Take a branch from the fire and ignite the border. The branches are drenched in lantern oil, so they will blaze at the slightest ask.

'When the border is on fire, help Eve and Gaston mount. Only then, should you mount your horse. They're responsible for the horses. You're responsible for our guides. Take charge. Keep them together. Don't let them flee.

'If we have to run, we'll take the unproven passageway. We'll hit it at speed, so make sure you have a torch, so your horse can see the track. Otherwise, they might hurt themselves.

'If you're hungry, there are meat cuts in a sack over there. Take one. It's not much, I know, but full stomachs make heavy eyes. Breakfast in the morning is going to be a feast. If you're hungry later, drink some water and dream of breakfast.

'Most importantly, keep the fire burning as bright as it is now. There's a stack of logs over there to feed it with. Where's your axe?'

'Here,' since the start of the howling, William imagined himself using the axe in combat. He slept with it in his hand and still held it.

'Hopefully you won't need it.'

After patting him on the back, Richard went to lie down near the fire.

'Any howls tonight?' William asked.

'Nope.'

Why not? He wanted to reply but stopped himself. *How would Richard know?*

Illumination from the campfire spread over the borders up to the far trees. Sparks floated through the camp, into the woods. William thought through his brief. Memorised every word Richard told him.

He kept guard duties since they left Saint Constantines. Usually, the biggest struggle came from the tiredness of the day. Tonight's responsibilities sat differently in his stomach and stressed his thoughts. *Please, God, let me do everything asked of me.*

He walked across to Thunderwind and stroked him while he finished the hot water. All the horses remained saddled. *They move more when they're fearful,* Richard told him. Though sleepless, they appeared calm.

Argus approached as William opened the sack of rations which contained a salted ham shank and two salted beef joints. He took the shank. While he ate, he scanned the dark gaps between each tree, from the far side, over the border, back to himself. Here, he picked up his patrol.

On his first round of the camp, he chewed on the shank's best meat. Firelight extended his vision into the intruding dark between the trees.

During his second round, he picked at the rest of the shank. Afterwards, he gave the remains to Argus. *That's a small price for your company,* he thought while placing the bone into the hound's mouth.

Though he tried to focus on looking over the camp, William developed a habit during previous duties. At least twice an hour, while passing Eve, he took quick, furtive glances at her face.

After giving Richard enough time to fall asleep, he decided; *Now's the time to look at her.* He resisted the urge to rush into a viewing position. *If Christopher or Richard catch me, they'll deem me unable to control my urges. They'll say I'm unfit to become a squire.* He feared. *All my hard work and all my dreams will be lost.*

William continued his route around the border. Outwardly, he appeared to be continuing as before, but inside he became excited.

His heart became a bird, instead of singing a tune; it beat its wings excitedly. He pretended to look into the woods, twisted and scanned the camp. *No one is awake.* He looked at her.

Despite everything she slept peacefully. On top of his attraction, he also admired her. Through his covert observation, he registered things about her. She liked horses as much as him and always showed eagerness to learn how to ride. She worked hard. While doing so, she often smiled to herself.

At night, he found himself revering her more often. At peace, her face possessed a gentleness and softness that never existed in his life before.

Already racing, his heart pumped his body with a curious excitement. He imagined lying next to her, sharing her warmth, feeling her skin on his skin, his lips touching her lips. Goose flesh went up his arms.

Awakened by a glance, he justified the distraction. *I feel more alert*, he told himself.

For the next two turns of the hourglass, William tended the fire and made tours of the camp. He walked the route around the barrier and back to the horses again and again. He turned and walked in the opposite direction. Without planning, he would cut across the camp to inspect silent patches of the woods. All the while, he toyed with his axe.

William turned the hourglass for the third time. *If I can finish this last hour,* he thought, *we will make it to the mission.*

For a change of scenery, he peered upward. Light spread into the canopy's bottom, but like the abyss did not penetrate far. Something white stood out against the dull tones. As he concentrated, he recognised the bird he saw moments before the howling started. The one Eve called an omen.

Argus growled. A branch snapped. *The boy,* he thought, *no, not now, please not now.*

William followed the direction of Argus' snarling muzzle. Beyond the border stood a man who wore hides so filthy they merged into a matted mess.

Terror surged through William's veins like a winter wind which turned morning dew into numbing ice.

'OY!' He challenged. *You sound scared and pathetic. Do something. Do it now.*

The man snarled. His teeth brought a fierceness to his face reminiscent of a beast.

'Halt!' William raised his axe and moved towards the figure. *What am I doing?*

The man ran at him. *He's going to leap the border and attack me.*

William wanted to run to meet him, to defend his team and do his duty, but the tension in his stomach acted like a force working against him. He walked, trying to muster more courage.

Preparing to leap over the branch border, the man entered the campfire light. Argus, sprinting to the camp's defence, leapt and hit the savage in the waist at full speed. The savage landed on the branch border. He tried to stand.

William prepared his axe and rushed forward. Before he could reach him, Argus bit down into the savage's neck and ragged his mouth from side to side. The savage tore at the hound. They became entangled on the ground. Entwined in a death roll, they took their screams and snarls into the dark.

***

'William...WILLIAM!' Christopher's call retrieved the page from the distracting shock of the violence. Mounted on Bucephalus, the knight's helmet muffled his voice. 'Speak boy. What did you see?'

'A man,' William pointed, 'over there.'

'Put your hand down,' the knight said. Firelight penetrated the helmet's viewing hole, revealing the composure of the eyes within.

'Don't panic. Think. Do your duties; wake the others. Ignite the border.'

Things happened too fast for William to think through. His mind could not form an internal voice. The command Christopher gave him animated his body.

He ran to wake up the others. Richard put on his chain mail. He must have called Ash because the horse approached him.

Snarls came from William's right. *That's Argus,* he realised. Frightened for his friend, he wanted to call the hound back from the fight.

'William,' Richard said, 'the defences. Quickly!' The squire jumped on the saddle. 'Ignite the border.'

Having visualised this task whilst patrolling, William drew on the mental planning to help him cope with his rising panic. He sprinted to the fire, grabbed a burning branch, dragged it, twisted and swirled it into the barrier. The blast of heat hit initially in the centre but spread rapidly sideways. The page raised his arm to protect his face.

The increase of light revealed figures moving beyond the barrier. *I can't hear Argus anymore,* he realised.

Eve and Gaston rushed to opposite sides of the camp with torches. Every time they punched the barrier a rush of flames ignited.

A howl came from the direction of the stream. A ripple effect occurred, as howl after howl came from close by. The accumulation of sound made one matter clear; we are surrounded.

A three-pace-wide gap in the centre of the main barrier would not set alight. *I have to do as I am instructed,* William decided with the grit in his guts as much as the words in his mind. *I have to finish lighting the border.*

'Mount your horses!' he instructed Eve and Gaston, who complied.

William grabbed the thickest branch from the fire, hauled it from the flames and dragged it to the gap in the border.

One of the savages ran for the same spot. *It's going to jump. My axe! Where's my axe?* William made the mistake of looking into the man's wild, demented with savagery, eyes. Intimidated, he hesitated. *What am I doing?* The savage cleared the border and came straight at him. William lifted his burning branch to create distance and back-footed away from the attacker.

Ash rode behind the savage. A metallic slash reflected flame light. Blood sprayed through the branch, covering William's face. The savage slumped to the ground.

'Don't stop, William,' Richard said while he turned his horse, 'get the border burning.'

He reached the gap as fast as he could and plunged the branch into it. It did not take. William turned, sprinted to the campfire, grabbed the two biggest branches and hauled them towards the weak spot.

A wild man jumped through the passage. Ash intercepted him. The wild man leapt up at the squire. Richard dipped his shoulder, grabbed the man's groin, pulled him close, head-butted him then ran his sword through his gut. Shuffling closer to the border, the squire dumped the wounded savage on the flames.

Sweat poured from William. The close fires burned his skin. He twisted, threw his weight into the branches and got them over the weak spot. *The border's complete,* he thought, *and it's working.* Like horses trying to escape a paddock, wild men ran around searching for a way into the camp.

A group of savages approached the borderless side of the barrier. Christopher and Bucephalus waited for them. A vision of calm within the storm, the armoured knight looked huge in comparison to everyone else.

Now the page understood why they treated Bucephalus better than the other horses. The war beast subtly shuffled like a courser, ready to run a joust. Each movement highlighted his pedigree for battle. *He isn't moving because he's nervous,* William noted, *he's excited.*

The knight's shield hovered over his left thigh and his sword stood vertical, both flushed with firelight. Despite the urgency and danger of the moment, anticipation surged through William as he realised; *I am going to see my master's sword, Reprobus, unleashed.*

***

A savage ran from the woods with sole minded, aggressive intensity. They leapt at Christopher. A simple backhanded slash-separated their head from their body.

An attacker came at the knight's left. His shield punched away grasping hands before his sword thrust straight in and out of the savage's chest. Their scream became gurgled with blood.

Christopher punched his shield into a duo of attackers to his left, forcing them to grab hold of the defence before he lifted it. He used his thigh armour as a platform for the flat side of his sword and thrust underneath his shield. As he retrieved his weapon, their lifeblood oozed through his armour, padding and over his flesh.

One savage still stood despite the holes in his abdomen. *That's the first time I've seen that,* Christopher thought. He lifted his shield, angled it, and hammered the rim onto the man's face.

A wild man sprung from behind the falling body. Christopher allowed him to catch his shield. The man's hand tried to gain purchase against the knight's shoulder armour. A shocked groan came from his unwilling acceptance of steel through his flank.

A savage leapt onto Bucephalus' side. His weight trapped Christopher's elbow, so he could not pull Reprobus clear of the dying man slumped over the blade. A frantic forearm beat at his helmet. Fingers reached into his viewing hole.

The knight used his shield to push the dead man from his sword. He twisted his wrist, so his sword's shaft pointed over his neck, then dropped his shoulder to bring his attacker's weight onto his weapon.

He sprung upright and flung his enemy to the ground. Bucephalus rocked backwards. Christopher understood, *the horse just stamped on the savage's skull.*

A savage on his right rushed forward. A sideways slash of sharpened steel opened their chest. The breath freed from within their lungs created an explosion of blood.

Christopher held his shield in front of his viewing hole and used the mirror-like strip across the shield's top to complete his 360-degree view of the battlefield.

One approached his right flank. Two came to his left.

He swung his sword up and flicked the weapon into the air. The handle rotated around his gauntlet. He caught it in reverse, its pommel next to his thumb and forefinger, and drove his arm back. The speed of two connecting forces drove the savage two feet onto the blade before his knees collapsed, and he fell backwards.

The knight anchored his weight into his saddle. His sword looped over in an arch, cleared his horse's head, then pointed down again. Its razor edge sliced through the wrists of the man who reached for Christopher's shield.

Screams in his ear provoked a war rhyme; *True terror derived from true pain. Tell me, poor soul, what is my sword's name?* Christopher plunged his weapon into the screamer's neck. Sliding his palm around Reprobus' handle, he grabbed it in the orthodox position.

An attacker lunged from beside the screamer. Christopher punched him with his shield. He thrust his sword forward. Steel eased through the soft flesh of the savage's windpipe. His chin bounced off the sword's shaft. As Reprobus withdrew, the dying man's hands clamped over the cut. He made eye contact. *There's something childlike in his fear.* Christopher perceived. *Animals in life, men in death.*

More came at his left and his right. His moving blade sliced through a forearm and swept upwards before diverting momentum into a downward hack. Reprobus divided a screaming savage's neck and shoulder, before slashing across another's upper arms and chest.

He tilted his shield and lashed out with its curved bottom to steel-punch the brow of a left-side attacker. Blood spurted out of his broken nose.

A slower savage, who charged on his shoulder, panicked and tried to stop. They lifted their hands to keep their balance. Bucephalus' mouth whipped sideways and bit their hand. He made to snap again. The savage stepped aside. The knight's shield crashed into their face. Teeth flew from their mouth. They fell to the floor.

The screams and blood of their carved-up comrades made the wild men weary of the danger of the knight's sword. They hesitated, stood back and regrouped.

When they decided to attack, they numbered two in front, three to the right, six to the left and four behind.

The two in front charged. Focussed on the knight's sword, shield and armour, the front runner was shoved by Bucephalus as he leapt. Christopher sliced their head off. He hacked into a second savage who charged off the first's shoulder.

Fingers dug into the metal at the top of his armoured collar. A savage tried to unsaddle him. Christopher used his shield's reflective strip to direct his sword over his shoulder. The weight fell away.

A hand reached around his waist to grasp his groin. He thumped his shield down to clamp the forearm against his thigh.

Fingers grasped the top of his shield. Reprobus sliced between the attacker's knuckles.

Back-swinging right, Christopher slashed through three men's upper bodies. The sword sliced back, criss-crossing the first cuts.

He released the crushed forearm near his groin and jabbed the savage's face with the bottom of his shield.

More and more wild people rushed at him. The surrounding circle squeezed closer. Another jumped from the mass. Reprobus cleaved through them, drenching those close by in blood.

Another attacked his rear left flank. He lifted his shield and thrust his sword through the gap. A woman screamed. His sword cleared. His shield dropped. Bodies slammed into it. He slashed at the savages building up on his right. Though he killed at will, they continued to use their superior numbers to surround him.

***

Despite being in the centre of dangerous territory, William paused in awe at the spectacle of a knight amid combat.

At all times seated stable on Bucephalus' saddle, his master moved rapidly and decisively. His sword cut. His shield punched. Savage after savage fell.

William's focus changed from the centre of the fight, with its eruptions of blood, to the crowd surrounding the knight. *Their numbers are too many,* he thought, *he cannot kill them quick enough.*

Do something, William's inner voice said, *they are surrounding him.*

Richard fought two savages. *He cannot help.*

Do something! The circle around his master compressed. *It's too late.*

Bucephalus' head plunged forward. *God, no, Christopher's falling.*

Two savages at the back of the crowd slammed shoulders-first to the ground as Bucephalus bucked and kicked behind him. Clearing a route out of the crowd, the destrier reversed out of the mass of savages. Christopher's sword and shield continued their constant motion.

'Mount your horse, William,' Richard ordered. 'Protect your riders. Do your job.'

It's my job to guard them, William glanced at Eve and Gaston, who mounted with torches in hand. *But where's my axe?* He scanned the campsite until he spotted a glimpse of red reflected from metal. Resting on its head, standing vertically, his axe lay next to the fire.

He sprinted, collected it at pace, pushed off his foot and ran for Thunderwind. Eve passed him the horse's reins. William missed his stirrup, but pulled himself up one-handed, using the pommel. The fear in Eve's eyes stretched across to him like hands. Their icy fingers scratched his skin.

Stay calm, he told himself.

The camp changed. A charged sensation, like expecting lighting to strike close, filled the air. William forced his eyes away from his master's fight to search for the cause of the change. Nothing happened beyond the border. *Look up,* the voice of fear which must have whispered in Eve's ear, now spoke into his.

Something is in the abyss. High in the trees, firelight reflected off a metallic, Christian cross, which hovered within the darkness, as bright as a full moon on a night with no stars.

Against the reflection, the blackness deepened to a humanoid form of perfect shade. *The abyss is coming to life.* The shape dropped from the tree. It landed soft and as soundlessly as a shadow.

As it stood, as tall as Christopher's mounted height, firelight exposed its monstrous features; a muzzled mouth, taloned hands, and eyes, which glimmered like light at the bottom of a deep well. A Christian cross, engraved within the beast's chest, shimmered.

Savages, upon seeing its arrival, scattered back to the tree line.

'Chris,' Richard said, 'behind you.'

'Behind you!' William echoed.

Christopher grabbed his pommel, leaned forward and turned his horse.

The living shadow stood like a man but moved like a creature. It stepped forward, crouched then sprung itself into a sweeping talon. The connection rocked Christopher. Reprobus flew from his hand. His body swayed.

The shadow went from one swing to prepare for another. Before the killing blow landed, a body of fur barged into the beast. Argus, making the creature miss, placed himself in front of Bucephalus.

His snapping and snarling bought the horse time to retreat. With a desperate blend of fear of the beast but an innate willingness to fight, the hound wagered his life to save his master.

'GET CHRISTOPHER OUT OF HERE, TAKE THE TRAIL,' Richard screamed. 'RUN!'

The squire charged at the creature.

'Quick,' Gaston grabbed the reins from Eve's hand and led their horses towards the path into the woods.

A whimper caused William to turn and see Argus being flung into the abyss.

The beast turned towards Richard.

Bucephalus, with Christopher, slumped in his saddle, backstepped to the far side of the camp.

Are you going to be the man you always wanted to be? The voice within which urged him to do something challenged him. '*Come on,*' it said, '*do something.*'

The beast clamped Ash by the neck and lifted the horse onto his back legs. Richard hacked at the beast's arm.

Are you going to be the man you always wanted to be? The voice repeated.

'YES, I AM,' William answered himself. He held Thunderwind's reins in the same hand as his axe and charged through the camp, towards Bucephalus. He grabbed the horse's reins, saying, 'Come on,' before pulling him towards the path.

As he crossed the camp, he glanced towards the fighting. Ash fell on his side. Blood pulsed from three long gashes down his neck. Savages rushed in for the kill.

Richard, having escaped his horse's saddle, backstepped. His sword parried the beast's talons.

Savages rushed towards William.

Past the burning barrier, the light dimmed. Further ahead, a torch lay on the ground. *Make sure you have a torch,* Richard instructed earlier, *so your horse can see the track. Otherwise, the horses will hurt themselves. In the darkness both horses would fall.* William feared but acknowledged, *I'm being chased.*

William tried to stop the horses. They ignored him. He whipped his leg over his saddle and dropped to the ground. The momentum sent him rolling. His weapon came out of his hand.

He found his feet and continued running. Before him, stood his axe, the torch he needed to collect and an onrushing savage.

William converted his momentum into aggression. He collected his axe, grounded himself and swung with every inch of power within him. The tip of his weapon hit the oncoming, lunging savage underneath his armpit. William leaned on his outside foot, planted his leg and flung his enemy to the ground.

A scream came from behind him. *That's Richard* he realised the beast won their fight. Though he wanted to turn back and help the man he idolised, his sense of duty pushed him to pick up the torch and run.

PROLOGUE
Part Three

For six days, the sun turned in the sky with rays of burning light. Lucius spent each second waiting for death. An insignificant surrender, he no longer controlled any aspect of his life. His captors, not he, made his decisions.

The substance they gave him to drink throughout the short periods between the sun's setting and its rising kept him alive.

At first, Lucius tried to resist. He received brutal punishments. Half of the blood they forced him to drink came from craters within his mouth created by lost teeth. Thereafter, he submitted and drank without resistance.

After the forced feedings, they allowed him to slump to the ground, curl his malnourished legs into his skin-tight ribcage, and sleep.

The blood in his stomach seeped sourness into his thoughts. He did not dream anymore; he entered a midway of semi-asleep, semi-awake visions. In them, he stood naked in the moonlight. The witch fixed her halfway eyes on him.

Reversed, her living eye now held the murk of blindness and her dead eye possessed a living surface; like a body of water which held an aquatic world inside. He anticipated something edging closer to the top. Something coming for him.

***

Lucius unclenched his blistered eyelids. He opened his dried lips and tested the dampness of the late evening air. Suspended in the trees, he managed only shallow, instinctive thoughts; *Night is coming*.

Excited by this recognition, he swung softly in preparation for dusk. The dehumanising torture transformed him into a creature of reaction. The fact that they fed him blood no longer mattered, just the relief and the lessening of his pain, which came from the feeding.

At first, he drank to submit for the reward of respite; the time alone looking up at the reassuring moon. As his slow death continued, he grew to desire the comfort of substance.

Torture eroded his once-established mind. The wealth of knowledge gained from years of study toppled swiftly. Elaborate thinking and the ability to problem solve gave way to a sole desire. His characteristics, personality and memories no longer existed. Addiction, to the experience of feeding, ruled him.

Recognition of being lowered caused his mouth to water.

His stomach, which inverted beneath his ribs, sucked inwards with hunger cramps. Deepening heartbeats shook his frail chest. The burnt skin of the ruined arms from which he dangled, tingled with goose pimples.

Lucius squinted at the crowd of blazing torches that waited for him. The barbarians, the people of the woods, his masters, gathered in greater numbers than ever before. A mass of hands picked him up from the undergrowth and hauled him to the feeding tree.

Tonight, they made him wait. His heart pounded with urgency. His frustrated body shivered with sweaty desire. He twitched with agitation.

'Azz-ta,' he pleaded. No one listened.

'AZZ-TA,' he shouted. The barbarians' term for blood, replaced the majority of a once vast vocabulary. Someone within the crowd repeated 'AZZ-TA.' Infectious and exciting, the two syllables provoked the wildness of the people. They chanted louder and louder.

A corridor opened. Torches lighted both sides. *Where is she?* Lucius longed for the witch to approach. *I can feel her looking at me.* Only the two of them mattered. The other voices infused into a background beat around them.

Tonight, like always, she appeared as a creation of the dark. Lucius breathed erratically. *GIVE IT TO ME*, the addiction, which ruled his internal voice, screamed inside his mind. The witch and the padre's exchange of glares had once been a conflict of sanity and insanity. Now, his hazed stare and her halfway eyes met each other with equal measures of madness.

'Azz—Ta,' she said. The structuring of this word came as a struggle to her, yet she repeated herself. 'Azz—Ta.'

The crowd's voices reinforced hers. The barbarians squeezed closer. Lucius squinted against the increase of light.

At the height of the crowd's excitement, the witch's hand snapped into the air to produce silence. An inhuman heart dwarfed the hand she gripped it in. A relic of the flesh, old but not rotten, withered and dry. She mumbled again in her confused language of wordless sounds. Madness reached from her living eye, merged with blind hatred of her dead eye to create a power that gripped his skin.

She angled her hand into his mouth. Driven to physical desperation, Lucius lunged at the offering. Anticipating a punch of fluid, he bit into hard muscle. A tooth, weakened by his diet of blood, worked itself loose against the barren meat. Blood seeped from his gums over the heart. Vibrations tingled through his lips. Somehow his blood brought the heart to life. It beat in the witch's hand.

Lucius became more savage than the uncivilised people around him. He tore a mouthful of flesh clear. A rush of energy resonated from his stomach. He used the new, increasing strength to devour the rest of the unnaturally beating heart.

Lucius tilted his head back. *Mother,* he thought as the moonlight fell on his face, *Protector. Goddess.*

Needles exploded from his heart. Shards spread through his veins. His ribcage shattered from the recoil. His lungs collapsed and expelled breath from his mouth. He fell from his captors' grasp and hit the ground.

This is death, he thought. Despite being the moment, he waited for since being taken captive, he still could not help panicking. He lay motionless, observing every detail of the moment; the fires, the faces of the people watching him.

Coldness advanced from his toes, through his foot, up his legs, along his body, like a lake losing its surface to the winter's ice. When it hit his mind, it froze his last thought before it formed.

***

Heat throbbed within Lucius' chest. Lingering cold quickly smothered the rebel heartbeat. Like sparks of flint before a fire, the heat surged until his heart ignited with a new, forceful energy. Pounding, hard and deliberate, it drew in his dead blood, purified it and forced life back through his veins.

Lost strength tingled with the sensation of being reclaimed. Cold numbness faded away in pulses. Body heat spread with the flow of his blood until warmth reached his toes.

In his resurrection, his body reversed the effects of the suspension torture. Pain indicated his reclaiming of his arms. He braced against the agony until the only sensation in his limbs came from the squeeze of his fingers pushing into his palms.

Lucius turned onto his front. He hopped onto squatted legs and lifted himself with thigh strength. When he stood, his shoulders felt as though they continued to lift higher.

Though his body found new strength, the wrenching in his stomach found a new, demanding hunger which raged for substance. The hole, from his dislodged tooth, antagonised matters by weeping with the source of his craving.

The crowd squeezed tighter around him. The faces of the people who beat him night after night became clear in new, vivid detail. The curiosity they expressed stressed they expected something to happen.

The witch's mumblings rose to a high pitch. Her eyes bulged. She clutched at the crucifix on his chest, which over days of cindering sunburn became grafted onto his skin, and made it clear this is what invoked her hate.

Bones decorated the rags she wore. She plucked from them a claw. Lucius remembered a massive, black hand emerging from a hole in a cave.

The witch cut open her furs and exposed her bare, left breast. In one wild, forceful movement she thrust her arm out and then plunged the point of the claw through her skin. She dragged it down from her shoulder, across her chest. Her eyes remained locked on Lucius' eyes. Her screams continued to curse him.

She dropped the bone and rubbed her hand, which ran red with her blood, over the crucifix.

'AZZ-TA,' she screeched. Frail from her agony, she repeated the word until she inspired the crowd to chant it. Lucius grabbed her, pushed his mouth into her wound, he gorged on her blood. Its warmth, the exhilarating rush of feeding his stomach commands, released him from his pain.

The witch lost the strength of her legs but did not fall to the ground. He held her with a feat of strength far beyond the capacity of his weakened arms.

In the ecstasy of the moment, Lucius experienced a vision. The woman stood before him. Reversed, the living eye now dead, the surface of her dead eye, now alive, swirled. It drew Lucius closer until a clawed hand, massive, black and strong, lunged out of the eye, grasped his head and pulled him into the lifeless pit of the witch's pupil.

Outwardly, nothing altered. Lucius still held the witch to his lips. His eyes still glared with delirium. He appeared to be the frail, fightless man the wild people took captive and tortured.

Internally, the new heart establishing itself in his chest drew strength from the witch's blood and used it to bring change to Lucius' body.

Chapter Seven.

The flame light flickered as William pumped his arms. He charged along the path invoking speed with every step. Each breath thrust heavy air out of his lungs.

They are not far behind, he imagined other feet following his, breaths echoing his and hands reaching out to grasp a hold of him. He dared not check behind.

Thunderwind and Bucephalus waited for him. *You need to keep going*, he told himself, *you must get them moving.*

Thunderwind approached him. William's difficulty came from ascending the saddle without burning his mount with his torch. His energy unsettled the horse, who started to move uneasily.

'Calm down.' *Am I talking to Thunderwind or myself?* Speaking settled the horse but played with the page's uneasiness. He checked the outer limit of the firelight, expecting savages to rush forward. *Well don't wait for them*, his internal voice sounded like Richard.

Thank God you are with me, he thought as he pushed Thunderwind along the road.

'Christopher,' he called as he approached Bucephalus. Crouched forward, the knight gave no response but made breathing motions. 'Master?' Silence.

Designed for jousting, a stabilising beam at the front of Bucephalus' saddle prevented the knight from falling. Scratch marks ran along the horse's side. The blood seeping from them captured the flame light.

The savages will be catching us up, William reminded himself. He guided Thunderwind in front of the destrier and started a light trot. The war horse followed. Every time he checked the stalking darkness, he expected something to advance on them. He pushed the pace to the limits possible to maintain light between both mounts.

An earthquake of emotions tore William's insides apart. He began to weep. Tears flowed so strongly they burnt his eyes. Tremors shook his shoulders. His heart hammered against his chest as though trying to break free. The physical reaction came from the understanding that; *Richard, Ash and Argus are dead.*

He recalled Richard's final scream, his death call, which propelled from the camp with percussions of agony.

It should be me, not Richard. William's mind reverberated with regrets, *I should've done more, if I raised the alarm better Richard would have survived...*

Though untrustworthy and unwelcoming, the abyss absorbed William's grief with non-judgemental silence. He did not want to explain himself to someone. *How could a person understand that Richard was the man I wanted to be, yet I allowed him to die in my place? I was the person on duty so I should be the one who died.*

William stopped the horses. His fading torch needed replacing.

'How long have we been running away for?' he asked the mounts. They offered no opinion. Darkness encroached.

Just do it, he told himself after a final check of the lights border. He dropped from his saddle and searched for a suitable branch on the ground. *There are none.*

The savages will catch us up soon. Fear whispered. *But you need more light,* logic countered.

Without my axe or one of the wood saws, I'll have to snap a branch off a tree, by hand. William searched for a movable branch, found one and ragged at it. Frustration grew as it wouldn't snap free. Tension twisted in his stomach and built towards rage. The branch snapped.

In the soft glow of his weakening torch, he checked the path constantly. William ripped cloth from inside his furs and wrapped it around the new branch. He remounted before he lit the torch.

Something came into the new light from in front. Though expecting an attack, it still caught him off guard. He gasped. The shape became Springly, one of his master's rounceys. The horse approached him for comfort.

'Why are you alone?' William said while meeting the mount with an open palm. Other than being scared, the horse appeared to be fine. William used a coiled line Springly carried to attach the saddles.

He continued along the road, clueless as to what pursued him or what lay in front. His sense of time disappeared inside the silent isolating abyss.

A yellow dot ahead became a dim light. *It is still too dark for sunlight,* he reasoned, *so that must be Eve and Gaston.* By how they waited, both side by side blocking the path, he understood they expected him to take charge of them. *They pushed their mounts too hard,* he thought.

'What do you think you're doing?' he challenged them.

'Pardon?' Gaston said.

'Riding the horses to near death and leaving one of them behind.'

'I am sorry, we were scared, I...' William interrupted,

'Sorry is not good enough. They are your duty...' He glared at Gaston. 'Change mounts, give them a rest.' William untied Springly and passed his line to the monk.

'I'll ride in front,' he said.

'Is Christopher okay?' Gaston queried.

'I don't know,' William answered, 'He is breathing, but he is not responding. What does that mean?'

'I need to examine him. Can you take his helmet off?' Gaston positioned himself on the other side of Christopher.

Despite William's anger, the monk acted calm. Shame flushed through William. He handed the monk his torch while he removed his master's helmet. Christopher appeared to be sleeping. Gaston inspected the knight's head for bumps or breaks.

'The helmet saved his life,' he said, 'But he is not out of difficulty. We need to get to the mission.'

William put the helmet back on. He rode to the front of the riders.

'Where is Richard?' Eve asked. The question acted like a dagger in his heart, it hurt so much.

'Richard is dead,' he needed to lift each word from his mouth. Tears come to Eve's eyes. The page turned away before he started to cry. *Now is not the time for weakness,* he reminded himself. 'We need to keep moving.' He spoke as though he did not cry, but he did.

'The mission will not be far now,' Gaston said. 'You are doing well, William.'

William ignored the comment. 'If you detect anything,' he instructed, 'call out, and run.'

The ride offered solitude. Between waves of intense feelings, William's mind became stressed under self-review of the night's events. How the savages appeared from nowhere. How Argus responded instead of him. How the hound placed himself in front of his master's horse. How the beast lifted Ash onto his back legs. How Richard spent his last moments fighting. How brave and honourable the squire acted.

He considered his actions; How he killed a man with an axe. How he then ran away. He escorted the horses, *but was that the right thing to do? Should I go back?*

To each thought, he fantasised about an alternative set of events, where he behaved braver, smarter and more decisive. He imagined himself as a better person. The one who engaged with the first savage. Who charged the beast and gave his life. *Could I ever do that? Could I ever be so brave?*

Richard's valour inspired him to think of the words engraved onto Christopher's shield, 'May God Guide Me.' Shame filled him.

I am motivated by revenge. Richard died for something greater than himself. If I died, as I should have, it would have been for nothing.

William considered; *how much better would my life be without my desire for revenge? How much lighter would my soul be without the weight of hate? I must honour Richard by how I live,* he decided, *I must take a new moral course.*

The riders came to a hole in the overhead where snowflakes fell through. A scream came from some tormented part of his mind. He visualised himself in the camp. Ash lay on the ground, surrounded by attacking savages. The beast held Richard. The clawed hand punched into his stomach. Its arm pushed up. Blood spurted into the air. Richard's agonised expression changed into a puzzled one, which asked, where is William? He is the one on duty. He should be the one here, not me.

A cold chill ran along the page's spine. Anger and grief fought a war within his heart until he decided; revenge, not faith or honour, will be the thing which guides me.

***

The subdued illumination which created the eternal shade within the abyss, brightened to indicate both morning and a thinning of the vegetation above. A light-blue, predawn sky seeped through the overhead. Used to witnessing many transformations from night into day, William thought, *it's strange that no birds are singing.*

When William recognised the end of the passage, he inadvertently tightened his reins but stopped himself from riding away, not only to escape from the tunnel but to also end the worst night of his life. The tension caused by the trauma of the night, built within him as he neared his escape.

The bright whiteness of the opening came from the combination of snowfall and sunlight. A cold wind met them at the exit. A large, thick beam came into view. Only a glimpse of something much larger, drew his attention as he left the woods. As tall as the surrounding trees, the structure's arms spread out from four-fifths of its height.

'A Crucifix,' Gaston said. Dark brown in the dawn light, snow clumped in a windless spot on its right arm. At its base, stones piled around it. Snow started to build over the body of a pig. A frozen waterfall of blood came from a slash across its neck and stained the stones below it.

Smaller, six-foot-tall, imitations of the crucifix stood at the entrance to the passageway and in a circle around the enormous one.

Beyond the circle of crucifixes, ran a long line of spiked fencing. Behind the human settlement, the faint outline of mountains confirmed for William; *we've reached the mission and the end of "The Abyss of Trees".*

'This way,' William led his team passed the giant crucifix.

'WHO ARE YOU?' The clear tone of an unseen man's challenge threw William. For a moment, he believed himself to be in Christendom, then the wind struck his skin, and he knew by its sting that he remained in Barbarous.

'THEODUS,' Gaston shouted. 'WE SEEK A MAN CALLED THEODUS.'

The gates for the spiked fence opened. The crowd who gathered to see them wore tailored sheepskin leggings and tunics. They are just like the villagers back home, William noted.

The majority of the crowd expressed curiosity. One man stood beside the gate and glared at him. Broad in a labourer's sense; thick everywhere, rather than toned through discipline, his beard hid half of his face. He squinted. William understood when their eyes locked. *This man thinks I'm a threat.*

Gaston leaned across, pointed at someone who emerged from the crowd and said, 'This is Theodus.'

The same height, with the same thick grey hair, he resembled the man William most wanted to see. *He even walks like Monroe.* He reassured himself before sliding from his saddle to convey respect by talking to Theodus at an equal height.

'You've come far,' Theodus said while approaching. His eyes fixed on Christopher.

'Yes,' William replied, stepping forward. 'Very, very far. Father Monroe sent us.' The words punched Theodus. He stopped to try to control himself but was lost to the turmoil. Deep creases around his eyes channelled the tears down his cheeks. He wiped them away as they reached his chin.

'Please.' Theodus held his hand open in a silent request for the page's name.

'William.'

'Please, William, before we talk of anything else, tell me something of my brother. Tell me of Monroe?'

'Should we not go inside first?' Gaston asked.

'There is nothing to fear during the day,' Theodus said. 'The shadow of the woods sleeps in the light. It is the night that wakes it.'

'Monroe took me in when I was very young,' William smiled as he remembered the old man. 'He is my father. I miss him.' Theodus nodded tearfully. 'He is always happy. He spends his days tending his flock. At night he creates beautiful books, or he reads. He smiles often. He is the most loved man in the village.

The day before I left him, he became a Bishop. When he received your letters, he wept. To know you are still alive brought him joy. He sends you his love. He misses you.'

Clumsy with his happiness, Theodus' eyes squeezed tight as though guarding his thoughts from the world. The group remained silent until Theodus gathered himself.

Curious about how the missionaries survived, William spotted the hand-ploughed field on one side of the village and the lake on the other. Wheat and fish, he summarised.

'As you said, Brother, we've come far to be here,' Gaston ended the silence. 'No harm befell us until last night. First, men of some kind attacked us. Then something else came.'

The happiness left Theodus' face. *I hope you enjoyed your moment,* William thought.

'You know what Gaston speaks of, do you not, father?' The page pressed.

'You are too young to have come here, William,' Theodus expression conveyed apology.

'Your master, is he;' Theodus attention lifted to the knight, 'did the night claim him?'

'Christopher took a blow to his head,' Gaston explained. 'There is bruising, some bleeding but no injured bone, and no damage to his skull. He needs to be laid down and examined.'

'You're from Saint Constantines,' Theodus realised.

'We both are,' Gaston indicated towards himself then Eve. William recognised a moment of shocked recognition which unbalanced Theodus' composure.

'The knight who came to you, where is he?' Theodus talked to Gaston but continued to examine Eve. She flushed red with embarrassment.

'I'm sorry to tell you this, but after he delivered his message, he died.'

'Then at least you laid him to rest inside Christendom,' Theodus spoke with a sad smile. He turned to William and added, 'Your coming is a miracle, as is your master's survival. He is the first person to escape an encounter with the shadow of the woods.'

'Christopher lived,' William's voice shuddered as he replied, 'but others died.'

'Then the Lord did not grant your master the mercy he deserves. We should take him inside, but beforehand...can I make a request of you?'

'Of course.'

'Your master is an embodiment of hope to my people. I do not want them to detect him rocking on his saddle. Could you do something to steady him, please?'

'Eve and I will ride either side of his horse and steady him,' Gaston suggested.

'That should do it,' William agreed.

'Thank you,' Theodus said before leading them towards the mission.

As they approached, the crowd parted and stood in front of a line of thatched-roof buildings. Some expressed hope. Others glared with mistrust.

Livestock wandered throughout the village; cows, pigs, sheep and geese. Chickens chirped somewhere out of sight. Without the threat of the woods, this village would be more prosperous than the one he grew up in.

The spiked fence, which appeared to border the whole village, went ten paces into a lake. The lake's vast expanse produced foot-high waves. The snow created a haze. The view better reflected the weather and geography than the weatherless, stale, shaded world of "The Abyss of Trees".

William's attention focused on the far side of the lake. A figure, bright despite the haze, stood on the shore. *If you fight you have a chance* Richard's voice confirmed for him, the person looking at him through the haze, to be the dead squire.

'William,' Theodus brought his attention back to the present, 'please wait while I open the church doors.'

William looked back across the lake. *There's no one there. Maybe there never was.*

The wooden church stood tall and wide. Each of its timber pillars, spaced ten paces apart, boasted spiral carvings as immaculately chiselled as the figurehead on the Thetis. Of all the decorations of religious symbols, saints and crucifixes, and naturalistic features of trees and animals, a half-shaded crow caught his eye. *If you fight you have a chance.*

Before entering, the page checked his master. If unaware of Christopher's condition, he would presume him conscious.

The crowd stopped. In contrast to everyone else around her, who measured Christopher, one woman stared at Eve. Gusts of emotion rippled through the soft, pretty, familiar features.

A hair's breadth separated Christopher's helmet from the top of the doorway. Once inside, Gaston and William shut the doors.

***

William struggled to free Christopher from the saddle. He weighed too much. Recognising this, Bucephalus knelt. The knight swayed forward.

'Thank you,' the page said to the horse. Gaston and Theodus helped the page pull his master clear of the saddle onto the ground. William untied the armour's steel plates. They moved him to a bed in a small room. Gaston and Theodus inspected his head. They opened his eyes and checked their reaction to the light.

'We must keep watches, in case he wakes,' Theodus said. 'William, would you like to go first?'

'Would you do it please Gaston? I must take care of the horses.'

'Of course,' the Monk replied.

'Do you have a barn or stable?'

'A barn,' Theodus answered. 'I will take you there.'

Outside, the snow fell thicker. Visibility only stretched halfway across the lake now. He led Bucephalus. The other horses followed in a direct line. The waiting crowd stood back to measure William and the horses, but the focus remained on the church with the knight inside.

'Make way,' Theodus commanded. 'Our guests came a long way and need to rest. Come back tomorrow.'

They went to the only building on the lakeside of the path. It differed from the barn in William's village, by being larger and more circular. Smoke seeped out of the chimney that broke through the top of its thatched roof.

Inside the large room, the light came from the fire inside a stone chimney dug into its centre. Their arrival brought eight boys, aged between ten and fourteen, to them. *They've never seen a horse before*, William realised as they took the mount's reins with puzzled expressions.

'These boys are orphans of the shadow of the woods' Theodus explained. The page looked around at the group. *In another life, I may have been one of them.* He at once envied their unity and pitied their circumstances.

'They tend to the livestock,' Theodus continued, 'and they do a very good job of it.' One of the boys smiled at Theodus in gratitude for the compliment.

The boy's beds sat on a shelf beneath the thatched roof. With the livestock inside, the ground would be full of animals. It smelt both of burning foliage and muck.

'Girls and younger boys,' Theodus explained, 'live with families who lost their children.'

'How many people has the beast taken?'

'Too many.' The question provoked sadness in the priest's eyes. William regretted asking so bluntly.

The boys conferred over what the saddles could be. William showed them how to work the various straps.

'You've never seen anyone riding a horse before, have you?' he asked them. None of them mustered the confidence to answer him.

What would Richard do with you, he wondered. He remembered the night before he departed from the village. The knight and squire took children on horse rides. He left Lunar saddled.

'Follow me,' he said, leading the horse outside. Snow quilted the ground. Missionaries, who went about their daily routine, stopped to stare.

'Here,' William lifted the smallest boy on Lunar's saddle. He kept hold and walked the horse. The boy laughed to the others who mirrored his amusement. More small children approached. *This is what Christopher and Richard would do*. William reassured himself.

The boys and girls asked him questions; *what is the horse called? how old are the horses? How fast can he run? What is his favourite food?* They asked things about him also. *Where did he come from? How long he would stay? Would he leave Lunar behind for them to ride?*

The weather deteriorated until visibility faded to a stone's throw.

'We must return your horses to the barn,' Theodus said, 'then take the livestock inside. The weather is becoming much worse.'

***

Christopher awoke to a squeezing pressure at the back of his head. He touched the area to inspect for signs of injury. *A bit of bruising but nothing too severe,* he judged.

He sat up. A flow of dizziness, thirst, hunger and nausea made an internal contrast of sensations. The knight braced himself with his arms and concentrated on his breathing.

Light seeped into the room through the gap between the door and its frame and outlined someone sitting next to him.

'Thank heaven you are awake.' Christopher did not recognise the speaker.

'Theodus?' he guessed.

'Yes.'

'What happened?'

'You survived an encounter with the shadow of the woods.'

Sparks intermittently illuminated the room until flames caught within a lantern which smelt of burning oil. The room revealed itself.

'You look like your brother,' Christopher said. He left out the older, more exhausted part of his observation.

Theodus passed Christopher his helmet, back to front. Dents and scratches aligned with the part of his head he inspected for injury.

'Explain everything to me, Father,' he said. 'Not just what happened to me, but everything, every event since you came here.'

'We came here,' Theodus said, 'to help the people of the woods. The first two years, we cultivated the land and built the mission's homes, the barn and this church. There were many more of us then. We felt safe. We made bonds with the half-starved wild people. Fed them, bathed them, cared for them. Love bonded both peoples together. When it came time to teach them the way of the Lord, our new brothers and sisters surprised us. They already knew, and feared, the symbol of the cross. When we asked them why? Why do you fear the cross? They said one word; "Azzta".

'They tried to warn us. We ignored them. We...*I*...presumed to know better. To convince them to convert, we built the garden of Christ. A circle of six-foot-tall crucifixes surrounds a forty-foot-high one in the centre. We wanted to show them that our faith should be rejoiced, not feared or rejected. We were the ignorant ones, not them. They understood the evil we provoked. If only I listened, I could have got my people out...

'The mass baptism of the wild people took place after our first successful harvest. We picked a perfect day, no wind just a pleasant calm. We celebrated into the night. I recall how bright the moon shone, and the stars twinkled.

'It started with a woman's scream. I ran towards the noise as more screams joined the first. The sight I encountered startled me.

I thought Mary floated in the air. Then I noticed the shadow, so powerful, so confident and big like a man is to a boy. It held her like a child holding a straw doll.

'One of the men I baptised that day pointed at the beast. He said,"Azzta". I learned the truth of their fear, as I saw an aged silver crucifix the demon bore on its chest. That is why the people of the woods feared the crosses we constructed. Mary's husband led a group of men in pursuit of the shadow into the woods. They never returned.

'A month later, a little boy, Logan, disappeared. We built fences, and men stood guard, but it took him anyway. Logan's uncle commanded our knights. He took all but one of our fighting men to retrieve his nephew.

'Days later, we found our knights in the garden of Christ, impaled on the crucifixes, their hearts ripped out and their guts torn from their bodies. Panic spread throughout the village. Many of our missionaries fled back to Christendom. Each morning, we woke up expecting to find them as we found the knights. We did not. For two months, we trusted in hope.

'The next full moon, the children who fled with their parents came back, alone. Dirty, and distraught, wild gazes possessed their eyes. Despite it being night, we opened our gates and rushed out to them. They attacked us. They tried to take a little boy and girl from their mother. We fought them off. We drove them back into the abyss. That is the only time I ever used my hands for violence, and it was against our children.

'Now the gates we built to keep them safe are used to keep them out. The lost children of our mission, the savages, the soulless, bodily remains of what was once innocent and right about our coming here, are the ones who attacked you.'

Regret thickened the atmosphere. Christopher said nothing. He allowed Theodus the leadership of the conversation.

'When you are strong enough to leave the church,' he continued, 'you will see the garden of Christ, and the cross that stands as high as a tree...the monument of our arrogance. That is where they gather. They do this because that is where we feed them. It keeps them at bay, though if there is a full moon...Azzta's moon, then perhaps, someone will disappear.'

The long silence emphasised the potency of the confession.

'When this first began,' Theodus looked away, 'I gathered my people into this church, and I told them to no longer expect a Christian burial. I cannot commit them to the ground, knowing their body would take the place of a living person. Giving prevents the Shadow from taking.

'So far, I have refused forty-seven souls their rightful burial. I have knowingly dammed them, and myself, to purgatory.'

'Your faith has not forsaken you, Father.' Christopher said, 'Hope is here.' He swung his body around and let both feet rest on the floor.

'Can you fetch my squire, Richard, please?'

'Only William, Eve and Gaston arrived with you.' The sensation of nausea struck Christopher's gut harder than a joust. *Richard must be dead,* he realised. *Apart from my clothes, the ground is empty.*

'No hound, either?' he asked. The sympathy on Theodus' face answered him. Though the pain inside could not be more intense, the knight did not show his emotions; discipline denied them. Advice, once offered to Richard, now echoed in his mind, *You must never show weakness, not even to yourself.*

The knight reached for his clothes and began to dress.

***

With the horses taken care of, William returned to the church. Inside, he took off his outer layers and hung them over the pew closest to the altar. He knelt on a stage before a wooden crucifix, identical to the one beside the passage into the woods. Embedded into the only stone wall within the church, it created a symbolism; the rock being the eternal substance for the wood's spiritualism.

He pressed his palms together and rested his forehead against the tips of his fingers.

'May God guide me,' his softly spoken words sounded loud. The hall stayed silent, as did his mind. He did not want to stand up. It would be a struggle to do so. The fatigue, which stalked him throughout the day, ambushed him now. He closed his eyes, kept them shut and enjoyed the silence. Sleep swept through him.

You were on duty. Richard's voice came from within him, *You should have died, not me.*

The dream took William back to the attacked camp. He guided Bucephalus towards the path. The moment froze. Richard, defending himself, twisted to look at him. His expression conveyed many things at once, *why should I die? why are you not helping me? why are you running away?*

The crow William saw before the howling, then again before the attack, flew over the squire's shoulder, towards him. It grasped William's axe and pulled him backwards. William fell from his horse, through the ground, through the red snow.

He opened his eyes, startled then gasped.

Soft fingers rested on the back of his hand. The touch startled him. He followed the hand along an arm until he stopped at Eve's eyes. The confrontation of his affection created an overflow of excitement. She turned to face the cross and stooped into a praying position. *Why didn't you go outside and meet the missionaries?* He wanted to ask her questions but his inexperience with the effects of his attraction stopped him. *You wanted to come here the most. You could have given the children horse rides and met some of the settlers.*

'When Christopher wakes up,' she whispered only loud enough for him to hear, 'Gaston will tell him everything you've done. He will be proud of you.'

William did not want her to leave, but he could not think of anything to say to her.

She leaned over so her lips hovered next to his ear.

'We shall stand side by side in the shadow,' she half-whispered half-hummed. 'In the darkness, we are the light each other shall follow.

'We shall stand side by side through the night. When darkness surrounds us, our love shall be too strong, shall burn too bright.

'I shall stand by your side beyond death. Should darkness try to drown you, mine shall be love's saving breath.'

The words and the impression of her breath on his skin startled a swarm of butterflies within his stomach. Her cheek pushed into his. Her mouth moved towards his. He turned to meet her. Their lips pressed against each other's. Neither flinched nor backed away.

The butterflies escaped his stomach and flew through his body. His heart thumped. His blood rushed.

Their soft movements progressed and became increasingly passionate. They twisted on their knees to discover each other's bodies with their hands.

Movement from a different part of the church caused them to part. Theodus entered the doorway.

'Christopher is awake,' he said. 'He wants to see you.'

William rushed to follow Theodus. Before leaving the hall, he turned to Eve. She faced the stone wall and prayed.

What just happened? he thought.

***

'Master, you're awake.' William said as he entered the room.

'How did he die?' Christopher asked while he dressed.

The relief of seeing the knight conscious switched to the shame of surviving when Richard died. William found words hard to say, so he chose the one he thought best.

'Fighting.'

William did not recognise the knight's brief expression. Gone in the blink of an eye, *is it grief or pain or heartache?* he could not tell because emotions did not belong on his master's face.

'Fetch my shield and sword,' Christopher instructed.

William and Theodus looked at each other, trying to decide how they should challenge the knight's intentions.

'You lost your sword when the beast hit you, lord—'

'The night is no friend to you,' Theodus added. 'Perhaps you should wait until the morning.'

'Theodus may be right master—' A look silenced William.

'You don't have to come,' Christopher continued to dress, 'but you have to do as I say.'

'This is madness.' Theodus challenged him. 'Why can you not wait until the morning?'

'Before Richard became my squire,' Christopher explained, 'he was my little brother. '

Of course, the truth of the statement hit William. He recalled their similarities, their size and build. He remembered the small exchanges between the two of them, how they thought so alike. Richard even made Christopher smile. *They cared for each other and fought for each other.*

Already sad for Richard, now William grieved for Christopher. Who, in becoming a knight, denied himself any relationship with a wife or family. *He brought to him the only person he could love, his brother. Now, that kinship is gone.* For William, a deeper resolve came in this grief's place, one which tears would no longer satisfy.

While Theodus brought Christopher outer layer furs, William told his master what happened the night before; the night of the shadow; how the shadow hit him, how Argus leapt to his defence and how Richard died.

'If you're going back into the Abyss,' he finished, 'then I wish to come with you.'

***

Christopher stepped outside into a world of winter. A sheet of white covered everything. Aggressive wind collected its chill as it swept across the top of the thick snow. Clouds flowed through the open sky passed the full moon.

The fresh, near-frozen air made Christopher's head fuzz with dizziness. *The sooner you get moving the better*, he told himself. Even before the years spent on the road, he preferred outside to indoors.

His belt kept fur covers close to his body. Despite his scabbard being empty, he wore it next to his dagger.

Ahead, William trudged through the calf-deep snow. Head down, he waded into the wind. Stepping into his page's fading footsteps, Christopher anticipated his horses having problems walking across the path.

If the wind did not keep its roof clear, the barn would be mistaken for a mound of snow. William pushed the door inward and held it open until Christopher came inside.

Warm and well-lit, the barn's size exceeded his expectations. Livestock of various kinds lifted their heads to inspect him, but none rose from the body heat they invested into the ground. Above them, boys slept side by side, on a shelf under the thatching. *They use the firelight for protection*, Christopher notice, *because they're afraid of the dark*.

The cold air that escorted them inside drew Bucephalus's attention. The horse walked straight across. Christopher cupped one hand under the horse's jaw, stroked his neck with his other hand and rested his head against the destrier's.

'We'll take the rounceys, Will,' Christopher said, still stroking his horse as he inspected a bandage down its flank.

'I cannot risk worsening your injury in the cold,' he said, justifyinghis decision to the horse.

Without speaking to each other, the knight and his page brushed down Stormpath, Lunar, Springly and Beck, put their fur covers on and then saddled them.

Afterwards, Christopher went to a bag of supplies which made it back with one of the rounceys.

'I'll be gone for the night. Go get some sleep, Will. I'll be back tomorrow.'

'You need me to show you the way.'

'There's a man on the gate. He'll lead me to the passageway, and I will find my way.'

'You look knackered. Plus, I need you to tend to the other horses. No...Stay here and rest.'

'Richard wouldn't have let you go without him. The man he wanted me to become would insist on going with you, my Lord. So, I must insist on going with you.'

You're right, the knight thought.

'Today, you are tougher than you were yesterday,' Christopher said, 'but just you mind your tone.' He patted his page on the back. 'Take your training sword with you. Tomorrow we'll spar.'

'Are you going outside?' a boy asked.

'Yes.'

'You'll need torches.'

'We can see outside,' Christopher replied. 'But we'll need them for when we go into the woods.'

The boys sat up and checked each other's reactions to what Christopher said. Some seemed shocked, others horrified. 'Can you fetch two unlit torches, please?

'Come here,' Christopher waved a small boy across to him. 'Tomorrow morning, tell the man or woman who came with us to tend to the horses. Can you do that?'

'Yes,' the boy smiled. An older boy gave them two torches with hay and twigs wrapped around the head.

Outside, Christopher used Stormpath as a windbreaker. They headed toward a light at the end of the village. The night watchman met them.

'Where are you going?'

'Out there.'

'Into the woods?'

'Yes.'

'Godspeed.'

The watchmen held onto a line that stopped the gate from whipping away as he opened it. It slammed behind them.

All black, the central crucifix grew like a towering shadow from the ground. A thousand winters would not knock it down. The wind reached its pinnacle on the march across the open country. The men and horses huddled closer and moved slower.

That makes a statement, Christopher thought as they approached the six-foot crucifix beside the dark tunnel, *what lies beyond is not a Christian country.*

The knight marched his team clear of the wind back into the familiar stillness of "The Abyss of Trees". He clamped a torch with his knees and struck flints against its head until it took to flames.

'We'll save the other one till this one gets weak,' he told William. He attached a line from Stormpath to the other horses, mounted him and led the way.

The abyss absorbed them into its stillness and silence. Hours of progress went by without deviation. Christopher used the second torch.

When they passed through the opening into the previous night's campsite, William pointed out the obvious,

'There are no bodies.'

Now a dead reflection of the night before, last night's boundary, and campfire made small mounds underneath settled snow.

'Go through the pile of branches,' he instructed William. 'Find four or five suitable for torches.'

Christopher dismounted to check the area where the fighting took place. Snow sat over the ground he wanted to see. He scraped it away with his foot until he detected ripped-up turf.

He moved around, following the trail of human footprints and horse hooves, until he found something different; an unfamiliar, almost man-like imprint. *Its toes are not round but pointed. There is also a break between the foot and the sharp nail marks.* He placed his foot inside the print. *The difference is the same as a boy's to a man's.*

It lifted Ash onto his back legs, he recalled William telling him.

This is where you braced yourself, Christopher thought, trying to understand the beast. *Otherwise, you're light-footed. You're quick, silent and powerful.*

The knight found a red stain near a groove which led to the woods. *Drag marks,* he decided.

After establishing a new torch, he gave his old one to William and instructed the page to stay with the horses.

Christopher went into the bush, his torch in front of him, his dagger poised by his hip, ready to thrust.

Snapping twigs warned him something rushed close. Christopher thrust the torch into the earth, took half-a-step back and prepared himself to counterattack.

A mass of bloodied fur burst through branches and leapt towards him. Surprised, Christopher dropped his dagger and lifted his hands.

'Argus,' he said as the hound slammed into him, knocked him to the ground and licked at his face.

'Thank God you're alive,' he said. Argus' whole body wriggled from his wagging tail. 'Why did I believe you could die, you tough bastard.' Christopher grabbed the spare skin around the hound's muzzle and rubbed it playfully. The hound growled to echo his desire to wrestle, but instead, barked and stamped his feet. *He's telling me to follow him.*

'Go on, lead the way.'

Christopher put his dagger away and picked up his torch.

Through the woods, he came to open ground, to a mound of rock half-covered with snow. Signs of a fresh struggle disturbed the white surface outside. Moonlight shone onto a cave. Metal sparkled within. Christopher's momentum stopped. He could not move forward without taking a steadying breath first.

'You're inside there aren't you?' He asked the still figure. *If Richard only answered me back.*

He knelt to stroke Argus.

You fought some of them off, didn't you? The marks in the snow indicated that three, perhaps four, of the savages returned to try to take Richard's body from inside the cave. Argus, who dragged the dead squire to a safe place, stood his ground and fought them off.

'You could have followed my scent to the village, couldn't you?' he asked the dog, who twisted his head in an attempt to understand, 'but you stayed to protect him.' He hugged Argus before crawling into the tunnel.

'Who gave you permission to die?' he asked Richard who lay on his back. Frozen flesh stuck to peeled chainmail. Pools of iced blood sat around the squire's ripped-open ribcage. *His heart, lungs and organs are gone.* Christopher recognised. *It knew what it wanted.*

Richard's eyes remained open, but the light of life no longer illuminated them. He leaned in, placed his forehead against his squire's, closed his eyes and imagined his brother heard him.

'If a man is judged by how he lives, then you are the best person I will ever know. Though your sword is irreplaceable, the laughter, and life you brought, will make the world a colder place now they are gone.

'You are my favourite thing about me being me. You are my brother. But more so, you are my best friend. Had you become a knight, you'd have been a better one than me. Heaven will feel a safer place with you in it. Farewell, Squire...brother...companion.' Christopher tried to close Richard's eyes, but the eyelids refused to move. *They will remain forever open.*

Tucked in beside the squire's arm he discovered two swords: Richard's blade and Reprobus.

***

'I'm not going to ask you to put your grief aside William,' Christopher said after they wrapped Richard's body, carried him to Stormpath's saddle and tied him down, 'but try your best to put on a brave face in front of the others, yes?'

'Yes lord.'

On the road back to the mission, William tried to find a method to follow his master's instructions. *You were on duty,* his sense of shame taunted, *why didn't you charge the beast? Why did Richard die, not you?*

What advice would Richard offer me? He thought. He remembered his teaching during his voyage on the Thetis, *Endurance means to keep going. Persistence means never giving in.* The squire beat this advice into him. *I'll do as you instructed,* he promised Richard. *I will endure and persist.*

Argus, walked behind Stormpath, maintaining a vigil over his fallen friend. *He looks like he's been through hell,* William evaluated the different coats of blood dried into the hound's coat. He remembered Argus colliding with the feral man.

The cold wind which swept across the garden of crucifixes awoke William from the half-sleeping trance he fell into. The cold found inlets through his furs, and he shivered. Christopher paused to scrutinize the giant cross. His torch blew out. Still, he looked. *What are you thinking?* William wondered.

The knight continued to the gate, which he booted rather than knocked. Cracks in the fence showed flame light approaching.

'Did you find what you looked for?' the night watchman enquired.

'That and more,' Christopher answered.

'Good.'

The gate opened.

'How long until morning?' Christopher asked.

'Not long,' the watchman replied, thought about it again before correcting himself. 'Soon.'

The knight nodded thanks; the watchman nodded to accept the gratitude. He and the page nodded in curtsey. The watchman stepped back when Argus passed.

Outside the barn, Christopher dismounted and took Stormpath's reins.

'Take the horses inside,' he instructed, 'leave them saddled, we'll eat something before heading back out. Tie them up, then come collect Stormpath.'

'Yes, master,' William glanced at the body lying over Stormpath's saddle before he turned away.

Inside the barn, both the animals and the boys slept. Large logs, smouldering inside the caged chimney, left the room chilled rather than warm. William did as instructed, then left.

Outside, stillness held the wind quiet, and a serenity sat over the village.

Flutters drew his attention to the bird, partly white, mostly black now. *Follow it* a phantom voice in his head instructed. The bird led him to the lakeside, before gliding downward to rest on the shoulders of a dark figure.

'Impossible,' William muttered while he approached. The spectre became more real the closer he got, until his belief became certainty that a ghost stood before him.

'It's time,' Richard said.

***

When Christopher shut the church door, reverberations ran through the building.

'I prayed for your safe return,' still awake, Theodus stood from his position in front of the wooden crucifix. 'It is a rare thing to have a prayer answered.' Argus left red paw prints as he ran around the church hall inspecting the scents.

'You met with danger in the woods?' The priest pointed at Stormpath's cargo.

He thinks this is William, Christopher realised.

'No danger,' the knight replied as he manoeuvred Richard's body onto his shoulder, 'simply sorrow.'

He walked to the altar and laid his brother down.

'Someone once told me "a sword only wins you burdens",' Christopher said. 'It is true. Death would be kinder than glory.'

Theodus took time to think of a response, 'The only way to make peace with the price your brother paid is to honour him.' He understood the language of grief. 'Ask yourself what would Richard want you to do? Let his memory, not your sorrow or anger, direct you.'

Christopher also considered his reply. 'Richard came here to help your people. He did not die for me. He died for them. You must honour his sacrifice. Bury him, Father. Give him a funeral.'

'I would like to do that,' Theodus said.

'Tell me, Father...' Christopher's concentration moved. 'In an abyss of trees, where does the shadow dwell?'

'You are looking for the road no one else will walk.' Theodus always talked to Christopher with an expression of guilt on his face. 'We settled next to the lake because we needed water for the animals and crops. The people of the woods used to live further inside the abyss. There used to be many trails, like the one you followed tonight. One runs beside the wheat field. If the woods have not claimed it, that trail will lead you to the mountain where the Shadow dwells.'

'We were far from the mountain when we were attacked. Do your lost children stay close to the settlement? Did the beast come because it heard fighting?'

'No.' Theodus shook his head. 'They all live in the mountain. The shadow only comes out when the moon is full. I don't know why the children come here...perhaps some part of them wishes to be close to us.'

Because you're their food, Christopher thought.

'A man, Corsedon,' Theodus continued, 'once witnessed the children going into a cave while he fished on the lake. He said they did not return. He said that a passage runs from the lakes through the mountains. That's why they come from the west, when the mountains are in the east. Corsedon can show you the way to the cave, if you wish?'

'There's no need,' Christopher said. 'It'll be easy to find. Your children will not cover their tracks. They've never been hunted before.'

***

'You're dead,' William's tone blended blame and regret with sadness.

'Men don't stop at death, little brother,' the phantom replied.

'I'm sorry you took my place.'

'My death was my death. I chose it, not you.

A moment of destiny approaches. Your heart is full of fear. It makes you weak. If you cannot put your past behind you, death will take you.'

'What must I do?'

'If you fight, you have a chance.' The crow leapt from Richard's shoulder, unbalanced him and toppled him backwards. As he crashed onto the frozen lake the squire transformed into a stream of blood which glimmered in a black reflection of the moonlight. The bird flew by the boy who haunted William's nightmares, and perched on an upright stake, embedded into the ice.

The ground will break, William reasoned.

'NO!' He screamed to express his desire to stop the events from unfolding. He launched into a sprint and took his stride from the firm ground onto the ice. Both arms pumped. His lungs sucked in cold air and spat out steam.

'Mum!' the boy said.

At full speed, William's foot slipped. He fell, right arm first onto the frozen surface. Pain shot up from his hand, along his limb and tingled his shoulder. The ice cracked with a whipping sound. Splinters shot through the surface.

I'm going to plunge into the red snow. He realised. *My nightmare is going to become real.* Fear increased his panic. *You've failed. Turn back while you can. You can still make it back before the ice breaks. Do it now; run for the shore.*

You cannot quit. A voice inside his head imitated Richards.

But it's too late. His reason countered.

The boy's innocence will be lost. The squire's voice encouraged. *Come on. Do something!*

THE ICE IS ABOUT TO BREAK! His fear manifested sensations, he shivered, and tensions cramped his stomach.

'NO!' he commanded his anxieties into submission.

'NO!' he repeated, rolling onto his knees before finding his feet and pushing himself into a run.

The boy stopped and looked down at the ice.

'NO!' William cried out as he closed the distance but remained too far to stop the inevitable from happening.

The ice broke under him. One foot went under the surface. William fell forward and reached as far as possible. The boy dropped.

William slammed through the cracked ice, into the water. Living needles pierced his flesh as he submerged under the surface. You're *about to die.* He bit down on his bottom lip as he struggled to get to the sinking boy.

The needles lost their rage as a deep burning reached under his skin to his bones. Too weak to create fresh thoughts his mind repeated the same one; *you're about to die.*

William grabbed hold of the boy, put him over his shoulder and fought his way up, out of the water.

He reached the surface and kicked to keep himself afloat. He grabbed the ice and pulled himself up. The ice broke. This time as he went under, he took a mouthful of ice water which froze his chest. He coughed against the pain of a spiking fire.

Endurance, like a sound or smell inducing a memory, the pain brought Richard's lessons to mind, *Persistence.*

You're about to die! Fear screamed inside his mind.

Endurance, he thought back, *Persistence—*

YOU'RE ABOUT TO DIE!

William held the boy with one arm, shuffled his elbow through breaking ice with the other and kicked with both legs. He believed if he could reach the perched bird, then the boy would be safe.

The exhaustion of the freezing water drained his will and energy like nothing he ever experienced before. In the moment he could not rationalise the level of pain he suffered. Every time the ice broke, the cold within the water became hands which dragged him down.

Endurance. He kicked and struggled. *Persistence.*

YOU'RE ABOUT TO DIE!

His reaching arm stroked the stake sticking up from the ice. He grasped hold and pulled himself close.

There is no energy left, his body told him as he willed to move. He took a lung full of air, intending to give himself strength, instead, he coughed most of it back out.

William reached into a reserve of willpower he did not know existed and pulled himself close to the steak. He rolled the boy onto the ice before slipping and smacking his chin against the surface.

With his mission complete, the echoing encouragement of endurance and persistence ceased. Before he could let go, the boy coughed. *Help him,* he thought. William squeezed himself into the bird's perch and rubbed the boy's back.

He closed his eyes as a lifetime of sleep, lost to nightmares, descended on him. Small, warm fingers pushed his lips into a smile. William forced his eyes open. The boy's head lay on the ice next to his. They gazed into each other's eyes and smiled.

William took another long blink. The boy stood on the ice, looking down at him.

'Thank you,' the boy's voice sounded innocent. William laughed. *I forgot I ever sounded like that.* For the first time in his life, he thought; *I am ready to go to sleep now.*

His dream came to him as a sensation of being taken away.

'WILLIAM...'a distant voice screamed, 'WILLIAM.' They sounded familiar. *It's Richard, coming to take me?*

After the next long blink, he found himself, laid flat on his back, being dragged backwards, across the surface of the lake. *I have the crow's perch in my hand,* he realised.

Before dropping out of the strange dream and descending into sleep, he leaned forward to view the ice around where he entered the water: *it's no longer red,* he thought, *it is pure, beautiful and innocent.*

***

In a smaller side room, Christopher hung his outer layers beside a fire. Theodus fetched him two bowls of soup. The knight stayed from having any. He intended to wait for his page and acknowledge his efforts over the last two days.

The wait lasted longer than expected. Argus, who lay in front of the fire, stood and ran to the church doors.

'What are you trying to tell me,' Christopher asked as the hound looked from him to the door and then back again.

The knight collected Stormpath on his route to respond to Argus' urgency. The hound ran out into the night.

Absorbed into a surreal peacefulness, the barks enforced the message; *something is wrong.* Alert to his surroundings, Christopher wondered; *What happened to the wind?*

Drawn to the lake, he found Argus stood on the border of shore and ice, directing his body at a patch of broken surface forty paces ahead. Arms surged out of the water.

Someone's out there. Christopher took the rope from Stormpath's saddle. He tied one end to the horse's pommel, fed himself some slack, and stepped onto the lake. He tied a flexible loop at the end, and small circles which would unravel once thrown.

That's William, he realised. *He's clinging to a post on the ice.*

'William...William!' Christopher said before he threw the end of his rope towards him. It landed in the water as his page dipped below the surface. As he reeled it in, William resurfaced. Christopher made more loops and threw the rope again. The end fell over the post and his page's neck and chest.

At the top of his voice, Christopher shouted, 'HAA!!' The sound swept across the lake. Stormpath trotted forward.

'Can you hear me?' he asked as William slid toward him. He untied the rope and inspected the page's face. *He's dazed, faint and bloody cold.*

Christopher lifted the page over his shoulder and charged to the closest building, the barn. The water which oozed between his shoulder blades and down his back stung his skin with a raw frost.

Christopher booted the barn door open. The dimness inside highlighted the weakness of the fire. He rolled William onto the floor. Whatever the page carried fell to the ground.

Christopher ran to his horses. One by one, he untied their saddles, took their fur cover and slung them on top of William.

The barn's keepers, woken by the excitement, gathered around.

'Pile your covers on top of him, lads,' Christopher commanded them. A boy took a quilt from around his shoulders and held it to Christopher.

'Lay that over him,' the knight said.

'Richard...' William mumbled, 'I saw Richard...' *Ramblings and delirium are better than silence,* Christopher decided, *they're an indication his mind is still working.*

On the floor, beside the page, lay the thing he dragged out of the lake. *That's our cutting axe,* Christopher recognised it, *but what was it doing in the lake?*

Chapter Eight.

Already tired before entering the ice, William slept heavily. He stirred but resisted opening his eyes. A stranger to the territory of thoughtlessness which the mind entered before becoming fully awake, he lingered in the moment. The tranquillity could not last. Nor did he want it to. He simply wanted to enjoy it for a while.

Someone's lying next to me, a gentle, feminine scent, which emphasised cleanness, purity and vibrancy, confirmed their identity; *It's Eve.*

He remembered his duties. *I should be busy.*

William patted a bedside table, found a beaker, dipped his finger inside, ensured it contained water, lifted it and then drank.

'Why did you go onto the lake?' Eve asked.

'I had to.'

'Why?'

'I just had to.'

'When we were in the abyss...' she leaned closer to him. 'I listened to you struggling in your sleep. Once you talked about red snow, another time, you said something about falling through ice. That had something to do with what you did last night, didn't it? I know it did because now you sleep peacefully. Something has changed. Please, tell me what it is?'

If not for the dark, the physical closeness to Eve would have created turmoil within. Unable to see her, he concentrated on the compassion in her voice. *I can trust her,* he decided.

'The dreams come from my childhood,' William said. 'I think I had two sisters. I recall playing games with them, though I've forgotten their names and their faces. My mother, I do remember. She was a graceful woman, and my father...he was very big, very strong. He hunted. He must have shown me how to ride because I have always been able to, but Father Monroe never taught me.

My first real memories are of a red haze in the distance. A morning sunset that lasted the whole day and into the night.

I remember my family, and other families waving goodbye to the men from our village. They joined a long line and went towards the endless sunset.

We went home and waited. Each day, the red light came closer. One morning, I awoke earlier, dressed and went outside. The sunset had arrived in our village. I fled into the forest and hid.

Near nightfall, I grew scared of the dark, so I returned home. The snow turned the forest white but, in my village, grey ash fell in the air. I called to my mother. She screamed my name. I went to her but became confused because of the burning houses. I stepped on something strange. Redness seeped through the snow at my feet and raised up my legs. The ground gave way. I dropped through a sheet of ice, into a puddle of blood so deep, I could not stand. I nearly drowned.'

'How did you escape?'

'Christopher saved me. He took me to Father Monroe, the man who raised me.'

'But all of this is a memory and does not explain why you went onto the ice last night?'

'While returning from the barn I saw the bird.'

'The one from the woods?' Eve guessed.

'Yes. Only last night, its feathers seemed blacker than before. It came from nowhere and perched on Richard's shoulder.' He grabbed her hand, asking physically, *believe me, please, listen to everything.* 'Richard's ghost told me to face my fears.' The phrase *If you fight you have a chance echoed in his mind.* 'So, I went onto the ice.'

'Is that where you found your axe?'

'What axe?' he said.

Eve left the bed and opened the door to let the faint light from a nearby fire into the room. He admired her exposed legs as she bent to collect something from the ground. *I should look away,* he thought. But he did not.

Eve sat beside him. *She looks tired,* he thought. She passed him the cutting axe he used throughout their journey, which he embedded into a savage on the night of the shadow. Confused at first, he understood when she handed it to him.

'The bird perched on this when it left Richard's shoulder,' he said, 'it stuck out of the ice.' As his fingers gripped the axe, a wave of energy flushed through him. *This axe is no longer a tool,* he realised, *the axe wants to be used in battle, wants to become a weapon.*

'How did I escape the water?' He only remembered going through the surface and his struggle to save the boy.

'Christopher rescued you.' Eve glanced from him to the axe and her expression changed.

She recognises I am someone different when I hold this axe.

'They carried you back from the barn to the church this morning,' she continued. 'Gaston tended to you first. I took over at noon. It is night again now.'

'What about Christopher? Where is he?'

'He went back into the Abyss.'

'Then his hunt has begun.'

***

Better prepared than the night before, Christopher loaded torches and overnight rations. He fur-wrapped his two chosen horses, Stormpath and Lunar, before setting off at dawn.

He walked around the settlement's border until he found the wheat field. Hewed stalks pushed up out of the snow, rotten but frozen, the chaff left from the harvest crumbled underfoot like thin ice. Argus led him to a circular entrance into the woods, which seemed almost like a passage underground, like an animal's warren.

Inside, he removed his hood to improve his view rather than light a torch. Out of the wind, the air became stale. Christopher deducted from the reduction of large trees which allow more natural light to filter through; *This must be the border of the abyss.*

He brought a foot-long, curved hewing knife from the barn with him in anticipation of weeds or rambles blocking his way, but he found the path almost preserved from its previous inhabitants, the savages converted by Theodus. Able to mount, he made good progress.

Four times, he dropped from his horse to break branches obstructing his route. Once, he needed to navigate around a pool of water, twice he passed through clear grounds where the wild people must have once lived. Nothing remained. Snow swirled in the pockets of wind.

In the third open ground, the outline of the mountains poked above the trees. He paused and took four cuts of salted beef from his rations, which he shared with Argus.

Christopher took in the change of scenery ahead. Where the abyss stretched into depths of darkness, the mountain became a product of the open sky. Clouds drifted into the stone tops and hid the head of the mountains within a sheet of white.

In a moment like this, we would discuss tactics. In his mind, he spoke to Richard. The realisation of not being able to discuss his plans with the one person who could understand his thinking birthed a loneliness within him. The mountains suddenly became as isolating as they were vast.

Keep moving forward, his disciplined mindset prevented him from following an internal conversation about grief and revenge. *Do what you have to, to get the job done,* he instructed himself. Christopher tossed his last bite of salted beef to Argus, remounted and set off.

The sides of the trail after the second clearing grew wider. The wind blew through. Light overtook the shade.

Christopher pushed Stormpath to a canter. It felt good to be riding with purpose after all the slow trots and walks.

The woods are ending, he judged by the introduction of steadily inclining stone against thinning trees, which allowed wider vision. The base of the mountain came into view. The landscape lifted and dropped like gigantic frozen waves. Wind, which behaved differently in different parts, swept snow down some passages while allowing other patches to sit undisturbed. Frozen walls in one part contrasted sunspots in another.

If Christendom is the land of men, he thought, *the abyss the kingdom of shadow, then this is a frontier of something else. A land of stone and wind. A land of winter.*

The compass of discipline pulled him back from his reflections. He stood in the middle of a crossroads. To his left, the path between the trees and rock followed the mountain, which curved away. To his right, the rock line came inwards. This way would lead to the lakeside cave.

Argus found a scent in the wind. He indicated for them to follow left. *They must be that way.*

The sun sat in the middle of the sky. *May God guide me,* rather than a prayer, the mantra requested luck.

Before returning to the settlement, Christopher reminded himself of his objectives, *I have to scout my enemies and their terrain, formulate a plan and have a firm idea of where and when I want the conflict to take place.*

The first step is to measure my enemies' strengths and weaknesses. They hunt at night. They'll be asleep during the day. Now is the time to find them.

He swayed Stormpath to the right. *The terrain must be evaluated first,* he decided. Argus paused to disagree, *the enemy is the other way,* he indicated. A swift whistle convinced him to run by Christopher and take the lead. The hound ran in and out of the woods, inspecting the trees.

They followed the trail beside the mountain until a rock wall cut across them. Argus found a track that cut up the steep rock. Christopher dismounted and ran up the track.

Another wood sat within the mountain step. The trees here, with their thick bottoms, thin tops and needle-green pine leaves, seemed more natural to their environment than the colossal ghosts which haunted the abyss.

'Tchtch,' he ushered his horses. They climbed the steep incline.

Christopher hiked close to a mountain that ran back towards the lake. He scrutinised the rock line. Accustomed to the constant conditions, he heard a change in the wind. It developed a scraping texture, as though being constrained and stretched. The noise drew him to a cave. Lower and smaller than he expected, the horses would not fit through.

He took Argus' harness from Lunar's saddle and attached it with a short lead. The hound went inside first. Lighting a torch, Christopher followed.

Above him, the cave's height varied from seven feet to twelve. Two paces wide in some parts the walls became tighter in others. The ground declined. Fifty paces inside, the tunnel narrowed to give just enough room for one person to hold their ground.

*Fifty paces...*In his mind, Christopher saw himself riding a horse, running a joust and colliding at the halfway point. This marked the distance in his memory. He followed the corridor.

Argus stopped at the edge of a steep, seven-foot fall. The knight dropped his torch, knelt, dropped off the edge, landed and squatted.

'Come on,' he instructed Argus who dropped into his arms. The ground continued to decline in varying degrees.

Someone with a strong knowledge of the cave can run through here very fast.

Faint yellow sunlight spread along the left side of the tunnel. The path opened up into a cavern, then continued through to the outside. On the right, the ground sloped down into frozen lake water.

It took him minutes to get from one side of the mountain to the other. He wondered, *why would they come to the mission this way when the other way is easier.* He then guessed—*they were taken as children. They would have thought of this as their secret passageway. They never needed to change their route.*

Outside, he re-entered the abyss. The rock cut through his right and into the frozen lake. Wind collided with its solid surface, picked up shards of ice and swept towards the mission. From this distance, he could not see any activity taking place.

In a straight line, the mission is less than a mile. He judged. *Going around the lake, it will be four, possibly four-and-a-half miles away.*

The first part of his plan formed in his mind. He used the char at the end of his torch to mark the closest tree with a cross.

***

Christopher arrived back at the crossroads in mid-afternoon. *I don't have much sunlight left* he judged. He dismounted and trekked ten paces into the woods. Argus pulled tight on his lead and sniffed the air. A danger detector, the hound led them alongside the mountain.

When Argus growled, Christopher knelt beside him and held a hand over his muzzle.

'Shhh...' he whispered. The hound obeyed. The horses stamped and moved more flippantly. *They're on edge,* Christopher read their body language. He marked the closest tree with the ashy end of his extinguished torch before leading his team away.

Further inside the woods, he tied both horses to solid tree branches and fed them a carrot. Their erratic movements stopped.

He felt satisfied, *they're calm now.* He chose the horses because throughout the howling they reassured each other and kept themselves steady.

'I need you to stay solid tonight boys.' He said before leaving them.

Fifteen trees along from his marked point, he detected a noise which he interpreted as coming from many voices contributing at once, like the sound structure of a beehive. He hushed Argus again as hairs stood up along the hound's back.

A further twenty trees, the mountainside cut inward in a V shape. Sunlight faded along two cliff walls until it became swallowed within a cave. *That's the Shadow's lair,* Christopher's gut told him.

He retreated further into the woods before getting in line with the lair. He edged closer, careful not to be uncovered. He stopped a step short of a line of bright sunlight.

The outline of a tunnel remained dark because rock walls on either side created deep shaded cover. On the ground, snow gave way to broken, off-white shards, pressured into a solid pathway. *That's human bones,* he realised.

A savage walked out of the entrance. The knight gripped his hound's muzzle. Argus' silent growl vibrated in his hand. Slouched and filthy, the savage looked like a ravaged imitation of the settlers. Its matted hair is entangled with ragged clothes. Stretched intestines held its garments together. *He's more animal than man,* Christopher thought.

Neither he nor Argus made a sound, but the savage glanced in their direction. Disciplined kept him still, but in his heart, he wanted to be seen, wanted to draw Reprobus and to take compensation for his brother's death with his steel.

Fresh noise came from the tunnel. From booming echoes, the sound broke down into individual voices. A mixture of sizes, sexes and body shapes, the savages emerged as a pack. *There's twenty of them.* After establishing the size of their group, he measured their habits. They kept their jaws loose, then grabbed each other's chins and grunted with their throats. Occasionally, they made chesty gasps, like a laughing sound.

Affectionate with each other one instant they became aggressive the next. Moments of sudden tension, when violence seemed inevitable, dissolved without explanation.

Daylight dwindled, but Christopher stayed to scrutinize their movements, catalogue their wounds and work out each individual's weaker side. He noted which ones moved faster. He identified their leaders.

Sunlight gave way to moonlight; the savages stayed close to the cave. While a group of them fought, Christopher capitalised on their distraction to adjust himself into a more comfortable position.

Lying with his back against a tree trunk, with Argus lain across his legs, his increasing comfort seduced him into a shallow sleep.

He awoke as Argus' lead slipped from his hand. Creeping forward, the hound prepared himself to run at their enemies. He gripped the lead, brought controlling tension into the leather and narrowly prevented the intended attack.

Moonlight penetrated the cave better than the sun. The savages gathered around something inside.

The horses, Christopher's mind jumped to the worst circumstances.

No, what they're eating is too small. He wondered. *What is that?* Christopher crept closer until he spied beyond the savages. Bodies hung inside the tunnel. Treat like lumps of meat, dangled from their feet, their arms drooped straight, their rib cages were all ripped open. *Their hearts and other organs have been taken,* he noticed, *just like Richard's.*

Christopher stroked Argus' head. *Thank you, brother,* he thought, *for saving Richard from the fate of hanging in this cave.*

What they're eating comes from one of the hanging bodies. He looked away from the lump of flesh they argued over. *Not only do they eat human flesh, they eat the flesh of their kin.*

Their group activity centred around the moonlight. When it faded, they became lethargic. Indications of the sun, blue tones coming across the sky and light further up the mountain, pushed their numbers further into the cave.

Soon, only one remained. The runt of the pack, this one sported a long untreated injury which deformed his hand. He hesitated by one the hanging bodies. *He's too scared to go inside,* his watcher recognised. Step by step, he edged further into the cave. Small movements and occasional flinches, indicated fear.

A much larger savage lunged out of the tunnel, catching even Christopher by surprise; they crashed into the runt and knocked him to the ground. The bigger savage grasped the runt's wrist pulled it to its mouth and bit.

The runt, screaming with pain, pushed at the attacker's jaw, as though asking him to let go. Instead, the larger savage lifted the runt and slammed him to the ground. The runt curled up to protect himself. The other threw his fists up and then powered them down. *There is no technique to this attack, only the ambition to cause pain.*

Thank you, Christopher recognised an opportunity, formulated a plan and under the cover of the runt savage's scream, he slipped away.

***

Christopher pushed his rounceys hard to halve the time of the return journey. He arrived back at the mission at mid-morning.

A line of four labourers worked the wheat field. Despite the frost damage from the snow sitting over the crops, it would still make livestock feed. Working with them, the night watchman called to Christopher.

'GOOD HUNTING?'

'THERE WILL BE TONIGHT,' he called back. They bid each other farewell with a nod.

The settlers inside the village wore silent questions on their faces; *can you stop the horror? can you free the mission from torment and fear?*

A group of children gathered in front of the barn. Christopher drew Reprobus and threw it, spiralling, into the air. The children's eyes followed the blade as it lifted and turned. They did not see the knight slip from his saddle. He caught the blade by its handle, took its momentum away with a smaller spin and returned it to its sheath. He walked ten paces from the children, spun on his heel and shouted 'RAH!' They ran away laughing.

Christopher waved over a boy he recognised from the barn.

'Can you take my horses to the barn please?'

'Yes. Of course.'

'Place them with the other horses.' As he handed over the reins, he patted the boy's shoulder. 'And offer them some water. Thank you.'

He allowed light into the church as he entered and approached the altar where Richard lay. Christopher knelt before him, placed his sword on the floor and pressed his hands together. The scouting rewarded him with a plan of action. Now, he prayed for its success.

Someone stood behind him. He finished, stood and turned to face William.

Something is different about him, Christopher recognised. His page held the axe he retrieved from the frozen lake. Before, the axe had been a tool and a training aid, now William held it like a weapon. *That's the difference.* The knight realised *he wants to use the axe in a fight.*

'I'm sorry for going out onto the ice, Master,' William said.

'How are you feeling?'

'I'm not sure,' William replied. By remaining quiet, Christopher forced him to elaborate. 'I feel strong and like I am excited for something.' *You want to use your axe.*

'Thank you,' he changed the subject, 'for saving my life.'

'We are even,' Christopher said. 'You saved mine. Now I saved yours. We do that for each other.'

'That is the second time you saved my life...The second time you've pulled me from the ice.'

Before becoming a knight, during the first days of "The Burning", Christopher wanted to become a soldier in the service of Lord Spearhouse's common army. He ran away from Father Monroe and found a path made by a horde of horses and marching men. A gut intuition told him to take a shortcut through one of the many burning villages, whereby chance, he found the boy struggling to swim in the pool of blood.

'We have an hour before we must leave,' Christopher said.

William's eyes betrayed his thoughts by glancing at Richard's body. He looked away, unwilling to challenge his master, he left a question unasked.

'Richard's funeral must wait,' Christopher justified his reasoning. 'The only way we can win is to press our advantage. As things stand, we have light. The weather is manageable, but that will likely change.

And as for Richard, he knew, as I know, you would give your life for him. I would too. We cannot take these things back. Cannot change places with him. But we can honour him. The way to do that is with victory. If we fail, his death will be in vain.'

He grasped the page's shoulder.

'Tonight, we fight for Richard's funeral honours. I for one want to send him to the grave with glory.'

'Me too,' William agreed.

'Then my sword and your axe shall have a busy night.'

***

Thunderwind maintained a consistent canter. Christopher resisted the urge to ride faster, which would either exhaust the horse or leave Argus behind. Bred to run, the horse managed the pace with ease and energy. The courser reminded him of Ash. *No better a runner*, he remembered the other horse, *but a far greater friend*.

At the crossroads, he tamed the steed to a walk. Rather than cut through the trees, they made a trail through the centre of the snow which separated the mountain from the woods.

He stopped when the cliffs that protected the shadow's lair came into view. After he dismounted, he tied Thunderwind to a branch. He took his sword but left his shield. He tied Argus to a tree and muzzled his mouth to prevent barking.

'Shh,' he instructed the hound to be silent.

Christopher stalked diagonally, aligned himself with the cave then crept forward. He encountered no signs of any savage inside or outside. He gently shook a branch. Nothing happened. Calculatedly, he amplified his efforts to bait the woods with the sound of the rustling branch.

A savage emerged from the tunnel to soundlessly skulk forward. *His movements are impressive.* Christopher thought. *If he stalked me, I would not know it.*

Sunlight hit the ground stronger in some parts more than in others. The savage kept to the shade until he cleared the trail of bones. The runt's face showed the evidence of its beating. Swelling closed one eye. Dry blood sat around a cut on its lip.

The knight started to retreat from the cave's view but stopped. Thunderwind, dragging the branch Christopher tied him to, approached the cave. The runt paused. Predator and prey faced off.

Christopher's chest beat a deep, slow, war drum. *Everything will go wrong.* He anticipated the rest of the savages emerging from the cave and spoiling his plan.

The runt checked the cave before stalking toward Thunderwind. The horse retreated, which drew the savage further away from the cave.

Christopher stalked through the woods. He stepped in time with the savage while narrowing the distance to his target. He got behind the savage, drew back his sword and made a loud foot thump on the snow. The noise stopped both predator and prey. The savage made to turn. Reprobus struck first. In one swift slice the steel slashed through the runt's neck. The head fell to the snow first. Followed by the savage's body.

***

Christopher's orders, with their weight of responsibility, placed William into a race against time. Rather than trek back to the campsite where the shadow attacked, and try to track the savage's trail, when he left the village, he followed the outline of the lake. The attempted shortcut proved difficult as obstructive rock formations interrupted the shoreline.

'That is the reason why the savages came from the stream side passageway,' William reasoned to Gaston before he redirected them around the rocks. *They also have the luxury of time, which we don't,* he kept his thoughts to himself.

To save time he decided to cut across the stream as close to the lake as possible. To convince his team to follow, the page stamped down the ice which rimmed the stream and stepped into the flowing cold water which continued onto the lake. The chill grasped his lungs as he began his twenty-metre wade across the diversion. Springly, loaded with planks of wood, bags of hay and three sacks of hard lard, followed him.

'Good boy.' He reassured the horse as the water lifted to his upper knees. Gaston guided his horse, Beck, also loaded with donations from Theodus, into the stream.

As they returned to the shoreside of the lake, the shade from trees evidenced the approaching sunset. Shadows developed over William's nerves.

'AT LEAST WE HAVE A CLEAR PATH TO THE CAVE,' Gaston needed to shout over the wild, screeching wind.

Earlier, when William left the mission, the monk ran to catch him up.

'I would like to go with you.' Gaston said. 'The night will be long. If I go, we can keep watches. I will aide you as much as I can.' Not in a position to decline help, William took a promise from the monk before he agreed.

'You'll have to do as I say.'

'I will.'

'Swear in his name.'

'I swear in Jesus Christ's name, I shall do everything you ask.'

Now as the wind placed a barrier between them, William recognised the monk's truth. Again, he kept his thoughts private; *I could never control both horses on my own. Without Gaston's help I would not have got this far.*

On the lake, spirals of snow twisted around the frozen surface built upwards then beat against the treetops. *It is nearly dusk already.* His master instructed him, to be ready for sunset. *I still haven't found the cave. Time is running out.*

The shadows stretched long across the ice when they found a three-foot thick branch smashed through the lake's surface. Snow drifted against it. He recalled his master taking him to the lake, pointing across to the cave and instructing him, 'Follow the lakeside. The cave is by a tree marked with ash. *'The distance did not seem so far then,* he reconsidered, *but it does now.*

The sky entered a dusk tone of blue when William spotted a black line on the trunk of a tree. An internal sand dial quickened, and the last grains poured through. He ran ahead until he spied the cave.

Gaston rushed behind him as they went inside. The frozen lake merged into most of the cavern. A path broke off into the tunnel Christopher described to him. Strong winds gusted in from the lake.

William guided his horse as close to the tunnel as possible. He took a length of timber from Springly's saddle and smothered it with lard then coated it with hay. Gaston took the lengths from him and placed them into the tunnel how Christopher instructed; resting the tops of the prepared wood against each other, carpeting the ground with hay and using branches from outside to wedge between the walls and block off the passageway.

They finished as dusk passed into the first grips of darkness. *I have no fire yet,* William panicked as the grains of sand of his internal dial fell.

William wiped the grease from his hands onto some hay and built a tripod of twigs around it. He leaned over to protect it from the wind, then struck flints until he produced smoke. He built the flames until it grew into a healthy fire.

William took a torch to Gaston, who watched over the tunnel.

'Be careful no embers start the fire early,' he warned.

William rested a pot on the fire. Inside contained the last sack of lard.

When Christopher briefed William, Theodus listened in. He took the Page and horses to a woodshed and then brought other men to help load the cargo onto Beck and Springly. While they did so, Theodus showed him the three bags of lard.

'Take this pan with you,' he explained. 'Boil as much as that lard as you can inside. When you torch your fire, chuck the boiling oil onto it, and then,' Theodus lifted his hands upwards and outwards, 'THUM!' the gesture and sound conveyed his meaning 'BIG FIRE.'

William sliced the three sacks he brought the lard in, into fifteen strips, which he wrapped around thick branches.

Nerves remained, no longer because of decreasing time, but now for the coming conflict. The hour of the axe approached. *I'm ready.* He thought. *I just need to fight. If anything goes wrong, I'll fight*...Doubt whispered to him, *but are you brave enough? Will you be swift enough? When you saw the savage before, you hesitated.*

Not tonight, he chose to believe, *tonight I'm going to fight.*

***

Christopher rolled the runt's head outside the cave. His need, for the others to see it and take the bait, necessitated the risk of being spotted.

A trail of blood followed Thunderwind, who dragged the runt's corpse. The horse impressed Christopher with how easily he towed the body, especially when they reached the steep rock shelf.

From the murder scene, with its pool of hot blood, which oozed through the snow, the trail of red thinned into a weak pink line and then drained to occasional droplets by the time they reached the cave. Horseshoes, paws and footprints added further visual persuasion.

Weakening sunlight caught within the rock gleamed in a vigorous orange as Christopher diverted his team of three deep into the woods. After dumping the runt's body, he led the horse further away and double-secured Thunderwind to a trunk. Though the steed freed itself last time, and by accident made the perfect bait, he could not afford a repeat accident. *You cannot endanger the mission again,* He thought.

In the faded blue of dusk's last light, he returned and with sweeping motions used a bushy branch to erase the tracks which led

away from the cave. Christopher and Argus crawled under the cover
of the branches of a close tree. The wind, which further covered his
tracks, and hid most of the blood trail, varied in strength. Strong one
moment, still the next; sometimes gusts came from the mountain,
other times out of the tunnel.

The sky turned from blue to moonlight silver. Cloud shadows
crossed the passageway. *They will come,* his anticipation remained
set until he detected an unnatural movement to his right. His hand,
which sat over the hound's mouth, tightened. Neither of them made
any other action.

The savage crept by, close to the tree the knight hid under. *They're
stalking the tunnel,* other figures came into Christopher's peripheral
vision.

The wind blew across the cave. A savage stepped into the current
of snow. Tall, compact, slim and cleaner than the others, they moved
with the grace of a hunting cat. *This one's a woman,* he thought. She
went into the cave.

More figures emerged from the woods. *They're like spirits of the
woods.* Christopher admired the stillness of their movements. The
wind whistled louder then they moved and the silence they brought
with them forced the knight to doubt his eyes. Nineteen of them
entered the cave.

Christopher waited, counting each second as a pace. After sixty
seconds, he moved. Not seeing the beast, he trusted what Theodus
told him; *the Shadow only hunts at the full moon.* Tonight's moon
sported a crescent.

Christopher crawled clear of the tree, He prepared his sword
and shield as he darted across to the cave. Fifty quick shuttling steps
forward put him in position.

With his trap set, the night's success now rested in William's
hands.

The wind, which caused William problems all night, blew his torch out again. He rushed from guarding the tunnel to the fire by the entrance. He dipped the torch into the lard and then again into the fire. A blaze brought the torch back to life.

He ushered the torch low as he returned to the tunnel. A stream of firelight swept along the ground. The barricade remained undisturbed.

Where are they? The deeper the night became, the more doubts developed. He expected the savages hours ago. 'Be ready at sunset.' Christopher instructed. Dusk long since passed. Full darkness settled within the tunnel. Still, nothing.

'Let me take over.' Gaston stirred William from something close to sleep, as he stared at the unmoving barricade with no thoughts passing through his mind.

'Thank you,' he said whilst handing over the torch. He picked up his axe, which rested beside his leg before he walked away. William checked the horses first. Huddled together near the fire, they appeared to be comfortable. Accustomed to the cold, he appreciated the relief heat brought to his numbing hands.

They should be here by now, shouldn't they? He glanced at the tunnel obsessively. *How late is it?* he wondered. William left the fire to check outside. A fingernail-sized crescent did not stop the moon from dominating the sky.

A sound similar to bird wings drew his attention to the lake. *Not again,* he expected to see his flying omen. Instead, an approaching tide of snow shards swept towards him. William turned to tell Gaston to guard the torch. The wind swept over his voice. It blew out the main campfire.

Gaston who did not hear William, leaned into the tunnel, as though he identified something approaching. The monk lowered his torch to ignite the barrier. Before he could, the wind blew it out.

The darkness echoed with knocking wood.

'DEAR GOD,' Gaston cried, 'THEY ARE COMING!'

William ran up the dark path. Gaston, who approached from the other side, accidentally kicked the cooking pot. A blaze of heat and light filled the cave. William stepped out of the way of the bolting horses and leapt over the fire.

Light from the blaze of the campfire shone through the tunnel and onto the face of a savage who crawled over the wood.

'BRING A TORCH!' William commanded as he raced passed Gaston.

The savage leapt clear of the tunnel. William, who prepared his axe while he sprinted, met them with the swinging head of his weapon. The wild woman whelped. Blood gushed up William's arms and axe. His weapon slipped from his hands. The savage landed on lifeless legs, went limp, and fell face-first into the ice beside them.

More savages came through the tunnel. The closest created a large silhouette. One inner voice asked *what are you going to do?* Another replied, *If I fight, I have a chance.*

Gaston rushed up and plunged a torch into the now messy pile of logs. The flame spread and built rapidly. Caught inside the fire, one savage rammed his way through the hazardous branches. The others turned back.

If you do not run away, you will be in a fight to the death, the startled fear inside of William insisted. He took one step forward and told himself, *this is where I stand my ground.*

'Gaston, get me my axe.' William instructed before he lunged, forearm first into the wild man who came out of the tunnel. The connection shoved the savage toward the fire. Next, he launched his right fist twice from his shoulder into his foe's cheek.

The savage grabbed his collar and pushed him back. About to lose his balance, William pushed off one foot and flung his head forward. His forehead collided with the savage's chin.

Still being held, he punched quick and hard. The savage ragged him from side to side, trying to take him to the ground.

Unable to punch, he planted his feet and whipped his head sideward into his enemy's chin. He thumped a forearm down and broke the grip of the arms holding him. He punched the savage's left eye, while he stepped away to the right.

'My axe, Gaston, get my axe!' he said as the wild man slammed into him.

Anticipating being driven into the ground, William wrapped his arm around the savage's head, flung his legs into the air and directed his weight to his shoulders and back. They smacked into stone. A rock scratched William's side. The impact made him grimace, but the fall injured the other man more.

William rolled away. A hand grabbed his right ankle. He lifted his left leg, his knee to his chest and thrust his foot into the bleeding face. The hand let go. William stood and backed away. *I need my axe!*

The savage began to rise. *I should charge*, he thought, *but I need my axe.* Gaston stood back with an expression of horror on his face. William pointed at the dead woman on the ice.

'MY AXE!' He ordered.

Though not as tall, the man's maturity gave him more bulk. His hair entwined into his beard in a matted mess. The savage came at him again. *If I fight, I have a chance.*

The page swayed back to avoid the savage's attempt to grab his chest. His cocked right hand swung up into his foe's chin. He drove another uppercut into the man's beard, while he stepped back to avoid the hands that tried to grab him.

'MY AXE-'

The savage's palm shoved up into his mouth. His bust lip tingled and bled. A hand scratched across his face. Jaws lunged at him. William shuffled back. He shot out an elbow into the man's cheek but sharp teeth snapped and squeezed above his wrist.

William drove his other elbow onto the savage's head, flung his fist into his eye and kneed his groin. More animal than human, the teeth only clamped harder.

The teeth pushing against his bone drove William into survival actions. He bit down on his enemy's nose. The blood which seeped into his mouth mixed with his own from his broken lip.

The savage let go, blue in the face, gasping for air. William spat blood into his foe's face. He grabbed the man's matted hair and forced his head down. He released a rage of close uppercuts. His fist bounced off the bearded chin then returned over and over again. The wild man lifted his head and backed away from the fury.

Gaston gasped as he entered the freezing water. The monk hauled the wild woman onto solid ground.

An elbow darted into the page's nose. Blood blocked his nostrils. His eyes went wet and fuzzy. Strong arms drove his head downwards. Fists thumped onto his back.

William hooked an arm under the savage's right leg and yanked it inwards. The savage fell back.

William punched the face into a bloody mess. He made the eyes swollen and discoloured.

A hand worked its way up the page's chest, latched onto his throat and squeezed. Already tired, William struggled to breathe. He tried to pull away, but the handheld. He dropped, his knee slammed into his rival's abdomen. The hand released.

William stood, staggered back then fell backside first to the floor. While he drew in much-needed air, his enemy rolled onto their knees and started to rise. Gaston stared at the savage, amazed and horrified.

'Throw me the axe,' William said, standing, holding his hand out. Gaston's throw went off target. The page ran forward to catch his weapon. He took it in both hands, planted his feet and swung with purpose. The axe's head sunk into the savage's upper chest. He fell backward. Blood ran down onto the ice.

William slipped down onto his backside, then onto his back and lay panting. Sounds of collision echoed from beyond his engulfed barricade. *My fight is finished,* he realised, *Christopher's is just beginning.*

***

The blaze burst to life without warning. Adjusted to the darkness, Christopher's eyes flashed over white.

Shrieks indicated the success of the surprise. Approaching silhouettes confirmed the knight's trap worked.

Crouched behind his shield, Christopher brought his sword's crucifix-shaped handle to his lips and began to pray. 'Blessed be this blade,' he said. 'May it grant me the Lord's protection. May it give my enemies the mercy of a swift death.' Outlines drew closer. 'May all those who meet its steel, find forgiveness upon it.'

Christopher surged into a strong standing position. His shield collided with a savage, who slammed to the ground. Reprobus shot forward to pierce the fur rags and soft skin of a second savage's gut. The steel stretched and then retracted.

The knight placed the sword's pommel against his shield and allowed the next arrival to charge onto its tip. He knelt back, scooped low then converted the oncoming momentum to throw the runner over his shoulder. Argus met the savage with growls and snarls.

Christopher dropped his blade's tip through the chest of the wild man he floored with his shield. A fourth savage tried to rush past on his left. Christopher pressed them into the cave wall and slid his steel across their throat.

Pressure built within the cave. A stampede approached.

Reprobus flew forward in an overhand stab. The weapon pierced underneath a collarbone. The savage it embedded into slumped to the ground. Forced upwards while being pulled free, the sword slowed against the resistance of flesh. By the time the blade finished its course, the savage's scream became muffled with the gargles of rising blood.

A different body pressed into his shield. Christopher resisted before positioning Reprobus lateral across the line of their neck. He stepped back to let them push themselves onto his weapon. Blood pumped along his sword's fuller and over his hand. The body hit the floor with a thump.

The muffled screaming savage got to her feet and retreated into the flow of escaping savages. *They have realised they are caught in an ambush,* Christopher judged by the motionless figures, outlined by the barricade's light. *Now they are waiting for a leader to emerge and launch an attack.*

Blood-hungry, Argus tried to push past his master. Christopher trapped him against the wall with his knee then shoved him back with his hand.

The savages roared. Some made shrieks, others rumbled growls.

The first of them to hit his shield reached for his face. Christopher held them against his defence. He brought Reprobus up from his knee into the inside of his adversary's chest, killing him instantly.

Others pushed into him. He used his shield as a platform for Reprobus and thrust twice, each time taking a life.

He shoved his shield forward, pushed bodies into supporting savages, planted a foot on solid ground and darted Reprobus forward two times.

Two savages came at him, side by side. He sliced through one. Shield punched the other. The weight of advancing numbers forced the injured savage onto the knight's shield. He stepped back and surrendered ground.

A wild man swooped inside his sword grabbed his neck and dug its claws in. Christopher head-butted his nose, kneed him in the groin, then again in the face as he creased forward. Christopher punched his shield up and stood over him.

Argus grabbed the floored wild man's ankle and dragged him away, screaming.

Cutting down, Reprobus hacked into the neck of an approaching silhouette. With the last of his strength, the mortally wounded man drove his shoulder into the knight's abdomen. Christopher kept his footing and thumped the curved bottom of his shield into the man's back. The savage's arms sprung out as they winced.

A charging savage hit him on his exposed side and unbalanced him. Christopher, anticipating a fall to the ground, quickly placed Reprobus flat. The savage landed on his shield. The knight lifted his defensive elbow along with all the weight on top of it. He drew his dagger and buried it into his tackler's neck. Blood gushed over his face.

An escaping savage stamped on both of the men. Christopher reached out and whipped the wild man's ankle, tripping him. He rolled free, grabbed Reprobus and as he stood reciprocated the steel through the man's chest.

The knight paused, poised to strike. The moans of the dying reassured him of success. He retrieved his shield and dagger.

Outside, the moonlight and weather remained as before. A path of disturbed and discoloured ground showed where Argus dragged two savages. A dying mess of ripped skin, the one still alive suffered the worst fate of the encounter.

Christopher used his heel to push the hound away. Argus ran into the tunnel. The knight put the mauled savage out of his misery.

The screams from inside the tunnel reached pitches of terror. *Argus has found the savages who are not dead.* The knight remembered the blood on Argus's coat when he defended his brother's body. *These savages are the ones he fought off.*

The escaping screams became increasingly tortured. *I should end this*, Christopher thought, but then he understood. *Argus is fulfilling the promise he made when he dragged my brother's body into a cave. He is satisfying the vow he took when he stayed to defend the dead squire. Argus is taking Richard's revenge.*

***

William guarded the barricade until the savages' screaming stopped. *It is done*, he believed in Christopher's success.

'Gaston,' he said, 'we should make a fire outside, somewhere dry and out of the wind.' He walked by the monk who stared at the dead savages.

Cold and badly beaten, William took the pot outside into the woods. He dropped his torch into the remaining lard and fed twigs to the angry fire which arose.

The wounds on his wrist throbbed with increasing pain. He made awkward movements to compensate for the legacies of his fight; developing bruises on his back and ribs nipped when he swayed the wrong way.

After he collected a pile of branches, he tipped the pot over. Heat came through the white smoke. The warmth seduced him, *I could stay here,* he thought. Instead, he went to gather the horses.

Stood together, Springly and Beck, made dark figures beside the lake. They approached the page as soon as he called their names. Both shivered from exposure to the wind. He led them to his fire and made them comfortable.

Next, he went back into the cave to collect Gaston.

'There is a fire outside,' he said. The monk did not respond. He breathed in short breaths. He appeared pale, faint and shivered.

'You must follow me.' He grabbed his arm and led him to the fire. William, who wanted it to be hot enough to dry the monk, fed the flame more branches. Once all of his charges were sat within the warmth, he rested beside the fire, exhausted.

Throughout his work, he kept his axe close. His escort through the lonely act of taking someone's life, the weapon's iron head sported the dark red of dried blood. *The axe is bloodstained just like I am* he thought. The fight brought a mixture of guilt and triumph. *I did what needed to be done.*

As though hearing him, Gaston said,

'We did a dark deed tonight.'

'Well, what should we have done? Died?' William snapped, 'or should we have let Christopher do all the killing?

In our world, the choices we make need to be backed with action. You stand, you do not walk away. You do what needs doing.' William wanted to say more, but Gaston turned away towards the lake.

Initially unsure how to view his actions during the fight, the call to defend himself clarified his point of view. *He asked to come with me...* he thought, then, *what if he didn't come? He lit the fire!*

'Gaston.' The monk looked at him. 'I'm sorry you needed to do what you did. But if you did not come, I would have died.'

'You would not have—'

'Yes, I would,' William interrupted. 'You lit the fire. I couldn't hold them back and light it. You saved my life.'

Gaston sighed. *You did not think of it that way, did you?* The page realised.

'Where are you hurting?' Gaston inquired.

'Everywhere,' William said in all seriousness, but Gaston mistook it for a joke and laughed.

'We will treat your wounds one at a time.' The monk prepared a pot with boiling water to clean the blood away from William's cuts. He ripped a piece of his inner clothing to make a bandage for the bite on the page's arm, which seeped blood.

Argus came out of the dark and sat beside their fire. A thick gloop of blood stuck to his muzzle. *What happened to you?* William wondered.

'The two savages in the cave,' Christopher asked as he entered the campfire light, 'did you do that?'

'The wind blew our torches out,' William answered, 'as the savages reached the barrier. We lit it quickly, but those two got through. I killed the first one fast. But the second proved more difficult.'

'Why do you always pick the biggest?' William grinned at Christopher's teasing. 'First, the rat on the *Thetis*, which was bigger than Argus, now the giant inside. You need to be careful, or you'll get a reputation for yourself. Then what would Father Monroe say?'

'He would do the same thing to protect his scrolls,' William retorted.

Christopher laughed. For a second, he looked like Richard.

'He would not recognise you.' The knight held his hands out to the fire. 'He will be proud of you though, as would Richard, as am I. See, you didn't run, and that's what counts. You made the difference.'

The pride which flowed through William surpassed any pleasure he experienced in his life. Well-established negative opinions of himself coward against the euphoria which came from the complement. *I stood my ground*, having achieved what he hoped to do, he banished self-doubt, *and I did not run away.*

'How are you, Gaston?' Christopher enquired.

'I don't know.' The monk's tone expressed inner turmoil.

'I know you made vows of peace,' Christopher said, 'but the lord made it so you would be here tonight. Why would you be here now, for any other reason than the redemption you often pray for?

You're suffering guilt because of the death this night brought, but let me ask you, would your guilt not be worse, knowing your Lord offered you the chance to stop the horrors against the innocent, but you never took it?'

The knight squatted so his eyes met level with the monk's, 'Though I found my faith in the light, it was not tested until the darkness of that Holy Night.'

'The Lord's purpose brought you here, Brother. Remember that in the silent hours.'

Christopher waited for the words to sink in then instructed them,

'Take watches for the rest of the night. When the morning comes return to the mission. Tell Theodus to arrange Richard's burial for midday. Tell him afterwards, that I will need the whole settlement to help me prepare. Understand?'

'Yes, master. But where are you going?'

'I go to challenge the beast of the Abyss. Tonight, it's reign of shadow ends.'

PROLOGUE
Part Four

Before eating the inhuman heart, before draining the witch's blood, Lucius' agony came from the tortures of being suspended in a concentrated spot of sunlight with his body weight placing pressure on his limbs.

From the night of the ceremony, instead of absorbing the pain from an external source, his body inflicted agonies of its own. It reconstructed itself into something of superior size, with more physical potential than it ever possessed before.

His shoulder muscles tensed then twisted back to health. They extended along with the growth of his expanding arms, chest and his thickening neck.

Extending teeth grew new roots that screwed through Lucius' jaw bones. The mutating jaw, which throbbed against stretching skin, shattered then reformed like lumps of hot metal being shaped by a blacksmith's hammer.

Lucius's finger and toenails burned with the same sensation of being redesigned into something much larger and sharper.

Sensations below his torso felt like weights attached to his feet stretched his lower limbs. His legs not only became longer, they swelled in thickness. Sharp-cut, straight-edged muscles bloomed from his developing skeleton. No part of his anatomy escaped the agony of transformation.

The heat caught underneath the crucifix grafted to his chest intensified as his body tried and failed to reject the iron. The skin surrounding the foreign body swelled. Puss seeped from boils that burst against the corners of the crucifix. Replacement skin which grew from the boils toughened around the object to make it a part of his new body.

On the third night after the ceremony, the pain became bearable. A crusted texture of thick scabs that replaced his stretched, sunburnt skin, covered his body. In exchange for pain, it brought an unbearable itchiness. He rubbed at his inflamed legs with his opposing feet.

Later, when lifted his legs to inspect their condition, his skin appeared to be camouflaged by the night.

The fourth night ushered in the end of Lucius' nocturnal metamorphosis. He slept throughout the day and stirred as the sunlight faded against his skin. No longer dark to him, the night awoke a new world of awareness. Able to see further than he ever could during the day, shades of white now defined his vision. The abyss, previously hidden from him, now surrendered to his perception.

Alive in ways lost to the ignorance of human senses, the wind possessed new depths of scent. Though some odours hit more potent than others, as they came from a stronger or closer source, he discovered a new ability to focus on an individual fragrance the same way a human could concentrate on seeing an object.

The wind, with its changing air of intertwining textures, varying temperatures and thousands of flavours, brought motion to his immobility like a stream of water running over a rock.

Lucius, having endured death and rebirth, became aware of the power his new physique contained. He lifted his legs parallel. Even to his nocturnal eyes, they appeared a deep black. He inclined his legs onto their side and captured the moonlight in the ridges between their muscles.

Through his inspection of changes, Lucius realised the binds which held him in place no longer held him captive. He snapped his restraints with his teeth.

Despite the sudden drop, Lucius found himself instinctively prepared. He corrected his stance during the fall and landed in a braced position, his huge calf and thigh muscles absorbed the strain of the impact. He suffered no painful repercussions.

He raised claw-tipped fingers to the moon, rotated his hands and inspected them through the white light that caught between their lines and ridges. More weapons than tools, more like legs now than fingers, the ligaments near the clawed nails replicated miniature calf muscles, between the knuckle and palm the bulging muscles resembled thighs.

A branch snapped behind him. Four men stood a hundred paces away. He smelt blood in the bucket they brought with them. Since the night he ate the heart, they left him tied. When they lowered him, they poured blood into his mouth via a pole with a cupped end. They inspected his physical changes with torch lights yet did not dare to come close.

Now, standing on equal ground with them, he discovered himself to be two feet taller than the largest man.

Though he perceived them clearly, if not for the white tone they appeared to be standing in sunlight, they showed no sign of recognition toward him. He backed away with a silence alien to his size and weight. Light, from the torch they brought, tinted the surface of the surrounding leaves with colour.

The aroma of the blood they brought possessed him, he moved to take it. The expression of the man holding the buckets turned from inquisitive to terrified as Lucius entered the torchlight.

The fearful response took away the doubt which urged caution. Lucius understood his superiority over this smaller being. He forced a hand through the man's chest, picked him up, put a palm over his face then ripped his head from his neck.

The external growth changed his limbs into those of a predator, but with this, his first kill, he recognised internal transformations as his senses became overawed with information.

Lucius grabbed another man by his back and threw him upwards. His screams ended with a thud of a tree trunk. Another man started to run. Lucius, who caught him with a hand closed around his neck, lifted him and presented him to the moon. Wet silk flowed over his black arm.

He intended to hunt down the fleeing fourth man who he tracked with his ears. A change in the wind diverted his attention. The distinctive stench of stale death, of drying blood and decaying bodies overpowered the textures of the air. Visions sparked before his eyes of a cave entrance, a corridor and a tunnel. He understood that the wind came from a place of significance to his previous, human life. It called to him to discover its origin.

***

Lucius' feet moved as though guided by vision. When not running in firm lines, they pushed off strong branches, to gain height and clear unsuitable turf.

His arms swung in union with the momentum of his lower limbs. At first, they maintained his balance, but soon his upper limbs competed to play their part in this game of speed. He pivoted over obstacles and swung from higher branches.

The wind's scent called to him. Each action he took escalated the urgency to conquer the distance between him and the growing allure.

A passenger on his new body's voyage, Lucius experienced self-discovery. Making the air stream off the ridges of his body made it seem as though the wind submitted to him and acknowledged his superiority over it.

His proud chest allowed him to take deep, rich breaths. He drank in the fermentation of the wind; stale blood, decaying bodies, bloated flesh.

The denseness of the fog thickened between the widening gaps between the trees until he reached a wall of rock which glinted in a mosaic of moonlight shades. The mountain had a mouth, from it flowed the breath of a rotting air, thick with aromas of decay and death, which drew him here.

When Lucius entered the cave, he unlocked recognition from the man he used to be. He recognised the human remains from scents he detected lingering around their bodies. The broken spears, swords and shields that lay scattered outside triggered *deja vu*, as though what once existed within a dream come to life.

Alert to the scents, flavours, sights and sounds, Lucius invested concentration into every step he made. Streaks of blood and scratches on the ground and walls preserved the story of the men who failed to kill the creature within.

He descended into the tunnel at the end of the cave, headfirst. One motion at a time, Lucius climbed down so gracefully he did not hear his movement. His clawed fingers spread out to cover a wide area of surface. Their ability to support the whole of his weight revealed an advantage of their new design.

He reached the bottom. His fingers investigated the bodies of men, who lay crumpled on the ground. Of all of the distorted mess of bones and flesh, none of their hearts remained.

After retracing his steps to the top, he stopped below the soft cave light.

The night grew old while he waited. Hours of silence passed. Though his mind drifted into an absent numbness, his body held firm and remained ready.

An approaching, scratching sound shifted his trance into concentration. His breathing adopted the rhythm of the beast's movements. Lucius' lungs gathered his power.

A puff of dust spat down the well. Followed by stillness and silence.

A dark shape entered the lighter shade of the tunnel above. Lucius unleashed the patient power coiled in his legs, leapt up and clamped his hands into an invisibly black body.

Its roar ricocheted through Lucius' ears; his head throbbed as he braced against the acoustic attack. A speck of white showed where the beast's mouth opened. Lucius used the position of the beast's teeth to gauge where its neck must be. He snapped down with the widest grip his mouth could manage. Strong streams of blood gushed through the wound. Lucius swallowed fast to prevent himself from drowning for he would die before he let go.

The beast's roaring mouth became a fountain of spraying blood. The force of its voice vibrated through his throat to make Lucius' jaw quiver.

The beast lifted Lucius from the tunnel as it tried to escape. Lucius gripped tighter and focused on squeezing his teeth.

Dark claws swiped at him. One slashed his head. The other stabbed through the skin of his upper jaw and tried to pull him away.

Lucius squeezed his eyes shut, kept his jaws clamped and pushed himself further onto the beast.

A claw punched the side of his upper back. Still strong, his enemy's claws became ploughs as they tracked through his flesh. The pain would have been agony if not for the pleasure of blood flowing down his throat.

Unprepared, yet unwilling to surrender its life, the beast stripped a hunk of flesh from Lucius' back. It tried to tear a route to his heart.

Unable to reach the arm that attacked him, Lucius charged the beast sidelong into a cave wall. The beast pushed back. Both of them crashed into the rock. Lucius' jaws squeezed. The beast's claws dug frantically.

Lucius, who measured the strength of its pulse within the flow of its blood, felt the beast dying. The grip of his jaws squeezed tighter.

With the last of its power, the beast drove a claw into his ribs. A sharp pain came when he gasped. The pain stabbed deeper the more he breathed. Lucius struggled to hold the dying beast without functioning lungs. His victim stumbled, their combined weight became too much for its legs. They fell, embraced by jaw to neck, into the tunnel and disappeared into the darkness.

Chapter Nine.

Dawn light broke against the peak of a high-reaching mountain, creating a clear, fresh ambience to the grey-stone slopes. The light narrowed between cliffs to focus on a path of cannibalised bones but stopped at the cave mouth of the mountain.

Christopher left his horse and hound and walked out of the woods. Snow crunched underfoot until he trod on the bone carpet.

He stopped five paces back from the hanging bodies that lined the cave entrance.

He dropped the severed head on the ground, took his shield from his shoulder and beat it against Reprobus' handle three times. An attack on the stillness, the waves of noise went up the mountainside, into the clouds. The sound that entered the cave echoed as it turned to escape.

The stillness returned until Argus, tied to a tree, barked. *I'm being watched,* he understood this despite no indication of change from inside the cave.

A kick rolled the decapitated head underneath the hanging bodies. Darkness accepted his declaration of war with a twist of movement. The soft rolling sound quietened as it rotated across the floor.

'I call upon thee,' Christopher selected his words while waiting throughout the morning, 'who abandoned their soul, who is shadow, who deals in death, to meet me in the garden of Christ at nightfall. Tooth and claw shall meet shield and sword to decide who holds claim to these lands, be it my Lord God, or thee.'

Sunlight, reflected from his shield into the cave, caught momentarily on a seemingly suspended metallic crucifix.

'See my sword, demon,' Christopher pointed with his weapon. 'Its name is Reprobus. This steel is death. You are its prey. Tonight, it shall taste your flesh.'

The reflected light faded.

Christopher retreated, collected Argus and mounted Thunderwind. He glanced toward the creature's lair before he spun the steed around into a trot. Without looking, he slid Reprobus back into its sheath. There, the steel would wait for nightfall.

***

Above the frozen lake, high-reaching trees and mountains, the endless field of heaven grew its winter crop of snow clouds. Drifting peacefully, they appeared to convey respect for the mound of hard earth, open grave and surrounding stone wall.

It looks like a vision extracted from a dream, William reflected. A building buzz of distant voices, along with the midday sun, confirmed the time had come.

William returned to the church. Settlers gathered outside and obstructed the entrance. The gatekeeper commanded his fellow settlers to separate and form a path to allow William through. The Page nodded to thank him.

Richard's body lay stitched into a light grey cloth. His sword's handle rested on his chest, its tip on his knees.

Stood beside him, deep in thought, Theodus wore old yet little-used white robes.

Christopher stood when his page entered.

'It's noon,' William announced.

The knight and page positioned themselves at opposite ends of the board Richard rested on. Christopher lifted it by the head, William by the feet. After placing it on their shoulders, adjusting its weight and balance, they headed towards the lakeside grave.

Outside, the silent crowd separated into two lines of a path of honour. The settlers stepped forward to touch Richard's body as it passed. Shorter adults stood on their toes. Parents lifted children from the ground. Everyone showed respect.

William focused on walking in time with his master. *Their silent saluting is inappropriate,* he thought. *Richard always surrounded himself with noise, be it laughter, the telling of one of his stories or a lesson.* Regardless of his opinion, he still respected the settlers' emotions. *Their grief is as genuine as mine.*

They stopped beside the grave. The mourners gathered around.

'We have struggled to hold on for so long,' Theodus said, 'that we have come to believe we failed.

We have suffered more than any should have to suffer and lost more than anyone should have to lose. The abyss took everything from us. It stole our children, husbands and wives. Raped our religion and battered our beliefs and bestowed upon us this...this life of fear, and shame.

Yet it did not destroy us. Richard was such a man who had the strength to stand for the weak. He died to save us. We are gathered here now, because he succeeded. Not only did he rescue our hope but he has redeemed us from the sins we committed in the name of survival.

Richard will be the first person we commit to this earth since the Shadow fell over it. We must learn again that what has been lost must be mourned. Alongside Richard, we give our grief, our sadness and our unhealed pain to the soil. Yet his grave shall be more than a symbol for the things we lost. It will be our inspiration for the future. We shall follow his example. Never again shall we be tortured by fear. From this day onwards, we embrace hope.'

Theodus began to sing in a language unknown to William, a dialect of the woods. This song meant a great deal to the settlers. They sang with gusto and in perfect unison.

Unable to join the voices, William used the time to think about the things he would like to say to Richard.

Thank you for teaching me how to fight, he thought, *for helping me face my fears, for making me into a better man.*

From the corner of his eye, he noticed Eve looking at him. He did not look back. Richard deserved to be mourned without distraction.

When the hymn finished, Theodus indicated for them to lower the body by pointing at the grave with an open hand.

'We give to you, Lord, a good man,' Theodus said. 'A loyal servant of your cause. A redeemer of lost souls. May he rest in the kingdom of peace, until the day your love and your glory shall be shared by all. Amen.'

The collective of lowered heads echoed back, 'Amen.'

Theodus took Richard's sword as they lowered him. He presented it to Christopher once his hands were free. The knight plunged it into the ground to mark his brother's grave. Theodus placed his hand on the knight's shoulder.

'This is where the dead will be buried,' he said. 'This is where every child shall be christened, and everyone here baptised. Richard is our hero. This is our sacred ground. With your permission, Sir, the people would like to place a token with your brother. Each one represents a loved one they lost.'

Christopher showed he approved by smiling and nodding.

'I would like to lay a scroll with him,' Theodus added. 'On it are the names of each person who died for this cause. I would like your brother to know what he did for me, for all of us.'

'You may do so,' the knight replied, 'only if you lay your guilt with it.'

William recognised the first person to approach. An orphan from the barn, he dropped two flowers into the grave.

'These are for my mother and father,' he said. 'Father was taken by sickness, Mother by the shadow. She has golden hair and a big smile. Tell her to ask my father to follow you to heaven. He is stubborn, but he can never say no to her. Thank you, Richard.'

The boy stood beside Theodus. They recited a poem together.

Fear not, for I meet the unknown first,
Armed with your love, I shall bear its worst.
Though I am to the fox, a defenceless dove,
I am made strong, by the power of your love.
Though my path leads through strife, through pain,
I find strength in knowing, one day, we will meet again.

One after another, the settlers placed their tokens into Richard's grave. Many paused to say a prayer or some words. A few did not.

When everyone else left, William stayed behind. The grave overflowed with flowers. He could not see his friend's body, so he spoke to the memory of the man he missed.

'I will not doubt myself anymore. You taught me that. You set an example by how you lived, and how you died. You showed honour and courage. I will never forget you.'

When he touched the sword hilt of his gravestone marker, he heard a whisper that could have been a memory or could have been the wind. It sounded like Richard laughing. William smiled. That was how he wanted to remember his friend.

***

Though full of settlers who gathered to wait the night out together, the church felt empty. Unease clogged the air. Sat silently, they did not express their fears, nor shed light on the hopes locked within their hearts.

William's axe rested against the door. *Should anything happen,* he judged, *it will happen there.* With tensions already high, he did not want to carry the blade for no reason.

Exhausted, the settlers spent the afternoon preparing the Garden of Christ. First, they cleared frozen bones, weathered skins and pelts that cracked in his hands, away from the base of the towering crucifix.

Second, they replaced the surrounding stones with hay and timbers.

Third, two of the stable orphans climbed the cross and drenched its horizontal beams with oil.

By preparing the arena for a final conflict everyone in the church demonstrated faith in Christopher. If he won, if he killed the shadow, the settlers would be free. If he failed, he would be killed, but his troubles would be over. The mission's situation would become worse. They would have to pay a heavy blood price for their defiance.

Argus ran to the doors, barked and scratched to get out. The settlers watched the hound with dreadful curiosity.

'Faith is a candle,' Theodus said. The physical stresses on his face now conveyed wisdom. 'Man's duty is to do God's will.' The priest's voice filled the church. Everyone listened. 'That is why the Lord gives us the tools to see his tasks done. It is not a matter of fear. It is a matter of faith. Let me ask, do you believe in Christopher?'

'I do,' William found truth in his answer. *Christopher will do it.*

'The woods have drawn in,' Theodus continued. 'The night has made way for its master. Darkness has come. Now is the time to believe. Now is the hour of hope. Let the candle of our faith blaze.'

'FEAR NOT,' a boy's voice rang out, weak in tone, but strong in conviction, 'FOR I MEET THE UNKNOWN FIRST.'

The church's attention turned to the altar, where the boy stood.

'ARMED WITH YOUR LOVE, I SHALL BEAR ITS WORST. THOUGH I AM TO THE FOX, A DEFENCELESS DOVE.'

The other orphans added their voices to his. 'I AM MADE STRONG BY THE POWER OF YOUR LOVE.'

All in unison, they recited this poem, 'THOUGH MY PATH LEADS THROUGH STRIFE, THROUGH PAIN.'

Now the whole church recited alongside the boys, 'I FIND STRENGTH IN KNOWING, ONE DAY WE WILL MEET AGAIN.'

The settlers repeated the poem over and over again as a pledge of defiance and decoration of belief in Christopher, the man who came to challenge the darkness.

***

The towering crucifix burned from its base to its top. The fire, which blazed at first, pushed light and heat into the night and illuminated the surrounding tree line from trunk to leaves.

Christopher walked in a circle around the tower. He surveyed the tree front, settlement and wheat field. He checked beside or behind him. The knight carried his shield, sword and dagger, but wore no armour. He staked his life on speed, not strength.

Excitement for the coming fight stirred his blood. He desired to jog or run. Instead, to keep his focus, he swiped his sword, lunged and sidestepped.

After two hours, the border of burning crosses crumbled into heaps of embers. The giant crucifix stood as one glowing cinder. The abyss drew in, like the tide returning to an island. *The darker it gets, the more the enemy gains an advantage.*

To keep his concentration, Christopher made spontaneous visual inspections of shaded areas of the woods. Near the settlement, he caught a white reflection. *Something metallic moved there*, he judged. He resisted the urge to stop and look deeper. He continued to walk on his next passage, the shade appeared empty.

Tingles on his back told him, *I am being stalked.*

He walked his route four more times. The towering crucifix creaked. He glanced up at it. *Its arms will collapse soon.*

Christopher continued to walk and see nothing until the sensation of observation became an awareness of being stalked.

He turned around. The beast stood ten paces behind him. Seven-and-a-half feet tall from heel to skull, the creature's limbs, rib cage and torso sported a natural armour of pronounced muscles. Dark, even in the firelight, its face hid the eyes which measured him in return. Christopher lifted his sword. *This is what will kill you*, he indicated. The beast's lips drew back to show long, pure white teeth in a return declaration of malice.

'If we are each other's destiny...' Christopher said to provoke the beast further into the firelight, 'then let us end what fate began.'

He smacked his sword pommel against his shield. The beast roared and charged.

Christopher bounced on the balls of his feet as he read the rhythm of its steps. The beast's shoulder and left hand dropped to muster power before its arm swung upwards.

The knight stepped to the right. He slammed his shield into his enemy's upper arm. He used Reprobus as a dagger and stabbed it twice, first into its side, and then into its back.

The beast's arm swung around. Christopher angled his shield to deflect the attack. He stepped back while slashing his blade across the beast's side.

The beast turned. Christopher faked another evading step outwards, before ducking underneath its arm and moving inwards. His sword cleaved across its abdomen. It snarled. He slammed his shield up, underneath its left arm. While stepping around the beast's side, he kept his steel slicing. The beast turned. Its mouth lunged. Teeth snapped an inch from Christopher's nose.

Christopher lowered his sword hand and angled the blade at its chin. An arm flung around. He pulled away from the attack to defend. The impact which hit his outstretched shield, threw him with so much strength, he almost lost his footing.

After stepping back to keep his balance, Christopher continued to retreat against an onslaught of slashing claws. While hacking and retreating, shield punching and retreating, he kept speed with his enemy. *The beast's strength is the difference.* He realised.

Frustrated by the knight's movement, the beast tried to grasp hold of him. Christopher retreated but swept his blade into the position where the beast would expect his body to be.

Steel cut through the skin between its clawed fingers. The knight twisted the blade, trying to crack bones. It did not. A claw punched into his shield. The impact hurt worse than a joust. The same claw swooped again. The knight stepped back, leaned out of its way and hacked down onto the beast's wrists. His blade sliced through flesh. Bone, as strong as stone, stopped Reprobus from amputating the limb. The beast roared. Christopher hacked into its open mouth as he moved away. His steel sliced its cheeks before its jaws snapped.

The beast's left claw grabbed his shield. Christopher released himself from his defensive steel. The right claw came at his head. He gripped his sword with both hands and hacked down on the already injured wrist. The impact freed his shield. The beast lashed out. Christopher parried its claw.

An angry onslaught brought swift, strong movements. Christopher parried and retreated. *It is starting to dictate the fight,* he realised. *I cannot maintain this strategy of movement. I have to take a risk.*

The beast nudged closer. The power of its claws hit harder. Christopher nearly lost his sword. The beast planted its feet to muster its weight and power. *It wants to finish me.*

Rather than move his sword across to counter the coming blow, Christopher spun Reprobus in his hands, so he could rally all his power into a plunging thrust.

The beast's blow caught Christopher on his shoulder and flung him across the ground.

The knight ignored the pain as he rolled over onto his feet. With his dagger in his hand, he prepared for an attack that did not come.

The beast stood still. Flame light from the towering crucifix painted Reprobus' steel with fire. The sword stood half-buried inside the Beast's huge, black chest.

The knight's shield rested on the ground between them. Christopher sprinted across, picked it up whilst moving and ran for the beast. He leapt, threw all his weight behind the shield and collided with his swords pummel. The beast stumbled back but did not fall.

The heat of the tower behind the beast dried Christopher's sweat. His skin burned. He leapt again, to slam his dagger into the eye. Blood splattered out over his hand.

Christopher's shoulder charged his shield into its torso. He shoved the beast backwards. Hot ashes burned his feet as he pushed.

Close to the burning crucifix, he let go of his shield, squatted, grasped the beast's leg and threw his and its weight into the flame-weakened tower. The arms above collapsed. Burning timbers fell towards the fighters.

***

A thunderous crash stopped the settlers from singing. In the silence of a united-held breath, Argus' scratches filled the hall. A softer thump followed.

'That sound came from the barn doors!' a stable boy at the back of the hall said.

'He failed,' someone else added. 'Now the beast is slaughtering the livestock.'

'KEEP YOUR FAITH!' Theodus silenced their voices but not their fears. Everyone inside the church looked at William to do something.

'I'll check the barn,' he offered. At the door, he forgot to pick up his axe. A boy held it up to him.

'I do not need a weapon.' He declared his certainty. *I know Christopher won.*

Argus pushed his way outside and disappeared into the night. As the door closed behind William, Eve slid outside.

'Wait!' She grabbed his hand. 'I want to go with you.' The door shut behind her.

They said nothing to each other as they walked across to the barn. Crackling wood came from the burning heap beyond the settlement.

The barn doors sat open in an outward position, suggesting something came out. The calmness of the animals inside the cold, barely lit room conveyed safety. Thunderwind walked across to him, almost to confirm the inhabitants' well-being.

They closed the barn doors behind them. Still holding hands, they walked to the burning battleground. Red embers created a soft-lit border.

A black form startled William. He flinched and momentarily regretted not bringing his axe.

'Bucephalus,' he said. The horse recognised him and stopped his challenge. 'That must have been you who escaped the barn.'

Eve grabbed his arm.

'Look,' she pointed into the heart of the giant crucifix's cindering remains. Reprobus stood horizontally pressed into the bottom of the wooden beam. The weapon held the beast's charred body in place. Its mouth sat frozen in a wide-open, voiceless snarl. Like leeches feeding on a host, parasitic teeth sprouted randomly from its jaws.

The sense of relief which mustered his emotions halted. Argus sniffed at the ground, trying to find a specific scent. *Where is Christopher?*

William's stomach tightened to reject a horrible presumption, *he's dead.* Sweat on his skin absorbed the cold in the air. He checked the ashes near the beast's skeleton, ground further away and outside of the fire. *There is no sign of my master.*

Argus' first bark stopped his fear-like tension onto a wound. His second caused a rush of hope. The third brought joy. The hound ran to Christopher, who stood at the far side of the fire.

'YOU DID IT!' William released the pressure caught in his gut.

Christopher lifted his arm into the air and called out, 'FOR RICHARD!' Every emotion William experienced on his journey from Monroe's church to this moment, from the deepest sadness to the highest joy, rushed through him all at once. He could not cry for smiling, nor laugh for weeping. His master had beaten the beast and brought light to the darkness.

***

The settlers, who held hands and sang to comfort each other, confronted the remains of their tormentor together. The sight of the monster burning in the debris and ash brought a mass release of emotion. They cheered, hugged and kissed each other.

As Christopher prepared to address them, they hushed.

'The fear is over,' he announced, 'the horrors have ended. The long night has reached its dawn.

'Tomorrow, you will awake to a new world. Though I know you will toil to make it a better place for your children, I fear you have suffered so much that your thoughts will linger in the past. Do not let this happen. Forgive yourselves for the sins you committed to survive. The Lord is merciful, he forgives, and he understands.

'Take time to mourn your loss. Smile, cry, tell stories about them, but above all, give them peace. Do not disgrace the dreams they had for you.' The knight paused before locking eyes with William, 'Live in honour of them.'

The knight lifted his shield into the air, and sparked cheers as he said, 'To the glory of the dead!'

After the applause, Theodus approached Christopher. Speechless, the flow of his tears strengthened as layers of emotions built over a lifetime of trauma, dissolved into liquid expression. Becoming overwhelmed, he walked away without saying a word.

William, who stood beside the knight, revaluated his master. *He's physically grown somehow.* He wore the charisma of a man who achieved the impossible.

William recognised the same sense of awe in the settlers who visited with Christopher. The gleam in their eyes suggested they would remember this day for the rest of their lives.

Amongst the united joy, the page noticed the one thing out of place. An older woman cried with sadness. William went to help her. Theodus intercepted him.

'Monroe must learn of this moment.'

'I shall tell him about it. I shall tell him about everything. Why is that woman upset?'

'One of the savages was once her son.' Theodus explained. 'She is saying goodbye, that is all.'

William did not think of the savages as people before. He pictured the one he fought to the death but stopped himself from thinking about the other two he killed. Theodus grabbed his shoulder.

'Of all the victims of the shadow, those children suffered the worst,' he said. 'You—' his hand squeezed, 'and your master, set them free.'

'Thank you,' William smiled and then walked away from the priest and the crowd. The page waited for the fire to cool before retrieving his master's sword. Heat radiated through his boots as he stepped onto the ash. Reprobus stood as a part of a sculpture commemorating the death of the beast. When he pulled the blade clear, the monster fell apart into crumbling blocks of cinders. A chunk of iron broke free.

That's the crucifix William realised. He grabbed it with the makeshift protection of his sleeve.

He retreated out of the ash to inspect the object. A rim of ash showed where the skin grew over the iron.

Unsuited to the stillness, a sudden gust rushed through the ashes. For the briefest of moments, William recognised a foreign freedom and happiness. *The cross weighs less now*, he thought, *it's as though a weight has been lifted from it.*

'You've come far since leaving Monroe,' Christopher said as he stood beside him.

William looked at him, smiled, nodded and replied, 'It feels far.'

'I am releasing you from your oath.' The knight reached out for his sword.

'What do you mean?' asked William, who having exhausted his emotions, felt shocked, 'What did I do wrong?'

'You did nothing wrong, Will,' Christopher replied. 'It's the opposite. You surpassed expectations. Whatever debt you owed me with your oath, you have repaid tenfold. I could not ask for a better apprentice or friend.

'The fault is mine...I've come to care for you, see you like a little brother. That is why I'm releasing you from your oath. You have a choice to make. If you want to come with me, I will gladly take you. As a squire, not a page. You may lack the experience and knowledge of other squires, but you have proven yourself where it counts, and you can learn the rest.

'I realise there is an opportunity at another life here, with a woman you look to love. Should you choose that path, know that you're not going to change my opinion of you. You're a good man. Brave, loyal, trustworthy. I'll leave in spring. Take until then to decide. Right now,' Christopher patted him on the back before he walked away, 'I choose to go to bed.'

The knight took two steps and then paused. 'No one will ever understand what we did here,' he said over his shoulder. 'No one will ever appreciate what we lost. But we made a difference and that is all that counts.'

Christopher walked towards the church. Argus ran across to join him. The hound's tail wagged, and he bounced happily requesting the knight to wrestle.

A soft hand stroked William's forearm. He turned into Eve and met her lips with no reserve for his passion. His hands ran down her back with lustful wonder.

'We must join the others,' she said as they separated. A chorus of singing voices welcomed them to celebrate the end of a long night.

***

William ended his dreamless sleep with soft steps into awareness. First, he established; *I am in Theodus' church.* Then he determined; *I am laid next to Eve.* Lastly, he calculated by the lack of light and sound, *it must be early morning.*

William tried to fall back asleep but failed. The woman who cried when everyone else celebrated, haunted his thoughts. She reminded him of the innocent children the savages once were. *Their bodies should not be left to rot* he decided. *They deserve a Christian funeral. They deserve to return to God.*

William lay still until Eve stirred. When he told her of his intentions, she insisted on accompanying him. During the night, she shared revelations with him. She believed her mother brought her to Saint Constantines, but Gaston lied to her. He confessed to finding her in the woods, during an encounter with the beast.

Eve's mother had always been in the mission. The beast took her husband, son and daughter. They found her husband's remains on the border of the Abyss. Her son joined the savages. She believed her daughter dead, only to recognise her when she returned to the mission.

One of the dead must be Eve's brother, William realised.

They saddled Thunderwind and Springly, loaded Stormpath and Lunar with firewood, and left the settlement within the dawn hour. Argus followed, more interested in marking territory than keeping close to them.

High, ice-speckled clouds splashed the endless blue above. Sunshine shone brightly. The wind that swept off the lake denied the day of any warmth. The constant hiss from strained air kept them from talking and made their journey seem longer.

The cave in the mid-morning light appeared different to how he remembered. The two he killed lay pale and frozen.

'If you prepare a fire,' William suggested, 'I'll move them. Should you need my axe, it's tied to my saddle.'

He lit a prepared torch before going into the tunnel. A mess of frozen entrails stuck out of the first body he encountered. *There are wolves here,* he thought. But then he recalled Argus coming to the fire the morning after the tunnel fights, and the layer of blood around the hound's muzzle.

The mutilated remains of the savages matched the anguish and hatred on their faces. *Without a cremation, they would spend eternity like this.* The motion of picking up a body reminded him of back home, having to move sacks of grain.

He considered retrieving his axe to cut through the thin sinew which stopped one woman from being slashed in half. In another life, she would be deemed beautiful. Her dead eyes looked at him with a haunted expression. He tried to close them but could not.

Just like a sack of grain, he told himself as he dragged her body. Despite the cold, the hard work made him hot. With each new body discovered in the cave, he found a mix of his master's swift execution and Argus' premeditated mauling.

Eve collected branches and twigs and constructed a pyre.

'We'll do it together,' Eve said. The foliage burnt white smoke. They stood on the leeward side to avoid the smell of burning flesh.

When it came time to leave, Argus refused to come. He went to the tunnel and barked.

'I am sure I brought all the bodies outside.' William said.

'He wants to take us somewhere.' Eve replied.

William followed the hound, torch first into the tunnel. He helped the hound onto the upper shelf. Argus went ahead but waited by the exit.

When William reached him, the hound moved on again. He moved up the mountainside. William and Eve helped each other up the steep terrain until they came to the top.

Argus stood with his body pointing back over the Abyss, towards Saint Constantines. The view above the canopy which followed an endless carpet of coppery autumn yellows, browns and red leaves, submitted to the dominance of white smoke. A ridge of fire created an unnatural horizon.

The day-long sunset, William thought, his mind's eye recalled a nearly identical image from his childhood.

'It's like heaven is meeting hell, and the borders are being altered.' Eve said. 'Saint Constantines is beyond the smoke.

'*No,* William chose not to say, *Saint Constantines is inside the fire.*

'Come on,' William took her hand, 'we must tell Christopher.' They rushed unsafely down the rock side and rushed through the tunnel. William paused to help Argus down the drop. The hound dropped by himself and rushed ahead.

Eve stopped inside the cave. William pushed past her to take the lead.

In the middle of the cave, his axe stood upright. Perched on its head, the now completely black crow squawked at him, before leaping into flight and heading towards the burning horizon.

264

'The axe was on Thunderwind's saddle,' Eve shook her head in denial. 'I know. I saw it there. The bird could not have moved it.'

'The bird delivered a message,' William sighed.

'What message?'

'Without that axe, I would not have survived the savage's attack. The bird is reminding me I made a deal. It is telling me to go with Christopher.'

'Give the axe back,' Eve protested. *If I could, I would.*

'Destinies cannot be given back,' he said. 'I have to leave.'

They rode back to the settlement in silence. The happiness of the previous day now exchanged for the sadness of a coming separation. Their bond and their closeness seemed to fade. Within view of the settlement's dusk fires, Eve stopped him.

'You must go,' she said, 'I must stay.'

'I will come back to you.' William promised.

'I will wait for you,' she vowed. They sealed their pact with a kiss. Tears intertwined at their lips and fell to the ground together.

Epilogue

Christopher's body hurt when he moved. The hard-fought victory left him injured to his shoulders, back and chest. *Pain is the price of triumph,* the knight understood and accepted.

Given time to stay in the settlement, his body would recover. *I can no longer afford the luxury of rest.* Events elsewhere altered his plans. Despite not wanting to travel during winter, duty drew him home.

Exhausted, William slept on a church bench while his master and Theodus prepared the horses. With fewer riders, as Gaston and Eve decided to stay, their return to Christendom would be far quicker than their outward journey.

Though fully loaded, the knight asked Theodus for one more pouch of smoked meats. When the older man left the room, Christopher awoke his squire. He held a finger to his lips and ushered him out of the hall in silence. Though he denied Theodus the opportunity to say thank you, he saved him from becoming emotional again. *This way will be better.*

Outside, their mounts waited in the soundless blue light. A different attendant opened the gates as they approached. Christopher acknowledged Eve with a smile but did not stop to talk. He understood. *She is not here to see me.*

A smaller, less ambitious crucifix replaced the collapsed tower. Unpolished, and crudely cut, it operated as a frame for the silver cross which came from the beast. Christopher approved. The settlement needed to rebuild but not forget. Contemplating the importance of the past, he remembered something a friend once said to him; 'The past is a patient, omnificent hunter. Distances or situations are no protection. If a man lives long enough, his history will catch him.'

When William reported, 'Smoke and fire that stretched further than the eye could encompass.' Christopher recognised the mark of "The Burning". *The enemy of my past has returned.* He contemplated. *Holy armies will already be marching to meet the volcanic legions. The fight for Christendom is about to begin. Now, it is time for the church's champion to return, for Reprobus to rise, for the sword of God to reap its vengeance.*

About the Author

Sam is a Firefighter from Hull. He lives in Brough, East Yorkshire with his wife Kimberley and dog Robin.

www.ingramcontent.com/pod-product-compliance
Ingram Content Group UK Ltd.
Pitfield, Milton Keynes, MK11 3LW, UK
UKHW040900240225
455493UK00001B/105